THE COLLECTORS
PROGRAM

Michael Trzupek

ISBN-13: 9781735020303

Cover design by: Art Painter
Library of Congress Control Number: 2018675309
Printed in the United States of America

To all my friends and family that provided priceless feedback on every step of this journey. I could not have done it without you.

CONTENTS

CHAPTER 1

London, England

The town car slowly made its way through the affluent Lennox Garden neighborhood. The driver craned to read addresses in the darkness. After passing a few more buildings, the car stopped. The driver's door opened, the driver walked around the car and opened the rear passenger side door. From the back seat, a gentleman slowly stepped out carrying a briefcase. His suit fell perfectly, tailored to shoulders and waist. A flat-folded pocket handkerchief, a shade lighter than his silk tie, finished the look. He took a couple of steps before pausing to look at his phone.

Turning back toward the car and driver he said, "This may be a good time for you to grab dinner; I think this may take a while."

The driver nodded attentively and responded, "Yes, Mr. Roberts."

The gentleman turned and walked with determination to the entrance of the building. The doorman greeted him and extended his hand. They shook hands formally and the doorman asked, "Good evening, sir. How may I help you?"

"I'm afraid that I've come unannounced this evening, but I have a pressing matter I must address with Wilma Stone."

He took a business card from his suit pocket and handed it to the doorman who read the card and looked back at him with astonishment. "Yes, Mr. Roberts. She is in Unit Three, which is through these doors and around the corner to your right. Would you like me to escort you?"

"No, that won't be necessary. And please do be discreet about my visit."

The doorman replied, "Of course sir. They would not employ me, if not for my discretion."

"Yes, I would imagine so. Thank you very much."

Mr. Roberts stepped into the lobby. A foyer table with a large display of cut flowers anchored the room. He took a right and started down the hallway. A look of satisfaction came across his face. Art work hung on the wall and one picture caught his attention. He stopped and looked at it knowingly, smiling. Dropping the smile, he continued on and stopped in front of Unit Three. He rang the doorbell. While he waited, he took another business card from his pocket. He played with the card nervously. A young lady answered the door. She wore a conservative, yet form-fitting yellow dress and two-inch tangerine-colored heels.

"Hello," the young lady said. "How can I help you?"

"I'm sorry to bother you this evening, but I have a matter of some urgency to discuss with Mrs. Stone. Is she, by chance, available?" He handed her his business card and waited silently as she read it.

Looking up, she replied, "I'm Mrs. Stone. How can I help you?"

"I'm sorry," he explained, "but I'm looking for Mrs. Wilma Stone, I believe you must be Olivia Stone. Is your mother available?"

Olivia looked at him with a degree of surprise. "Yes, you are correct. If you will come in and wait here for a moment, I'll get my mother for you."

Mr. Roberts stepped into the entry. Olivia turned, her heels clacking across the marble entry as she disappeared around the corner. Two leather chairs book ended a half-moon table adorned with a crystal lamp and a Japanese Ikebana arrangement of flowers, leaves and willow stalks. The walls were a warm gray with no pictures or artwork on display.

The voices of the two women entered the room before them and grew in intensity by the time they stood in front of Mr. Roberts. Mrs. Wilma Stone wore a knee-length powder-blue dress with black heels. Her hair was gray and despite her age, she kept herself in good shape.

Olivia set about introducing Mr. Roberts. "Mother," she began, "this is Mr. Percy Roberts from the law firm B&R Solicitors. He's asking to speak with you."

Mr. Roberts extended his arm to shake Wilma's hand and addressed her formally, "Mrs. Stone, I'm sorry to call upon you unannounced this evening, but my firm has produced some information that directly benefits your family. I thought it prudent to bring this to your attention immediately and deliver it in person."

Wilma looked at him suspiciously, "This could not wait for the morning?" she asked. "Our family lawyer is quite well known in London and you could have brought the matter to him."

Mr. Roberts explained, "Yes, I understand this is all highly unusual, Mrs. Stone. But if I may, is there a place where we might sit and discuss this information? I think the reputation of my firm precedes itself. You must understand, I would have not come here tonight, if the matter did not demand it."

Wilma looked at Olivia and then back at Mr. Roberts. "Indeed, you are correct, Mr. Roberts. Please follow me to the drawing room."

The room had been decorated to the highest standard with modernized traditional furniture and, here and there, antique pieces. A very simple upholstered sofa and glass and chromium coffee table sat in the middle of the room. Half a dozen canvasses, each with gallery-style down lighting, hung on one wall. The room benefitted from floor-to-ceiling windows and on a clear night, the deep blue night sky and lights of Gladstone Park would have sparkled through. Matching Chippendale chairs and two mahogany end tables completed the room.

"Thank you so much, Mrs. Stone," Mr. Roberts replied. "I do think you will shortly appreciate the reason for my visit."

Wilma addressed Mr. Roberts. "May I offer you something to drink?"

"Thank you so kindly. A glass of chilled flat water perhaps?"

Wilma turned to her daughter. "Olivia, would you please bring Mr. Roberts some water?" She turned back to him. "I was not expecting a visitor this evening. I sent the staff home for the night, or else I would offer you more."

"Yes, of course mother," Olivia replied and left the room.

Wilma directed Mr. Roberts to be seated. He waited for her to sit first, and then looked around the room intently. Like its owner, it was an expression of aesthetic standards—classical proportion, restraint and elegance.

"So please, Mr. Roberts, do tell me what this is about," Wilma asked.

Mr. Roberts, who was on the edge of the chair, made sure he was sitting on his coat tails and sat up straight. "Mrs. Stone, as you are most likely aware, our team at B&R has a capability unmatched anywhere in Europe in the matter of thorough and insightful investigations of obscure documents and legal filings."

"I'm sure you do," Wilma said, "but how does this involve me?"

Mr. Roberts shuffled his hips and cleared his throat. He glanced momentarily toward the kitchen for the glass of water. "Yes, I'm getting to that Mrs. Stone," he said.

Olivia returned with a tray and three glasses of water and placed it on the coffee table. She took a seat on the couch next to her mother. Mr. Roberts took a sip of water and placed the glass on the table. Olivia handed him a serviette. He wiped his hands and placed the serviette under his water glass.

"Thank you, Olivia," he said before proceeding. "I was just sharing with your mother the reason for my visit this evening."

Wilma looked at Olivia and then back at him. "Please continue, Mr. Roberts."

"As I was saying, in this particular case our firm was contacted by the client I am here to represent. My client discovered in the course of his work, that your family has a fair amount of offshore wealth. It has gone unreported and nearly forgotten with your husband's passing five years ago. "

Wilma inhaled deeply at the mention of her husband and then leaned forward to reply, "I'm sorry Mr. Roberts but this is all quite irregular. Surely our family lawyer would have known about such a thing. I'm not sure why you have not addressed this with him first?"

"I understand your concern Mrs. Stone. However, we have reason to believe that your husband may have deliberately shielded this information from your family lawyer. The reasons are still unclear to us. I thought it best to bring this information to you directly and let you decide how to best proceed."

5

Olivia stuttered in disbelief. "I'm struggling to digest this, Mr. Roberts," she challenged. "Who is your client? Why have they not brought this to us themselves?"

Mr. Roberts nodded at Olivia's outburst and continued to address Wilma. "My client is in a unique position to have this information. At least for the moment, they wish to remain anonymous, until you have an opportunity to learn more about the matter."

Olivia said, "Mr. Roberts, with all due respect, this smacks of a third world financial scam. Why do you believe that this information is true?"

Mr. Roberts hesitated. "To be honest, I have worked with this client on other unrelated matters and his information has been unimpeachable. To directly answer your question, I can't be certain of the accuracy of this information without your help."

Wilma frowned. "And how exactly can we help you this evening?"

Mr. Roberts took another, longer drink of water before he responded. "My client has a piece of information that only your husband and you could possibly know. We believe this should establish the baseline credibility in this matter. If you would allow me to grab a piece of paper from my briefcase, it will be helpful for what will follow."

"Yes, of course," Wilma said.

"How much money are we talking about Mr. Roberts?" Olivia added.

He opened his briefcase and retrieved an envelope. After closing the briefcase and returning it to the floor beside him, he handed Wilma the envelope. Wilma looked at it with curiosity.

"If you will, please," Mr. Roberts said, "do not open it for a moment and let me explain further." He turned to address Olivia. "To your question, I will answer that once we have established the credibility of my client's information."

Both Wilma and Olivia nodded solemnly and replied in unison, "Of course." Wilma shot her daughter a disapproving glance.

"Mrs. Stone," Mr. Roberts continued, and then softened. "Wilma, to be clear, the question I am about to ask you may prove to be sensitive. You may wish to ask your daughter to take leave of us while we discuss this matter."

Olivia looked over at her mother, who never broke eye contact with their unexpected guest.

"Mr. Roberts, since my dear Frank left us, my daughter has been my solace. I have also entrusted her with the business in preparation for her to run it one day. There is nothing that cannot be shared with her."

Percy nodded his understanding and continued. "I appreciate your position Mrs. Stone. I felt compelled to share that what we are about to discuss is quite personal in nature. Something that someone of your high character would not discuss in such proper settings."

Olivia stood up. "Mother," she said impatiently, "would you like me to leave? I don't wish to embarrass you."

Wilma took Olivia's hand and gently guided her to sit down. "No, dear, I am much too old to think there remains some personal detail hiding in the shadows. Mr. Roberts, if you would, please do get on with this."

"As you wish, Mrs. Stone," he replied.

He glanced back and forth between mother and daughter,

cleared his throat and continued.

"Mrs. Stone, if my clients research is authentic, the correct answer to the authentication question is in that envelope. I had anticipated that you might wish to not voice your response. I took the additional step to provide a more discreet way to go about it. Upon hearing the question, you may open the envelope and nod if the answer is correct."

Wilma and Olivia both looked at the envelope, which Wilma now lifted from her lap.

"The question is 'Where is the location that you and Frank *actually* made love for the first time?'" he said.

Wilma's face turned a slight shade of red. She felt compelled to say, "Well indeed, Mr. Roberts, you continue to surprise me. I had not anticipated such a question. I now know why your firm's reputation precedes you. I would like to thank you for your thoughtful discretion in preparing this envelope."

Mr. Roberts nodded, almost relieved, "You are very welcome, Mrs. Stone."

Wilma slowly tore open the envelope and removed a folded piece of paper. She held the paper close as would a poker player, and read the answer. She refolded the paper and took the time to slip it back in the envelope. She handed the envelope back to Mr. Roberts.

"I trust that you'll properly dispose of that piece of paper, Mr. Roberts?" she said.

"Yes of course ma'am," he responded reassuringly.

She looked at her daughter with affection and said quietly, "Yes, the answer is correct, Mr. Roberts."

"Now what?" Olivia asked. A moment of awkward silence hung in the room.

"I would ask if you could join me in my office tomorrow," Mr. Roberts inquired, "so that we can walk through the next steps with my client."

"I don't understand," Olivia asked, exasperated. She took her mother's hand in her own and patted it, a little too hard to be reassuring. "You're not prepared to complete this tonight?"

"I regret that is not possible," Mr. Roberts explained, looking back and forth between them. "This was the first step in establishing my client's credibility with you. We will need to walk through the rest tomorrow."

"We can be there at 10 a.m.," Wilma answered stoically. "I will bring my lawyer as well."

Mr. Roberts put up his hand signaling his objection. "I'm sorry to request this. Until we can walk through the next step and understand your husband's intentions as it relates to your lawyer, I must ask that we exclude him for now. There will be plenty of time for his services, once you are satisfied as to the reasons for his lack of participation to date."

"I must say, Mr. Roberts, this is all highly unusual..." Wilma said.

"Nothing about this matter is usual," Mr. Roberts responded.

Wilma looked at Olivia anxiously. They stared at each other in silence. Mr. Roberts leaned back into the chair to give them the additional inches of personal space and waited patiently. Finally, Wilma turned to Mr. Roberts and said, "I will honor what appears to be my husband's request. I reserve the right to pull my lawyer in at the point that I no longer feel our rights are being protected."

"I would advise you to do so; I think it is a wise approach," Mr. Roberts responded.

He stood up to leave. "Mrs. Stone," he said, extending his hand, "I thank you for your time this evening and appreciate your latitude on this matter. I look forward to seeing you in the morning."

The three of them walked to the entry door and shook hands again. Olivia opened the door to the hallway.

"Mr. Roberts, you never said how much money we are discussing," she said, slightly barring the door.

"Ah yes, you are correct," Mr. Roberts nodded. "Well, now that we have established a foundation of credibility to this matter, I think there is no reason to obfuscate the details any longer." He looked at Wilma. "Fifty-seven million Pounds," he said, nodded, and stepped into the hallway.

Olivia and Wilma stood speechless with the door wide open as Mr. Roberts made his way out of the building.

Munich, Germany

Max Hoffman wore a black tee shirt, blue jeans, black shoes, and a frayed black cap. He sweated as he paced back and forth on the S-Bahn platform, constantly checking his watch. Around him men and women fanned themselves with magazines and brochures. A small child slept on top of two suitcases as her parents were immersed in their phones. A few men had their suit coats thrown over their shoulders or tucked under their arms. Their ties hung loose and low with the top several buttons of their dress shirts undone, revealing beads of sweat.

Max peered down the rail line. Finding nothing, he walked to the stairwell and looked over the banister. As he turned back toward the platform, he bumped into a young, attractive woman. He began to apologize but stopped and instead said, "Your luck running into me." The woman looked at him, confused, and walked deliberately around him. Max scanned the crowd to find nearly every eye upon him. He struggled to think what to do. Recovering, he shouted, "Your loss, baby." The young lady continued further down the platform, without acknowledging his comment.

The group of people nearest Max subtly increased their distance from him. Max ignored them and aimlessly shuffled his feet and checked his watch again. He stepped back toward the edge of the train platform and saw the slightest glow in the distance. He watched intently as the light gained in intensity. He returned to the stairs and yelled, "Lukas, you better move your fucking ass!"

Max continued to stare down the steps, fidgeting impatiently as the sound of an approaching train filled the air.

"Lukas," he shouted again.

The waiting passengers moved toward the edge of the platform. Max grimaced and let out a growl. He turned and headed back to the platform in the direction where the attractive woman had escaped. The train pulled into the station, ground to a stop, and the doors opened. A steady flow of people, most pulling luggage, spilled out of the train. Max stood close to the train, looking over his shoulder for Lukas. People had to maneuver around him and one man, in a suit, bumped into Max trying to get around him.

"Watch where you're going asshole," Max shouted intolerantly.

The gentleman turned and shot Max a glare but quickly merged into the exiting mass. Max watched the man disappear down the stairs and then turned to board the train. The blast of air conditioning shocked him and goose bumps broke out across his skin. Max stayed close to the door and watched the staircase intently. He saw Lukas running up the stairs and smiled. He was dressed like Max, except in a red tee shirt and no cap, his heavy gold chain bouncing against his chest as he took the stairs two at a time. Max leaned forward and blocked the train doors with his body. Lukas sprinted across the platform and into the train. Max stepped back and the doors closed.

"Where've you been, dude?" Max asked.

"My damn manager kept me to clean. Not going to pay me overtime either," Lukas panted.

Max looked around the train and smiled. "I'm glad you made it. There's some quality ass on this train - this one blonde practically begged me for it."

Lukas twirled around, looking at the people near them before he asked Max, "You talking about grandma over there?" leaning his head toward a woman that could have been either of their grandmothers.

Max shook his head dismissively and grunted. His eyes quickly scanned up and down the train car. Then he saw her, still waiting on the platform. As the train moved, he pointed in her direction and hit Lukas in the chest with the back of his other hand, "There she is."

As the train passed her and she saw Max pointing at her, the young woman flipped him off. Lukas laughed, "I think she gave you her number."

Max waved his hands indifferently. "Are you ready to party tonight, or what?" he said, changing the subject.

"Hell yeah," Lukas replied, "Are you working tomorrow?"

"Nope. And my old man has been a pain in my ass. Something big at his work. I need to get myself out of that house."

Lukas looked puzzled, "That sucks, but what does that have to do with tonight?"

"I will have to sneak my ass back in tonight, otherwise the parents will make my life hell tomorrow."

Lukas continued to stare at him, confused. "Never mind. You find anything good in the checked luggage today?"

Max scanned the train compartment nervously. "Shut the fuck up. You don't know who's on this train." He paused for a moment watching the reactions of the passengers before he continued, "Ever since Felix got busted, all kinds of cameras everywhere. It's going to be awhile until we do 787 shopping again."

"I bet that's crimping your cash. I can talk to my asshole manager and get you a job at the Blackbird."

Max just laughed, "No way I'm commuting my ass out to the airport every day for that piss ass bar."

Lukas looked down at his feet. He took a long breath in and then glanced at Max who was staring at him. "No need to rub it in," Lukas said meekly, "Since you are so loaded, I guess you're buying then?"

Max responded condescendingly, "You really think that's happening?"

Lukas' mouth dropped and he stared indignantly at Max. Max returned a glare that screamed "Try me." Gradually Lukas' face relaxed. "Where you thinking tonight?" he asked.

"Pete says the Hard Rock. Adorable American girls who find our accents hot."

"Drinks are too expensive to be blue balled, how about Barschwein?"

Max raised his eyebrow, "College chicks are a pain. But they love the wild thing with working boys."

13

"So, yes?" Lukas pressed eagerly.

"Sure. Your girl going to meet us out?"

A renewed look of astonishment broke out on Lukas' face. "Are you purposely picking on me tonight? You know Hannah and I split."

Max snickered, "This week. You two are impossible to keep up with. I'll take that's a no?"

Lukas moved closer to the window and looked in the direction the train was heading. He asked, "Is Pete picking us up or we going to have to bus?"

"Nah. Pete's got us."

The train slowed to a stop. Max stepped toward the doors and peered out the window. "Hey, there's Pete's piece of shit VW."

"Really?" Lukas replied sarcastically.

The doors opened and Max and Lukas joined the exiting passengers. Pete was waiting for them. He wore a solid black polo shirt, dark jeans and dress shoes. When he saw Max and Lukas, he flipped them off with a wide grin on his face.

"Nice to see you too, white boy," Max yelled above the crowd. Lukas shook his head and headed to the back seat of Pete's car. Max strutted around the front of the car and got in.

"How we doin' tonight, boys?" Pete asked once they were all in the car.

Max replied, "Just fine, but what happened to your A/C?"

"Give it a minute, asshole."

Max snapped, "Asshole? I didn't create the sauna in here."

Pete shot Max a look of disgust, "Really?" he said, with his hands up, "You can bus it to the Hard Rock if you want."

Lukas piped up from the back seat, "Barschwein is the new plan."

Pete turned to Max as he pulled away from the curb and asked, "I thought we were headed to the Hard Rock."

"Lukas here, decided he can't afford American women tonight."

Lukas glanced into the rear-view mirror. "Barschwein it is," he directed Pete.

Once they were underway, Max asked Pete, "Is your old man being a pain in the ass too? Something's going on at the university and it's stressing out my old man."

Pete weaved around a car before replying, "Nothing but the usual shit. Although...," he checked his rearview mirror before finishing, "... he said your dad is working on something that will change the world."

Max laughed. "I think my dad would like yours to believe that. He's been talking about changing the world since I was a kid. He should write me a fat check so I can move out and live *my* dream."

Lukas piped up, "You mean the blonde who left you her one-digit phone number?"

Max bristled. "Fuck off, asshole. Keep that shit up and you'll find yourself looking for your own way home tonight."

Pete glanced at Max, "You realize whose car this is, right?"

Max turned his head and looked out the window. "Don't you always fucking let us know it."

"Come now, ladies," Lukas coaxed from the back.

Pete slowed the car to make a point. "I should drop both of your asses off and let you take the bus the rest of the way."

Lukas tried to shift the conversation, "Hey, do we have a meeting with the boys this week or not?"

Max turned all the way around to address Lukas straight on, "No, and if you keep acting like this, they're going to kick your weak ass out."

Pete didn't wait for Lukas to respond, "You hear I got promoted?"

Max swung his head around to face Peter. "Are you getting a big bump in pay?"

"Pay and responsibility. You are looking at the newest line foreman."

"Damn, that's great Pete," Lukas said.

Max replied, "Shit, I don't know how much longer we'll be able to hang with you. You're all management and shit now."

Pete flashed a smile at Max. "You know you're always my boys. I'm just a richer asshole drinking better beer and chasing shorter skirts."

They all laughed before Lukas interrupted, "Hey we're getting close. Grab any spot you can find."

"Shit, I swear you guys think I'm your chauffer sometimes," Pete said.

Max placed his hand on Pete's shoulder. "I hate to break it to you my friend, but you are definitely our chauffer."

Pete shook his head and slowed the car, looking for a place to park. "Hey, there's something across the street. Hold on boys."

Pete pulled a U-turn in the middle of the street, which earned a honk from the vehicle behind him. Once he turned around, Pete shifted his car into reverse, eliciting another longer honk, this time from a BMW that was forced to brake and maneuver around him. Max rolled down his window, stuck out his hand, and flashed them the finger. Pete looked over at Max, unimpressed and not surprised. Max stared back at Pete and said, "BMW boy just needs to know who's boss."

"Excellent start to the evening," Pete responded sarcastically and slipped the car into the parking place.

The three friends got out of the car saying nothing more. Max walked between them and put his arms over their shoulders and declared, "It's time to get fucked and fucked up."

Lake of the Woods, OR, USA

Emily Dwyer sat motionless in her rocking chair beneath the overhang of a rustic cedar deck, her breathing was slow and shallow. A frayed gray flannel blanket covered her legs and a purple sweater with threadbare elbows draped from her upper body. The crack of a twig grabbed her attention and her eyes slowly turned to seek the cause of the sound. She stared down a well-worn dirt path which ran towards a waterfront dock, but whatever had caused the disturbance was not to be found. Her attention refocused on the lake which was gray and placid with impending rain hanging in the air. Months earlier the high-mountain lake would have been alive with activity and the air full of the sound of children and families at play. The cool fall afternoon had largely vanquished what few neighbors remained to the warmth of the indoors. Emily's husband Jacob had taken their girls, Ashley and Cindy, into town to run a few errands. Normally both girls would be in school back in Portland by now, but Emily had asked Jacob for the family to visit the lake while there was still time. A sudden gust of wind set the brittle autumn leaves into a chatter as if trying to share one last story with her. Emily closed her eyes and listened to the songs of nature playing all around.

Her earliest memory of the lake was when she was four. Her parents brought her and her brother to visit with aunties and cousins at their cabin, built years before by her grandfather. Each morning her father quietly woke her to make their way to the MasterCraft ski boat anchored on the dock. Too young yet to water ski, she sat next to her father with her hair whipping in the wind as her aunts skimmed the water one after another. The rest of the day she basked in the warm summer sun, alternating between naps on a cedar chaise lounge and dips in the crisp water of the lake. Vividly she recalled the aroma of her mother's fresh waffles made as a late afternoon treat. Heaping scoops of Tillamook French vanilla ice cream sandwiched between them, melting drop by drop onto the dock. As evening approached, the family retired to the cabin for showers and dinner. The adults dined in the oversized living room and the cousins around the corner giggling endlessly at the kids table in the kitchen. After cleaning up from dinner, board games and cards would almost always follow. But it was the night sky that filled her early imagination with what endless possibilities existed beyond this world. After gazing up at the heavens for four decades, the stars still made this place feel spiritual for her.

Emily opened her eyes and the ghosts of her past lingered for a moment upon the emerald landscape. She turned, ever so gently, in the direction of the empty gravel driveway. She watched as a bird landed and meticulously picked through the pebbles. She remembered her parents' station wagon parked in the same spot, covered in the sticky sap from the canopy of trees that surrounded the cabin. She glanced further up the driveway where her grandparent's Winnebago parked in the same spot every summer to provide overflow sleeping accommodations. After a few minutes the bird flew away and Emily returned her attention to the lake, a tear welling in the corner of her eye. She scanned the horizon and watched the countless pines sway as if silently declaring their victory of attrition.

Years of family trips paraded themselves in her mind in an instant. She recalled watching nervously as Ashley in her life jacket crawled along the dock. Emily's desire for carefree lake-side lounging all but a memory with her duties as a mother. Her mind jumped to Ashley and later Cindy on early morning boat rides of their own. She could still feel the joy of teaching Ashley the proper technique to get up on her water skis. There were the long hikes through the endless trails leaving all of them oblivious to the time of day. The recollection of Ashley's incredible ability to win repeatedly at cards each evening was her earliest indications of her daughter's intellect and instincts. Even as a parent it was the star gazing at night which was her most vivid memory. It was her favorite way of sharing her love with her girls. Ashley's belief that the mysteries of the universe were ours to know if we could only find a way to reach further, taught her there is so much to learn from our children when we only stop to listen. She yearned for the opportunity to watch her girls one day bring their children to stare upon the heavens. Emily's tears finally broke free with the regret it would be a moment she would never experience.

She stared at the fire pit where the previous night the four of them had made s'mores. In reality, Cindy and Ashley had done most of the work. Jacob had held Emily close, ostensibly to warm her, but the unspoken truth was that another autumn together was not in the cards. Emily had watched the girls giggling as the marshmallows blistered and browned. Cindy artfully propped the chocolate near enough to the fire to soften but not melt it. She assembled and proudly presented her mother with the first s'more of the night. Emily joyously bit into the treat, but could only enjoy a small piece before her lack of taste and appetite prevailed. She tried to hide the evidence but she could see the concern on Ashley's face as the desert went uneaten.

As Emily reflected on her family moving forward without her, she knew Ashley was the least of her concerns. Ashley had blossomed in middle school and found herself. Starting on the U-14 girls' select soccer team had brought her focus and a great group of girls with whom to share the unfairness of the situation. She hadn't yet dated, or at least Emily didn't think she had. Ashley was that rare, young teen blessed with girl next door good looks and the confidence of her self-value that comes with being connected to others.

Cindy was still young, only in the third grade. Her social orbits away from mom and dad had only begun to lengthen when the gravity of Emily's situation caused Cindy to spend little time away from her mom. It would deprive Cindy of a mother at a time when most girls begin to fully adopt and reflect their mother's behaviors. She had the spirit of an artist which Emily thought must have been a recessive gene passed on from generations long forgotten. For being so young, her wordplay and songs captivated Emily and Jacob even if sometimes the meaning was lost on them. Her heart was large and often she was the one consoling her parents. Jacob had taken long lunches with Cindy, their conversations inevitably returning to the vagaries of life. And as much as Emily appreciated their time together, there were just lessons that mothers shared with their daughters that would never be hers to teach.

But it wasn't either of the two girls that worried Emily the most. Jacob was more than Emily could have ever hoped for when they married. Even as she dealt with her bouts of depression and occasional poor choices with alcohol, he never left her side. Could Jacob let go and move on she wondered? Still young and with so many years ahead; how long would he punish and deprive himself of the chance to share life with another soul? She tried many times to discuss this with him but he shut her down as he said he wanted to treasure every moment with her. Letting any other woman enter his thoughts was too much, but deep down she knew it scared him.

Emily stared out on the lake, watching as the rain fell. Still lost in her thoughts, she recalled Jacob's first trip to the cabin, back when she called herself Emily Birch. Her parents needled her over her obvious infatuation. They had enjoyed a day, not that different from any other summer day at the lake. But on that day, she knew she had brought home the man she would marry. They were getting ready to take the boat out for an afternoon trip when the rain started. Instead, they escaped to the cabin and snuggled under a gray flannel blanket her mother had just bought. Beneath the blanket, Jacob's hands were restless with the energy of a new relationship. Emily's giggles led her parents to ask with faux naivety, what jokes they were whispering in each other's ears. The memory caused her cheeks to blush now just as they had that day.

It was raining harder now. The temperature had dropped and the air heavy which pulled her from her memories. She watched rain droplets hit the lake with increasing intensity leaving unbroken ripples in their wake. Each drop became part of the larger body of water, impossible anymore to distinguish from its origin. She felt deep sadness as the thought triggered a recognition she could not think of herself as one individual but part of a profound relationship. Her love with Jacob changed forever who she was. Yet in embracing death, it had forced Emily to recognize that she would have to face the unknown alone. No matter the strength of any relationship that moment of crossing over was one's alone to ponder and prepare.

Emily desired the energy to find her phone in the cabin. She wanted to listen to music and blissfully play back the soundtrack to her life. Something as trivial as forgetting to move her phone a mere ten feet had become a matter of profound difficulty. What if Jacob had decided to text? Or maybe she would want to listen once more to the voicemails she saved. They chronicled the sweet nothings he was fond of leaving for her. She had long ago lost his first message after meeting by chance at the Blue Moon on NW 23rd street in Portland. Jacob had been so hopeful she would answer so he could ask her out. But Emily was so flustered she forwarded his repeated calls straight to voicemail. Left with no choice he finally poured his heart out in a message and desperately waited for her reply.

The storm was heavy enough now that puddles formed and the lake seemed to vibrate from the rain bouncing on the surface. The old metal roof echoed from the downpour and Emily strained to hear much else. The other side of the lake disappeared in the storm's mist. Emily turned once again to see if her family has returned, this time worried about their safety. She set her feet to get up and find her phone. She anchored her hands into the armrest and pushed. The world spun around her and she let go of her grip and instead settled back into her rocker.

She remembered her grandfather's warning about the perpetual youth of the mind forced to grapple with the inevitable capitulation of the body. She'd become a prisoner of her body with no means of escape. She had desired to make love to Jacob with the fire and passion that audibly cracked the headboard. The tender love they shared was deeper than any time in their life, but to feel like a woman and allow Jacob to let loose with abandon was nothing more than a dream. Even something as simple as letting Cindy crawl into her lap and snuggle could only last for so long and almost always added a layer to the bruising on her thighs and chest. Regardless, the pain of lacking the physical side of love could never diminish one more moment of Ashley or Cindy's smile. Or to listen to Jacob breathe in the middle of the night. Or simply to hear "I love you" once again.

Emily took notice that the sound of the rain had ceased. She looked up and saw it was coming down in sheets. Perplexed, she strained to raise her head and understand where the sound had gone. She could feel the chill of the storm rising up her legs. Her breathing had become labored and she realized her oxygen deprived limbs were begging for more air.

Her thoughts returned to her parents. Her dad had perished in a car accident on highway 26 returning from a business trip to the coast. An impatient driver crossed over the center line to pass, instead bringing a sudden senseless end to both lives. But it was her mother's death of late stage kidney failure that became clear in this moment. Her family gathered around the hospital bed and her mother's recognition it was time to say goodbye. Emily would never forget her mother whispering "I love you" before she closed her eyes for the final time.

With a clarity that came but once and from some unknown source of knowledge, Emily knew she had reached her last moments. Like her hearing, her vision began to fail and the world took on a haziness as her eyes lost their focus. Agitation replaced what life remained in her beating heart as she wanted a chance to say goodbye to her family. She had written letters to be found, filled with hope and dreams but mostly love. But this was not fair, nor was it debatable. She strained to turn to the driveway, to see if she could find the girls once more. But the body had nothing left to give and she was left to watch the world fade before her. She could feel a great sleep upon her and was left with one thought. Perhaps a failing mind deprived her of the knowledge she was not alone but surrounded by her children. And with the last of her energy she mouthed, "I love you" with the desperation that Jacob, Ashley, and Cindy may have returned in time to share her final thought.

CHAPTER 2

Munich, Germany

Sunlight danced across Max's face as the wind bounced the half-closed Venetian blinds. Drool drenched his pillow as he slowly woke in the clothes he had worn to the Barschwein the night before. He let out a long, slow moan and grabbed his head. He closed his eyes and turned away from the window. The muffled sound of a television coming from somewhere in the house caught his attention. Without opening his eyes, Max pulled his foot to his chest and took off his shoe, throwing it to the floor. He paused to catch his breath before removing his other shoe. Cautiously, he swung his legs off the bed and sat up, then bent over to rest his head between his knees. He wiped his face with his palm and ran his fingers through his hair. He looked around his bed and then the floor before saying to himself, "Fuck, my hat."

He got to his feet and slowly emptied his pockets onto the desk. His wallet, phone, and keys were followed by some loose change and a well-worn, unopened condom package. Max took his clothes off at a snail's pace letting them drop to the floor indiscriminately. He walked to the bathroom and turned on the shower before looking in the mirror. He had a military style buzz cut which usually gave him a regimented, clean look, but not this morning. He picked a bit of white fuzz out of his hair and was about to get into the shower when there was a knock on the door.

"Max, are you alive in there?"

Max rolled his eyes and yelled back, "Hopping into the shower, Mom." The volume of his own voice caused him to wince in pain. He opened the medicine cabinet and rummaged around for a remedy.

"I'm heading out to the market. Don't forget it's Dad's birthday."

Max whispered to himself, "Shit," before moving toward the bedroom door so that he wouldn't have to yell. "I'm meeting Dad for drinks later."

"Oh, OK Sweetie. I love you!"

"Love you too Mom," he replied and then stepped into the shower.

Max stood in the shower for a good 20 minutes, maybe longer, using the heat and pressure of the water to induce his head to stop throbbing. He emerged feeling better. The bathroom was full of steam and the mirror fogged. Max tied his towel around his waist. He walked back into his bedroom and grabbed his phone.

"Shit," he said, seeing that it was dead.

He fumbled through his desk drawer and found his charger. He plugged in his phone and laid down on the bed. For a few minutes, he stared at the ceiling and then fell back to sleep.

A few hours later, Max woke to his phone ringing. He rolled over and grabbed it. "Dad" was on the caller ID. He glanced at the time and shouted, "Fuck," before answering.

"Hey Dad, be right there," he said before the caller could speak.

"I was worried you had forgotten me," said the voice on the other end.

"I'd never forget you on your birthday," Max told his dad. "I just got tied up. I'll be there in about 25 minutes. Can you wait?"

"Ummm...sure," his dad replied. "You sure the time still works?"

"Of course, Dad. I just got busy."

"Ok. I'll see you soon."

"Yep, let me get done here and I'll be right there."

"Love you Max," his dad said as Max hung up on the call.

Max went to his closet and dressed quickly. He put his phone, wallet and keys back in his pockets and threw the loose change and condom into his desk drawer. He opened his bedroom door and looked for his mother, forgetting she'd said she was stepping out.

"Mom?" he yelled.

He looked through the house and didn't find her. While in the kitchen, he grabbed a biscuit and started eating it as he walked out the front door.

After a short walk Max approached his dad's favorite pub. He opened the door to Baal and took a deep breath. It was a cozy venue, considered a favorite with locals for having quality service and thousands of books to read. Max looked around the dark wood interior before finally seeing his dad, and waved. Franz Hoffmann was at the horseshoe-shaped bar, dressed in a tweed jacket, dark pants and brogues. Max approached his dad and gave him a hug.

"Happy Birthday, Dad" Max said.

"Thank you, Max," he said. "Sit down." Franz removed the napkin he had used to hold the stool for Max.

Max sat down and looked around the room. "See anyone you

know?" Franz asked when he had his son's attention again.

Max chuckled, "Just a habit. Not likely in here."

"I imagine not," his dad replied. "Probably too many books on these walls for your liking."

Max looked at him disapprovingly.

Franz put his hand on his son's back, warmly, "I don't think that came out the right way."

Max relaxed and smiled. "Is that a Krombacker, Dad?"

Franz returned the smile and answered, "Of course, would you like one?"

"Hell yes, but the beers are on me tonight," Max said. "Happy Birthday!"

Franz motioned to the bartender. "Lars, can I get a Krombacker for Max?"

Lars was Franz's age and had the look of a man committed to a life behind the bar. Wearing a white shirt and dark pants, he was a tweed jacket away from being a professor. He turned to see Max and bellowed, "Look who the cat dragged in."

Lars extended his hand and gave Max a firm handshake. "You're here to celebrate the old man's birthday, he tells me."

Max nodded his head. "Absolutely. I wanted to make sure he felt every day of 51 with his attractive son drinking with him."

Lars grabbed a half-liter glass. Angling it below the tap, he pulled the handle. When the glass was half full, he tilted it upright, and continued pouring, finishing with an inch of head. He handed the beer to Max. "How's the construction job going?" he asked.

Max lifted his glass toward his father. "Prost!" Max and Lars said in unison, clinking their glasses. Looking his father in the eye, Max took a drink before turning and answering Lars.

"I'm working at the airport now," he said, taking another drink "The construction business is full of idiots."

Lars laughed. "Damn, it's been a while since you've been in here," he said. "Your poor dad is running out of books to read. You should join him more often. Be a good son."

Max shook his head, "I get to see him every day at home. I think he escapes to this place to get away from me."

Franz quickly defended himself, "Now that's not true. Max may live in my house, but I never see this boy other than when he's sleeping off work or beer."

Lars did a quick scan of the bar. "I'm going to have to cut this short; we're busy tonight and I need to fill orders. I'll check back on the two of you. Just holler if you need anything."

They both raised their glasses. Franz turned his attention to Max. "How are things at work?" he asked.

"You know, same old, same old," Max said. "My boss is always complaining about how slow we are at doing our jobs, but then gets pissed when we put a bag on the wrong plane."

"I don't understand how that ever happens. Isn't everything scanned these days?"

Max laughed, "Yeah, but Dad, you do know, in the real-world, things don't work exactly, not like the perfection of University."

"Ha," his dad snorted. "I'm going gray from all the damn things that go wrong. But seriously, how does a bag get lost?"

Max took another drink of his beer, scanning the crowd carefully over the top of his glass before he replied, "Sometimes, the scanner picks up the bag next to it. Sometimes, the software reads it wrong. And sometimes, you're a bag away from break and you don't give a shit where the bag goes."

His father shook his head. "Well, despite all our problems at University, integrity is one we rarely have to deal with."

Max felt the sting of his father's words hit his face. "Yeah, well, once again, I've disappointed the great professor."

"Stop that, Max," Franz said sternly. Softening he said, "You know that I love you so much. I just don't understand some of the choices you make."

Max dropped his head and shoulders over his beer and stared into the nearly empty glass with foam clinging to the side. "I can never live up to the perfect life you and Mom lead. And Lars wonders why I'm never in here..."

Franz sighed at the direction the evening was going. "Let's start again," he said. "What would you like to talk about?"

Max raised his head and looked at his father suspiciously. "How about we just lay off Max for a night?" and then changing the subject, he added, "What is Mom doing for you for your birthday?"

"I think she's planning on taking me to dinner and sneaking in a show, which is her gift more than mine," he laughed. "I've been at work so much in the last few months, I'd be surprised if she even gets me a card," he said, seriously.

Max was glad to move the focus off of him. "Are you and Mom having issues?"

"No," his dad replied. "Nothing like that. After 27 years together, she's used to the unpredictability of my schedule." He paused before continuing. "I've had some long days, but I'm working on something that could be quite amazing."

"Is it more of the that Society of Elders stuff?" Max asked.

Franz paused, looking at his son. "Well, if I was, you know I couldn't talk about it. But we are working on some amazing research. I think pretty soon I'll be able to have you over to the University and you can see for yourself."

"I don't know that the Technical University of Munich wants my type ruining the place," Max answered and took a drink of his beer. He waved at Lars and held up two fingers for another round.

"Now why would you say something like that?" his dad responded. "The team has always enjoyed having you visit."

"Uh-huh," Max muttered.

"Come on Max," Franz said. "You never know. You might find something there interesting. You might find your passion."

Max nearly spit out his beer, and choked on it instead. "I really doubt that they have much need for someone with my background except to clean up after all the smart people," he snapped at his dad. Lars brought two more beers and left them in front of the father and son without interruption.

"That's not true,' Franz said defensively. "You know, I work with this young guy out of Cambridge. No formal training. He had a friend working on one of our projects and this kid gets a crazy idea about how to approach it. He thought of a solution in a way all us 'smart people,' as you say, had not—and we'd been working on it for months. You never know Max, you might be surprised."

Max thought better than carry on his argument. He smiled sarcastically at his father. "Yes, I have to agree with the birthday boy; I would be surprised."

Franz jumped on the opportunity to turn the conversation. "Did you see that 1860 won two nil today? Perhaps relegation is not in the cards."

Max frowned. "I was hoping to be there today but I got busy."

"We should go to a game sometime," his dad suggested.

Max looked at his dad, then turned his head and looked at him out of the corner of his eye, "Are you serious?" he asked, incredulous.

"Absolutely," his dad said resolutely. "Don't you understand how much I love you, Max?"

"Dad, I know this. I just don't think you like me very much. I don't think you're very proud."

Franz leaned far back, momentarily forgetting he was on a stool and waved his arms to catch his balance. Once he had gathered himself, he raised his beer to toast, touched by his son's honesty.

"Let me reply to that, in a way you'll understand," he said, hoping they might see eye to eye on this confession. "A toast to my amazing son, who always makes me proud to be his dad."

Max smiled. Was he blushing? He wasn't sure. He raised his glass in return. "To my Dad, happy birthday to the most amazing man I know. May I, someday, make him prouder than his Society of Elders."

Franz shook his head but smiled. They clinked glasses and both took a long drink.

"Lars," Franz bellowed, catching the bartender's attention. "My son is driving me to drink tonight!"

Portland, OR

It was a brilliant fall day in the Pacific Northwest. Not quite as showy as New England, Oregon still put on a spectacular display. Big-leaf maples, the "King of the Northwest wood-

31

land," dropped their yellow and gold leaves which now carpeted both trails and sidewalks. The sunlight had softened and the temperature hovered in the upper 60's. These were the days locals didn't talk about, the dry days in the fall when the golden larches and vivid scarlet native huckleberry drove people to the mountains. This was the beauty they kept to themselves, preferring to propagate the myth of endless rain that discouraged outsiders from moving to this amazing and unique corner of the world.

Jacob sat on the couch in his bedroom, wound tightly with his daughters - what Emily used to refer to as a "puppy pile." The bedroom door opened and Emily's brother Wes walked into the room. Jacob's heavy eyes observed Wes. "Is everything OK?" he asked his brother-in-law.

"I was about to ask you the same thing," Wes replied.

Jacob struggled to force a smile, aware that it was more of a wince. "Just sharing stories about their Mom with the girls," he said.

Wes walked over to the couch and knelt down, placing his head at eye level to the girls. "Did your Mom ever tell you about the time we baked brownies for your grandpa?"

Cindy partially unwound herself from her father and looked at her uncle to answer, "No. What happened?"

Wes winked at her and began. "We wanted to show him we were all grown up. So, we decided to make brownies for him, which he loved. Now to be clear, we were pretty young and making brownies from a box but it was still a pretty big deal for us."

Ashley turned her head toward her uncle. "What happened?" she asked.

Wes looked at Jacob and then back to the girls. He smiled

before he continued, "So we pre-heated the oven, mixed all the ingredients in the glass pan, and put it in to bake, just like the box told us. Then we sat down for dinner. After dinner was over, we cleared the table. We were so excited for warm and gushy brownies! The timer went off to tell us the brownies were done. Your mom opened the oven. She put the brownies on the stove top to cool. I grabbed a knife to cut the brownies...and you'll never believe what happened."

Cindy was sitting up now in anticipation. "What?" she asked, all breathy.

"Well," Wes continued, looking at Cindy, then Ashley and back to Cindy, drawing out the suspense. "I couldn't cut the brownies."

"What do you mean you couldn't cut the brownies?" Ashley asked.

"That's exactly what your grandpa said! He couldn't believe we couldn't cut warm brownies, so, he stood up from the table and said he'll show us how. He started to cut--and he couldn't do it either; he couldn't cut the brownies. We checked the box, thinking we'd cooked them too long. It was your mom who realized what we'd done wrong-- we forgot to add water to the mix. We basically baked grandpa a brick."

"Is that true, Dad?" Cindy asked.

Jacob shrugged and made his eyes big

Wes finished with a chuckle, "It was so bad, we had to throw the brownies away—pan and all!"

Jacob was surprised to hear himself laugh. "That was one of your mom's favorite stories."

Cindy pressed herself back into her father and he wrapped his arms around both girls, pulling them closer.

Wes looked at Jacob. "Linda has lunch downstairs when you're ready."

"I'm not sure how hungry I am but it's probably good to eat something," he said over the girls' heads.

"What did Aunt Linda make for us?" Ashley asked.

"Your favorite, mac and cheese and chicken bites," Wes told her.

Jacob smiled warmly, "Thank you, Wes, for your help. Are you settled in OK?"

Wes patted Jacob on the knee, "We are great. The guest room is lovely as always, and Cooper loves the sleeper sofa in the basement." He turned to Ashley. "Ashley, Cooper says that the two of you are best friends, is that true?"

She smiled. "Yes," she said shyly.

"Do you know if my parents are in town yet?" Jacob asked Wes.

"Linda said that your sister called a while ago and all three of them are checked into the Heathman downtown," Wes informed Jacob. "They should be here soon."

"Is he talking about Aunt Carolyn?" Cindy asked.

"Yes, that's right," Jacob answered, "She's taking care of them, to make it easier around here for all of us."

"Speaking of easier," Wes interrupted, "Can I help any little girls get cleaned up for lunch?"

"I don't need any help," Cindy protested.

Wes put up his hands to signal retreat, "Right, right—I'm sorry I thought you might." He paused and looked to Jacob, "Should I tell Linda a couple minutes?"

Jacob nodded and patted the girls on the back. "Let's go girls, get cleaned up and let's meet downstairs."

Cindy and Ashley unclutched their father and stood up. Slowly and holding hands, they left their parent's room and moved down the hallway. Wes reached out a hand to Jacob and helped him up from the couch. He put his arms around Jacob and said quietly, "I'll always be thankful she chose you."

Jacob hung on Wes for a moment. "Thank you, Wes," he said before straightening.

The two men headed downstairs and into the kitchen. Jacob went directly to Linda and hugged her.

"Thank you for lunch. And the laundry. And the cleaning. And..."

Linda interrupted him by putting her finger over his lips. "Enough. We are family. You would do the same for us." She hugged him.

"I know, but..." Jacob said. Linda let him go and waved her finger at him lovingly. "Shoosh," she admonished.

They sat down to the table for lunch. The conversation was limited to praise for the mac and cheese and comments about the weather; everyone's thoughts were elsewhere. Finally, Jacob looked at the time on his phone. "We should probably start getting ready," he said.

Linda looked at her watch. "Why don't you and the girls get ready. We can get everything cleaned up here."

"Are you sure?" Jacob asked.

"Go on," Wes answered, "we've got this."

Jacob took a deep breath in and let it out slowly. He seemed to do a lot of sighing these days. "Thank you," he said to both Linda and Wes before turning to the girls. "Ash and Cindy, why don't you go upstairs and get dressed? We have to leave soon."

"Is it that time, Dad?" Ashley wondered aloud.

Jacob looked lovingly at his daughter. She has Emily's eyes, he thought. "It is," he told her.

The two girls went reluctantly upstairs, followed by Jacob. They walked slowly, delaying the inevitability of the afternoon. Jacob went to his room and on to the master bathroom where he undressed slowly. His suit was hanging on a hook on the back of the closet door. He found a dress shirt, took it off its hanger, put the shirt on and started to button it as he returned to the bathroom. He pulled on his slacks and tucked in his shirt before looking at himself in the mirror. He glanced down at the second sink and the small scallop-edged dish with its contents of earrings and a necklace. He sighed and walked back to his closet to find a tie. Slowly, he started to build a knot, but the length was too short. He pulled it apart and tried again. This time the knot was lopsided. His hands trembled at the third attempt and when the tie's tail fell below his belt, he undid the tie and started to cry. He was tired of having to repeat mundane tasks. Besides, it had always been Emily, even juggling a cup of coffee and a bowl of cereal, who would tie his ties.

Ashley walked into the bathroom dressed in a beautiful short sleeve, choker neck deep purple dress. He caught her image in the mirror and turned toward her. "What's wrong Daddy?" she asked, seeing his tears.

"I can't get this tie right," he said, looking down at the tie in his hands, hoping to draw attention away from his face. "Your mom always did it for me."

Ashley came over and stroked his hand. "Can I give it a try?"

He looked at his daughter with uncertainly but handed her the tie. She told him to sit on the edge of the bathtub and set about wrapping the tie around his neck. Slowly she built the shape of the knot and finally pulled it tight.

"Can you stand up, Dad?" she asked gently.

As he did, he caught their image in the mirror. The tie was perfect. He took her hand and squeezed it tightly. "So much like your mom," he said.

He let her hand go so that he could pull on his coat and shoes. As he pulled his shirt cuff from his jacket, he looked at his watch. "We need to get going," he said. "Will you please go find Aunt Linda? I'll make sure Cindy is ready to go."

When Jacob went into Cindy's room, she was sitting on her bed, talking to her favorite stuffed rabbit. He couldn't make out what she was saying before she became aware he was there and stopped her conversation.

"Hi, Dad," she said quietly.

"Hey kiddo, whatcha up to?"

She turned back to her rabbit and replied, "Just having a conversation with Hoppy".

Jacob came next to the bed and squatted in front of her. "What are the two of you talking about?"

"Oh, we were talking about how he is going to be my best friend forever. He says he will never leave me," she said matter of factly.

Jacob swallowed. He reached out and stroked the toy. "Is Hoppy missing mommy?"

Cindy looked sadly at her father, "Um hmm," she said. "We're sad she didn't say goodbye... to him," she added.

"I see," he started. "That is sad."

Through all of his feelings of sorrow, Jacob was finding it hard to think of the right thing to say.

He turned away from her momentarily. He bit his lip as tears made their way to his eyes. He closed his eyes and hoped they'd dry, before turning back to the little girl.

"I love you, Daddy," Cindy offered tenderly. She scooted off her bed and gave him a hug that toppled them both. Jacob pulled her closer and was overwhelmed by sadness, not just for what he had lost but for what his daughters had lost as well.

"I love you soooo much, Cindy," he said, drawing out the word. Jacob felt tortured by both love and loss.

Cindy looked at her dad in the eye. Using her chubby fingers, and a bit too much pressure, she wiped the tears off his face. "Daddy, why did mommy go away without saying goodbye?"

Jacob pressed his forehead to hers and answered, "Mommy didn't know when the time would come sweetie. But she wanted to say 'good-bye,' which is why she wrote all of us the notes we read last night."

Cindy considered his answer. "I know, but she didn't write one for Hoppy."

Jacob pulled her tightly to him. "She wrote your note for both of you" he said.

"OK," Cindy said, once again a believer in all good things.

"Your mommy loved all of us - and Hoppy is part of everything she loved," he said. "I'll tell you what! Let's bring Hoppy with us."

He picked up the stuffed bunny and spoke directly to it. ""You are most welcome to join us today, Hoppy," He said before handing it over to Cindy. He turned and kissed her.

Wes appeared in the doorway. "Jacob, it's time to get going," he announced.

This was it, the irreversible moment that he'd been dreading all year. "We're coming," he said without moving. He felt like he was being sucked into a hole.

"Of course, Jacob," said Wes, hearing his pain. "We'll meet you downstairs." He turned and left Jacob and Cindy alone.

Jacob put Cindy down and took her hand. "Ready to go?" he asked.

"Daddy, do I have to wear this?" she asked, pointing at her black dress. "Mommy and I love my red dress better. Can I please wear that dress?" she pleaded.

Jacob paused to consider. "Cindy, it's a custom to wear a dark dress to a funeral."

"Why?" Cindy asked. "Mommy would like it so much better. Cooper says she's in heaven and looking down at us."

Jacob shook his head at her tenacity. He was also frustrated that Cooper had brought up heaven. Jacob hadn't spoken in such terms to the girls. "Well, sweetie," he started, choosing to address God before dresses. "We don't know for sure what happens when people die. Some people, like Cooper and his family, believe that you go to heaven, but we can't be certain."

Cindy tilted her head to the side, trying to figure out if this meant she did or didn't have permission to wear the red dress.

Jacob could see the wheels turning in her eight-year-old brain. "OK," He said, "but make it quick."

Cindy let go of his hand and immediately threw off her black dress. She grabbed the red dress out of her closet and Jacob helped her put it on.

"You look beautiful, Cindy," he told her. "Good choice."

"Thank you, Daddy," she replied.

"OK, sweetie, it's time to get going," Jacob said. "Let's go find your sister. I think our car is waiting outside."

Holding hands, Cindy and Jacob walked downstairs. Wes and Linda were waiting, along with Ashley and Cooper.

Jacob asked, "Is the car here?"

Wes answered quickly, "Yes."

Without looking at anyone and with eyes straight ahead, Jacob said, "OK, it's time to do this."

All six people walked out the front door. Jacob was the last to get in the stretch limo. He sat next to Linda. Cindy moved to be closer to her dad.

"I want to sit next to daddy," she declared.

Jacob put his arm around Cindy, "OK," he said.

He looked over at Ashley, who was having a conversation with Cooper. The car started to move and Jacob watched the house disappear from view. He felt the autumn sun dancing on his face as it darted between pine needles and tree leaves. The cadence of trees going by created a lullaby and he slowly closed his eyes. For a moment, his grief left him, as his heart found a place to hide. He dreamt of his wedding day; the joy of that occasion. The garden roses in Emily's hair. How beautiful she looked in her strapless dress and veil. It was perfect, as if the Universe had said, "Love is the boundless possibility of what can be." Jacob could see her smile, and then his grief re-emerged and his body flinched awake.

Linda felt his body jump and asked, "Are you OK?"

"'Til death do us part," he recited.

Linda put her hands around his arm and grabbed tightly. "I'm so sorry, Jacob. We are all sorry."

Jacob mouthed, "I know," and then said out loud, "I just expected a long life ahead of us. Now I won't see her again, or hold her, or hear her tell us she loves us. I don't know..." he choked, "...what am I going to do?"

Before Linda could reply, Cindy interrupted, "Here, Daddy," she offered. "Hoppy says he wants to sit by you," and placed Hoppy on Jacob's lap. He pulled Cindy tightly into his side and kissed her on the forehead.

London, England

The chime announced the elevator's arrival at the 36th floor. Wilma and Olivia Stone exited and walked to the B&R Solicitors office. Wilma wore a black sheath dress and jacket with little in the way of accessories. Olivia had opted for a smart red jacket and skirt and a white blouse, casual, with just a hint of tradition. Both of them wore black heels although Olivia's appeared to have at least two inches on her mother's. Olivia held the office door open for her mother and they both walked up to the receptionist.

"Hello, welcome to B&R Solicitors, my name is Penny Smith," the receptionist said warmly. "How may I help you this morning?" She wore her long hair in a bun on the back of her head and sported a conservative black business suit.

"Good morning Ms. Smith. I'm Mrs. Wilma Stone and this is my daughter Olivia. We have an appointment with Percy Roberts."

"Thank you, Mrs. Stone. Mr. Roberts has been expecting you."

Penny stood up from the desk and led them down the hallway into a conference room. The room held a dark round table, and around the table were a half dozen leather chairs on wheels. On the table was a speaker phone. Pictures of various famous landmarks hung on the walls. A credenza held a pot of coffee and coffee cups as well as ice water and glasses. Below the counter was a mini refrigerator with a glass front revealing soft drinks and bottled sparkling water.

"Please have a seat and help yourself to some beverages. Mr. Roberts' assistant is out of the office at the moment. I will let Mr. Roberts know that you have arrived. It should be just a moment."

Wilma nodded her head. "Thank you, Ms. Smith."

Olivia walked to the window and looked out at the city. It was a simple room with a nice view. Wilma took a seat and beckoned to Olivia, "Please come sit down. You've seen the same view from our offices. I need you to be focused and help me with this meeting."

Olivia turned her attention to her mother. "Of course. What has you worried?"

Olivia took a seat beside her mother.

"There is just something odd about all this," Wilma answered. "Your father and I..., well, we shared everything. Why would he keep a secret like this from me? And if it's some scheme, why would a prestigious law firm such as this get caught up in it?"

Olivia put her hand on top of her mother's. "Mom, in my entire life, I've never seen anyone pull anything over on you. I have complete faith that we'll figure out what's going on."

A door they had not noticed in the wall panel opened and Mr. Roberts entered the room. He went directly to Wilma and extended his arm to greet her.

"Mrs. Stone, it is such a delight to see you this morning. Thank you for coming."

Wilma shook his hand, without getting up. "It is nice to see you as well."

Mr. Roberts stepped behind Wilma to greet Olivia. They shook hands and then he took a seat across the table from the women.

"Mrs. Stone, I don't wish to delay matters any longer. Shall we begin?"

Wilma looked around the room. "I thought your client was meeting us here today? Is that not why we came to your office this morning?" she asked.

Mr. Roberts nodded his head rapidly, "Yes, quite right. I'm sorry if it causes any alarm but my client will be joining us by phone. He has multiple investigations similar to yours. They require him to be away a great deal of the time. Unfortunately, he's unable to be here in person this morning."

Wilma looked at Olivia who said, "Let's see what he has to say. We aren't going to be forced to sign anything against our will. Are we, Mr. Roberts?" she said, more as a statement than a question.

"Certainly not, Ms. Stone. Our firm has a long history of integrity. As I've said, if at any point these matters are not resolved to your satisfaction, you are free to engage your lawyer. Might I remind you, however, that we are not yet satisfied about your lawyer's role in this matter. I do hope by the end of this call we'll have clarity."

Wilma leaned forward toward Mr. Roberts and said firmly, "Sir, it is only the professional courtesy your firm has earned which keeps me here. Let me be clear: I'll suffer no fools and your client is on a short rope and limited time at the moment."

"I understand. Let me dial in to the conference call and see if we can't resolve these matters to your satisfaction."

Mr. Roberts pressed numbers on the key pad and the phone began to ring. A male voice answered.

"Hello, is this Percy?" the voice asked.

"Yes, John, this is Percy Roberts. I'm joined by Mrs. Wilma Stone and her daughter Ms. Olivia Stone. Ladies, let me introduce Mr. John Waters from the private investigation firm of Endeavour Search."

"Wilma and Olivia, I am very glad to meet you. I am so sorry that I can't be there today to meet you in person. My work has brought me outside the city, but I believe I can come right to the point."

Wilma pulled the speaker phone closer to her. If John Waters had been in the room, she might have been tempted to grab him by his lapels. "Thank you, Mr. Waters, and I do appreciate you coming straight to the point. Also, I would also appreciate if you would refer to me as Mrs. Stone."

"My apologies, Mrs. Stone. I will of course address you as you wish."

Mr. Roberts jumped in, "Thank you, John." He didn't attempt to restore the phone to its original place and instead leaned forward and addressed Wilma and the speaker. "I've shared with Mr. Waters your confirmation of the answer, in the envelope last night. He'll now walk you through what additional information he can provide and the next steps, if you choose to continue."

John proceeded, "Percy, thank you once again. Mrs. Stone, we have good reason to believe that your husband has left you fifty-seven million Pounds. The money is being held at the Bank of Hegwisch in the British Virgin Islands. From the information we have gathered, there are two beneficiaries. The first is you. The second, upon your death, is your daughter. If both of you were to be deceased, the challenges would have escalated, but as both of you are in good health, we haven't pursued other remedies. The transfer can be completed quite quickly by Mrs. Wilma Stone appearing in person before the bank president with the account and security information, along with proof of identity."

Wilma sat back in her chair and looked to the ceiling. She looked over at Olivia and took a deep breath. "This all seems appropriate, but please tell me why you've asked our lawyer to be excluded from this discussion?"

John answered quickly, "From what we have ascertained, your husband had some reason to believe that your family lawyer may have created a legal approach to deprive you of these funds. It appears your husband moved the funds just days before his death. Unfortunately, he passed away before he could share the information and reasoning with you."

Olivia leaned toward the speaker and introduced herself. "Mr. Waters, this is Ms. Olivia Stone Can you tell us how you've come upon this information? I'm surprised that we are hearing about this for the first time and that our lawyer has never mentioned missing funds."

The phone was silent. "John are you still speaking, if so we can't hear you?" Mr. Roberts inquired.

"Oh, excuse me," John came back. "I'm getting feedback on this end of the line and put the call on mute. To answer the first part of your question. Our firm's success is based on the value that we create for our clients. We spend countless hours searching through records and official documents to find opportunities such as this. While I can't disclose our specific approach, I can guarantee you that if you choose to claim the funds, there will be no issues. As for the second part...," there was another awkward pause. Olivia asked this time, "Mr. Waters are you still there?"

John was coughing as he answered, "Yes, sorry about that. I had something in my throat and needed a drink of water. As for the second part, we have reason to believe that your father left a nominal amount of money in the original account to appease your lawyer and keep him unaware of the larger amount you would be inheriting."

"Mr. Waters this is Mrs. Stone again. I think I understand why we've been asked to come here today. Assuming your assessment is correct, is this the point at which we have to negotiate your terms to have you release our money?"

John laughed. "I apologize for the laughter, Mrs. Waters, but that was very direct and not entirely fair. Yes, we would like to collect our percentage for the work we have done. We are asking for three percent of the recovered funds, which works out to just over one and half million Pounds. We believe that's reasonable."

Agitated, Wilma replied, "Why wouldn't I simply go to my bank and explain the situation myself? I am certain there is some remedy for demonstrating that I am the beneficiary and immediately claim rightful ownership of the account without having to validate personal information you plan to share with me?"

John replied seriously, "Mrs. Stone you may do just as you say; there's nothing to stop you. I will let your conscious be your guide on this matter. I have, in all goodwill, brought you an opportunity that will provide your family in excess of 54 million Pounds even after my fee—funds you were unaware even existed. I would also offer this caution: banks don't take kindly to unusual requests and I think you may find it will cost you at least my fee in legal expenses to recover the money. There is the additional risk that your family lawyer may insert himself into the transaction, further complicating the matter and reducing your proceeds even further. I would implore you Mrs. Stone, to consider our fee as well within reason and the surest way to receive this inheritance, which your husband went to great lengths to protect for you. We have, in essence, delivered a gift from beyond the grave."

Wilma stared at Olivia. Olivia glanced back at her mother and shook her head. Wilma sat back in her chair again and looked to the ceiling. She sighed, took a deep breath and fixed her gaze on Mr. Roberts.

"Well, Mr. Roberts. What is it that we do now?"

Mr. Roberts opened the manila folder in front of him. Had he been holding it the entire time; Wilma couldn't remember. He presented a legal document to Wilma.

"Knowing that your lawyer was not going to be present, I have prepared a simple contract--perhaps the simplest contract you may ever read in your life. Please take time to read it start to finish, but it quite simply states that you agree to pay a fee of three percent of the total amount you find in the bank account. Upon providing your signature, Mr. Waters will provide the account and verification information for the funds. Your obligation to my client is for that account and that account alone. I do believe this quite well protects your rights."

Wilma looked around the room. She stood up, went to the windows and looked out at the city. "Oh, Frank," she said to her reflection. "Why did you put me in this awkward place? I wish you were here to direct me."

"I think quite honestly, Mrs. Stone, he meant this to be a gift and not an imposition," Mr. Roberts said.

She frowned and turned to look at her daughter. Walking back to the table and not losing eye contact with Olivia, she said, "May I have a pen, please?"

Mr. Roberts handed her a pen. Wilma looked down to the

document and put the pen to the page.

"Hold on, Mom," Olivia shouted, grabbing everyone's attention.

"Mr. Waters, I find it odd that you have never once called our lawyer by name. Maybe it's by chance, but it seems that if the story about the lack of loyalty is true, you would know his name. Can you, and not Mr. Roberts, please tell me what is the name of our lawyer so that I can put my intuition to rest?"

After a moment, John answered, "Of course, Ms. Stone. As the work here is a compilation of the efforts of several members of our team, it is understandable that I don't know your lawyer's name offhand, but let me look through your folder and find it for you. Please hold for a moment."

Wilma put the call on mute and beamed with pride at her daughter. "You are going to make a fine head of this family one-day Olivia; well done, dear."

Olivia smiled slightly, preferring to maintain the power she felt she now had in the situation, but pleased nonetheless. "Thank you. Let's see what Mr. Waters has to say."

Roberts took the phone off mute, "John, we would like to move forward on this matter. Can you please confirm the name?"

"One moment Percy.... I'm looking... here.... there are several pages...."

The phone was quiet.

"John, is there a problem?" Mr. Roberts asked again.

"Sorry about that Mrs. Stone. I have it right here. Mr. Walter Francis of the law firm Francis and Son's."

Mr. Roberts looked at Wilma for confirmation and she nodded. She returned to the page and signed the document. She passed it to Roberts who counter-signed it.

"Mr. Waters, I can confirm that we have a signed contract. Now, if you please, will you provide me the account information so that I can enter it and initial the addition to the contract?"

John replied, "Congratulations, Mrs. Stone. Percy, it is 7 9 8 4...."

CHAPTER 3

Seattle, WA

Ashley stepped into RN74 restaurant and looked around the bar area to her left as she approached the hostess stand. She was in a dark blouse and pants with her hair in loose waves on her shoulders.

"Good evening, may I help you?"

"Hi. I'm meeting my family. The reservation is probably under Jacob or Cindy Dwyer?"

The hostess scanned her screen and then responded, "Here we go. They are already here. Let me show you to your table."

The hostess led her through the maze of tables, before arriving at a rounded booth in the back. Cindy bounced her bottom on the seat, before jumping out of the booth to hug her sister.

"Ashley! You look so grown up!" she exclaimed.

Ashley looked Cindy up and down. Cindy was still shorter than her. She wore a striped sweater, dark jeans, and casual flats.

"It's so good to see you! I did peek in on you last night but you were fast asleep." Ashley said.

"I know. I had soccer practice until late and then geometry. I tried to stay up. Why didn't you wake me up this morning?"

"I tried, but you were out--it was like trying to wake the dead!"

she teased back.

Her father stood to give her a hug. He had a thick beard, his hair had streaks of gray. He looked good, in blue jeans, a slim-fit shirt and sweater.

"Dad," she said, drawing out the word. "I've missed you all day."

He smiled and put his arms around her, "Good to see you again."

Ashley winked at Cindy and said, "Dad loved me enough to make me breakfast this morning before my interview."

"He's trying to balance the score with all the breakfasts and dinners he's made me since you left for school," she replied with a wink of her own.

Jacob interrupted the two of them, "I see that the sisters haven't lost a beat. C'mon," he said sitting down and patting the seat beside him. "Take a seat. I'm excited to hear about the interview."

"I am excited to tell you all about it, but I want to hear how high school is treating our freshman!"

Cindy couldn't contain her excitement, "Well, soccer season is almost over and we're leading the conference. And I'm getting A's in all my classes including the AP classes."

Jacob nudged Cindy, "Isn't there more you want to share?"

Cindy blushed and Ashley noticed. "Oh--there's boy news!" Ashley squealed "You stinker, you haven't said a word in all the times we talked. Tell me, tell me, tell me."

Cindy shot a glare at her father, "Dad!"

"You should have seen her in her homecoming dress. Stunning!" Jacob ended with emphasis.

"Dad!" Cindy practically shouted this time.

"I love it. My little sister is going on dates! So, give me details."

"Give us both the details!" Jacob echoed.

Cindy sighed, "It's not a big deal. We went with a large group and had a great time. Now tell us about your job interview!"

Ashley pursed her lips and looked at Cindy. "Okay, I'll let you off the hook. The interview went really well. I'll be working on some cutting-edge technology related to memory computing."

Jacob raised an eyebrow. "Are you working on the Elders project?"

"I'm not sure. I think it could be related. They said I wouldn't find out the details until I started the internship."

"So, you excited about the opportunity?" Cindy asked.

"I am. How about you, Dad? How's work going?" Ashley inquired.

Jacob replied, "It's been good. The company's been great about letting me work remotely. We are doing a lot of collaborative work with our partners."

The waitress arrived and introduced herself. "Good evening, my name is Molly and I'll be your server for the evening. Have you dined with us before?"

Jacob smiled, enjoying her energy. "No, Molly, this is our first time here, but we have heard nothing but great things!"

"I am glad you decided to join us. Our chef does such an amazing job with the menu and I highly recommend the tasting menu, if you have the time. Is there anything I can get you to drink while you look at the menu?"

Jacob looked for a response from his daughters and hearing none responded, "I think water will be great for the time being. Give us a couple minutes to order; we're enjoying a little family reunion."

Molly grinned, "Oh, that's wonderful! Water will be right over and I'll give you a little extra time to look over the menu."

"How's dating going?" Ashley bluntly asked her Dad. Cindy's eyes grew large and she stared at her father.

Jacob chuckled, "The same Ash. It's hard. I go out every now and then, but there hasn't been anyone outstanding."

Cindy interrupted, eager to change the subject and avoid the image of Jacob dating. "What's your favorite part of the University of Illinois?" she asked Ashley.

Ashley knew Cindy was trying to change the subject and obliged with an answer but kept watching her father. "It has to be the Greek system. Don't get me wrong, the engineering program is amazing and as hard as everyone said, but rushing was fun, I love my 'sisters' and I have a lot of friends in the fraternities too."

"Don't take your eye off the ball, Ashley, there will always be boys," Jacob commanded. Ashley didn't think it was fair that they could talk about her boyfriends but not about Jacob dating.

"I know that, Dad, but there will always be work too. I love you and I think you really need to be open to letting someone into your life," Ashley responded.

Cindy made a dramatic gesture of dropping her head to the table and looking back and forth at them as if she was watching two tennis players rally.

Jacob answered as he always did, "Ashley, I know you mean

well. I loved your mother more than you could possibly understand. I love her to this day. She made life easy."

Cindy couldn't help herself, "How did she make it easy? I don't remember things like that."

Cindy's question softened Jacob's countenance and he smiled with the opportunity to reminisce. "Cindy, I could be lost in the middle of a bad day and she could touch me or say a word that made it all better. I could be struggling to console you or Ashley and she would walk into the room and make you giggle. Your mother was an amazing woman."

"It's not fair that mom was taken away from us," Cindy whined. Remembering was still painful to her.

Jacob put his hand on Cindy's back, "Sweetie, there is little about life that's fair. It's how we respond that defines us."

Ashley's mouth dropped open. She was speechless at the irony of his statement.

"Don't say it, Ash," Cindy pleaded, lifting her head up.

Jacob's voice lost its softness. "Say what?"

Tentatively, Ashley said quietly, "This is why you should date, Dad. Embrace the possibility of what could be."

Jacob dropped his head and looked to Cindy to say anything.

Cindy's face was sad and she knew it would be hard for all three of them to take in what she said next. "It's not fair that the Elders came too late for mom."

Ashley sat back into the cushion her gaze across the restaurant unfocused. Molly took it as her cue that they were ready to order and came over to the table. Jacob couldn't decide whether her timing was perfect or lousy. "Have you decided?" she asked eagerly.

"You know, Molly, we haven't, but what brought us here was the tasting menu. Can we do that for the table? Oh, and I think this conversation needs the premium wine pairing," Jacob finished, trying to smile.

Molly gave a knowing look, "Now, you two girls aren't giving your dad a hard time, are you?"

Ashley jumped in, "We think he's the greatest! Sometimes we just need to tighten the string around his little finger to remember that."

"Dads love their girls. Let me go get this tasting menu started and I'll have some champagne out for you, sir." Molly took their menus and left them alone again.

"Dad," Ashley started but Jacob cut her off.

"Ash, I need you to stop," he said firmly. "I am happy for you and your possible internship. I'm not sure if you are purposely being vague about the Elders project. Frankly, I'm not sure that I want to know."

Ashley tried to interrupt, "I really don't know, Dad."

Jacob lifted his hand to signal for her to stop.

"I love you girls. I love you so much. I've worked hard to make my peace with what happened with your mom. One day, perhaps, I'll find that place in my heart to let someone else in. But I don't know if I'll ever find a way to rationalize the inequity of the Elders project."

Cindy muttered, "I wish Mom was part of the Elders. I miss her."

Jacob saw a tear run down her cheek and used his napkin to wipe it away.

He put an arm around both girls and pulled them close. "Girls,

I wish a lot of things were different, but that's not going to change anything. And here's what's also true—it has been months since I've had the chance to have dinner with both of my beautiful daughters. Can we talk about something else, like, what Ashley had to do as a pledge and whether Cindy kissed her boyfriend at the homecoming dance?"

"Dad!" Cindy objected.

A server returned with a glass of champagne and amuse-bouche for the table. Jacob let go of the girls and grabbed a fork.

Molly reappeared. "Enjoy!" she extolled.

Munich, Germany

Max walked past the security guard and down a dimly-lit hallway filled with stacked boxes and exposed pipes. Two men dressed in jumpsuits and reflective vests and carrying large orange ear protection walked into the hallway. Max used their exit to gain access and scooted in behind them into the room before the door closed. Inside, a flurry of men were changing in front of numerous gray steel lockers. Max maneuvered his way to a locker on the far side of the room. He entered his combination and started changing into his uniform.

A couple of lockers over, someone said, "Looking a little rough this morning."

Max continued getting dressed without looking over. After he pulled on his pants, he turned and glanced over without answering.

"Too cool to talk this morning?" his co-worker asked.

Max scowled before turning back to his locker to continue getting dressed.

Ignored, the man, now fully dressed in his uniform, slammed his locker and walked toward the door muttering, "Whatever."

Max finished dressing and headed out to the tarmac. He grabbed a clipboard and ran his finger down the sheet until it stopped on his name. He moved his finger sideways to the flight information and then back up the sheet to find Karl Schneider's name. Max grinned and he threw the clipboard on the table. He put on his sunglasses and walked to a 787 bound for Moscow. Karl was moving a luggage ramp into position as Max approached. Karl was a large man with tree trunks for arms and steel girders for legs. Today he stood out as the only one in shorts.

"Karl, you beast. How you doin'?" Max bellowed. Starting with his hand above his head, he offered a wide exaggerated hand shake.

Karl chuckled, "Fuck, Max. You smell like the love child of mouthwash and beer and you look like your momma left you behind in the forest."

Max glanced around. "Life's too short to be good," he replied. "And my old man headed out on a flight to the U.S., so there's no one to kick my ass. How about you?"

"Couldn't do it. I needed sleep."

"Are you getting soft on me?" Max ribbed Karl.

"Do I look like I'm getting soft?"

Max grinned and moved closer to the plane to find a buggy full of suitcases waiting to be loaded.

"Are you running the conveyor or heading into the belly?" Max asked Karl.

"I'm heading up. You load."

"However you like it."

Max pulled the protective screen of the buggy back and began loading bags onto the conveyor. As the sun started to fully color the sky, Max frequently wiped sweat from his forehead and stopped to catch his breath. After a good hour, and some last-minute bags, Max watched Karl lock the cargo area of the plane and walk down the conveyor to join him. The two of them walked back toward the staging area.

"Can you believe that fucking purple bag?" Max asked.

"You mean the body in a bag, suitcase?"

Max laughed, "Yea, that one. It must have cost some asshole a fortune to send it."

Karl shrugged, "Why do you care?"

"My back…" Max started to answer, before Karl interrupted him to say, "Management at your 2 o'clock."

Max looked to his right and frowned. Under his breath he said to Karl, "Shit, here comes trouble."

In his early 30's and short enough to look up to Napoleon, the man barked, "Max, I need you in the conference room for five minutes before you jump on the next plane."

Max rolled his eyes at Karl, who bit his lip hard trying not to laugh.

Practically hissing, Max answered, "You got it, Stephan."

Max gave one last glance and then headed toward the conference room followed closely by Stephan.

"Max, why don't you sit down?" Stephan requested as he closed the door behind them.

Max took a deep breath and glanced around the room.

"Max, you and I haven't always seen eye to eye, but one thing we have in common is neither of us are bullshitters."

Max snickered, "I'm not sure why you think you have that in common with me."

Stephan gave Max a pained look, ignored the bait and proceeded, "Listen, I have to give you notice that we're letting you go."

"What the fuck did I do?" Max protested.

"You didn't do anything. Management has decided to install some new robotics and eliminate a lot of the baggage handling. You've been here the least amount of time and so you're first to go."

"Shit. I can't believe you are doing this to me. I have rights."

Stephan's face showed no sign of softening. "It's not personal, but regardless, you're still in the probationary period so we have the right to make the decision and eliminate your position." He sighed and added, "If you want to make an issue about it, I can get safety out here and ask them to take a blow sample."

"Fuck you, Stephan. You sanctimonious ass. Good luck proving that shit." Max fired back.

"Listen, you can walk off the job today and not get paid. I'm giving you notice and the opportunity to make money for a little while longer. Call me what you want, but I'm doing what I can for you."

Max stood up and slammed his fist into the table. "The only reason I'm not hopping over this table to kick your ass is 'cause your sorry ass ain't worth going to jail for."

Stephan started to say something but stopped as Max continued, "I also know you don't have power to do shit. You're the goddamn messenger for the stiffs upstairs."

"Max," Stephan pleaded.

"Fucking robots. There's always someone coming to take your money and now they're bringing in goddamn walking toasters. They keep finding ways to fuck us, don't they?"

"Hold on Max," Stephan shouted.

"No, you hold on. I've got a plane to load and I'm going to go do my job. Just stay out of my way."

Max pushed his chair back violently and threw the door open. Stephan sat back in his chair and took a deep breath. He picked up his mobile phone and dialed.

"Hey it's me. I just talked with Max. You can call off security. The guy didn't lay a finger on me. I guess I was wrong on that one."

Champaign, IL

"I would like to thank members of the media for joining us today. My name is Claire Rodgers and I am director of communications for the Center for Artificial Intelligence here at the University of Illinois."

Tall, blond, and with the slightest hint of a Bronx accent, Claire was wearing a black pencil skirt and white blouse and stood behind the podium.

"Today's press conference will include research leaders from Cambridge and the Technical University of Munich, as well as the University of Illinois. Joining us from Cambridge will be Dr. Ernie Clark, leader of the Neurologic Intelligence Institute. From the Technical University of Munich will be Dr. Franz Hoffman, leader of the Digital Intelligence Department. And from the University of Illinois, Dr. Ralph Cummings from the

Center for Artificial Intelligence."

Claire turned her attention from the throng of reporters before her and looked off stage. A gentleman glanced over at the three men in sport coats and ties and then back to her. He gave a thumbs up and Claire turned to address the reporters once again.

"There has been much speculation around the world regarding the reason for today's press conference. I would ask that you hold your questions until the three professors have provided their opening remarks, at which time I will return to the stage to moderate a Q&A. I now would like to introduce Doctors Clark, Hoffman and Cummings."

Claire stepped back and left the stage, passing the gentlemen as they walked on stage. There was an eruption of camera flashes. The three men took their seats at a white-skirted table, behind microphones and name placards, and waited for the press to quiet before they began.

Dr. Cummings cleared his throat and started.

"I would like to thank Dr. Clark and Dr. Hoffman for traveling so far to join us. I would also be remiss if I did not share our appreciation for the neuroscience, neuroinformatics and connectomics researchers around the world that we work with every day. In particular, I would like to thank the staff at Stanford University, who have continued their good work since developing retention technology almost 15 years ago. I would also like to thank the researchers from Tsinghua University, Oxford, MIT, Swiss Federal Institute of Technology, the University of Chicago, the University of Toronto, and the University of Tokyo. Their work and insights have helped lead to a breakthrough that we're going to share with you today. There are many others at universities around the world that have also contributed. Their work will be cited in the materials we distribute immediately following this press conference."

Dr. Cummings paused for a moment and took a drink from a bottle of water on the table.

"Fifteen years ago, for the first time in the history of mankind, Dr. Walter Grandstone's research team at Stanford University established the first successful transfer of human conscious-ness to a silicon-based substrate. This work eventually led to the Society of Elders who remain in residence in Virginia. Since that time, the program has been plagued by unexpected losses of digitally-retained individuals and frequent corrup-tion of their retained consciousness. In short, we had more success at transfer than maintenance. Several improvements have been made, the most important having been around portability and atomic batteries, which have reduced mortal-ity risk. Despite the improvements, the losses have made the digital conversion expensive and difficult to predict.

"To address these issues, over the last five years Dr. Clark, Dr. Hoffman, and I have collaborated, leveraging the various expertise within our research labs to try to solve the prob-lem. Our efforts have resulted in an unexpected discovery. I thought it...," Cummings corrected himself, "I should say, we thought the right person to discuss this discovery is Dr. Hoff-man from the Technical University of Munich. So, without further ado, I'd like to introduce Dr. Hoffman."

Dr. Cummings smiled and motioned for his colleague to speak. Dr. Hoffman adjusted his microphone and began.

"I would like to reiterate my colleague's appreciation for the universities around the world that have contributed to this breakthrough. I would also ask for your patience as English is my second language. While I am hopeful my prepared com-ments are well written, once we move into Q&A, please toler-ate my translations.

"As Dr. Cummings alluded, we have made a discovery that is quite outstanding. In our efforts to reverse the degradation occurring at the atomic level of the silicon, we discovered interactions which were not completely random. As we delved deeper, we discovered patterns within the digital consciousness which were unexpected. Guided by our discoveries, we worked to refine the understanding of those patterns and were able to improve upon many of the problems we have experienced with the Society of Elders. It's one of the primary reasons for their increased digital life span that many have noted in the press."

Dr. Hoffman stopped for a moment and took a deep breath. He surveyed the assembled press and then smiled at his colleagues sitting beside him. Dr. Clark patted Dr. Hoffman on the back and whispered, "You got this, Franz." Dr. Hoffman's shoulders relaxed. He looked back at his prepared comments and began again.

"As those patterns were better understood and tools were developed for interacting with them, we started to recognize there were impurities at the atomic level. We were able, at a very high level of sensitivity, to extract those impurities and found further patterns in them. Some extraordinary insights from researchers at Cambridge led to a breakthrough in the last year. It all comes down to this: what we thought were impurities were in fact other consciousnesses -- individuals not previously captured prior to death."

A collective gasp filled the room. Dr. Hoffman glanced up from his notes distracted by the outburst.

"If I may please finish. Using technology developed here at the University of Illinois and in Munich, we were able to successfully collect the consciousness of someone who had died but whom had not digitally transferred."

The clamor in the room grew louder this time. A couple of reporters ran out the back of the room. There was a crescendo of questions being shouted from the press, rendering them all incomprehensible. Dr. Hoffman leaned forward to try to speak but the clamor in the room persisted. He looked toward Claire in the wing with a look of helplessness on his face. She moved deliberately and approached the podium.

"Ladies and gentlemen, there will be...," she paused for a moment as the volume of voices started to decline, "...there will be plenty of time for questions. If you could please let the professors complete their prepared statements."

The room grew quiet again. Dr. Hoffman's eyes grew large-- the television screens off stage, just past Claire, were broadcasting the news conference. His comments were going live, around the world. Claire motioned to him to continue. He drew a deep breath in through his nose, his chest visibly filling with air beneath his suit, and then he leaned toward the microphone to continue.

"I would like to introduce Dr. Clark to complete the prepared remarks. Dr. Clark."

Dr. Hoffman reached across Dr. Cummings and shook hands with Dr. Clark. Dr. Clark looked relaxed in front of the microphone and began to read his comments.

"I share my colleagues' thanks for everyone who has contributed to this amazing discovery. In my comments, I would like to further update you on our progress since the discovery that Dr. Hoffman just shared.

"Initially, many of the problems we experienced with the Elders program were magnified and we were unable to retain a collected consciousness beyond 60 to 75 minutes. However, over the last year, we have been able to stabilize the results and have now successfully retained numerous consciousnesses to the point we have been able to communicate and identify them."

Once again, a buzz of excitement broke out in the room. Dr. Clark leaned closer to the microphone.

"Please let me finish," he demanded and after a moment he was able to continue. "Faced with the moral and ethical issues of reconnecting these individuals with their families, we felt it was time to make this announcement. We do so to begin reunification. I should be clear, while this is quite exciting, the number of individuals for reunification, to date, is small. Further, how it is that these individuals come to us is quite random; we do not know when or who we will collect. And even once we do, the process of identification is complicated and takes some time. We are, however, starting to accelerate collections and believe that as our abilities improve so will our capture and retention rates. With that I open it up to your questions."

A sea of voices started shouting. Claire took control of the situation.

"Nancy King of the *New York Times*, the first question is yours."

"Thank you, Claire. While I have so many questions I would like to ask the obvious one first: Did these collected souls report whether there is a God?"

The room grew deathly silent. Dr. Hoffman spoke, "I'll answer that question. I am going to be disappointing on this point, no doubt. We have discussed this with a handful of individuals that have reached the point of being able to have this conversation. The simple answer is that we don't know."

Someone from the rooms shouted, "How can that be?"

"Let me finish," Dr. Hoffman begged, "They describe a state of being unlike anything they have experienced or frankly I think expected. They are uncertain about what they have experienced and struggle to find the vocabulary to explain it. Universally everyone speaks of happiness, but beyond that... beyond that...," he stuttered, ".... let me just say, we plan, in time, to make them available for some members of the press to interview. But you need to understand, our ability to fully understand post-death experience has been, to this point, incomplete because there have been few cases of someone coming back... having been collected through our process. More to come, I promise."

A roar of voices exploded. Claire picked out another reporter, "Bob Harris from the *Wall Street Journal*."

"Thank you, Claire. This is to any of the doctors. How certain are you that these individuals are, in fact, who they say they are?"

Dr. Cummings took the question. "We interview them when they are ready and collect salient details about their past. We then use those details to verify their authenticity. Now that this has become public, we plan to validate this further by completing the conversation with living family members."

The press corps erupted again with a chorus of questions and raised hands. Claire pointed, "John," she said.

"Thank you. John Marks from CNN. I can appreciate the science community's interest in a controlled process but aren't these collected souls begging to be reunited with their families?"

Dr. Clark spoke up, "Not in the way you would expect, John. We don't know—we can't answer with any certainty what exists on the other side, and yet, all these "souls" as you call them, exhibit a high degree of calmness. They do express a desire to reconnect, but you have to remember that for them time is different—it's a different dimension than our experience. I suspect with no body; their experiences are happening without the constraint of time as we know it."

Before they could work themselves up again, Claire picked out the next questioner. "Wendy."

"Thank you. Wendy Jones from Fox News. Doctors, can you explain to us exactly how this can be possible?"

Dr. Hoffman addressed the question this time. "As we know from the Elders program the consciousness becomes energy transferred to silicon. Post death we never understood what happened to that energy. Now we believe, by chance some of that energy found its way back into the silicon of some Elders' units. Once we realized what it was, it allowed us to actively pursue and try to collect these consciousnesses. A good analogy might be thinking of them as raindrops and we have developed the technology to find the individual rain drops in the lakes after they form. But if you are asking how they exist after leaving the body, we can't begin to answer that question yet."

His answer fanned the flame of questions.

"Fred Sanders from the *Washington Post*. We obviously won't be able to get all our questions answered here today. What resources will you have after this press conference?"

"I'll actually take this one," Claire responded. "We will be distributing a media kit as you exit. It includes instructions on how to arrange follow up conversations with the research teams. As in the early days of the Elders program, this will follow a methodical process. The protocols and governmental interactions set in that program still govern this work. This is being treated as an offshoot of that effort."

The reporters erupted once again. Dr. Cummings covered the microphone with his hand and whispered into Dr. Hoffman's ear. "I hope you ate on the plane; we're going to be here for a while."

CHAPTER 4

Wailea, HI

The early evening clouds over the Pacific Ocean exploded in orange and ginger hues as the sun neared the horizon. The hazy outline of the island of Lanai could be seen in the distance to the east, while Kaho'olawe's burnt red and brown hillsides sat much closer to the south. The later, a small island snake bitten throughout modern history. Mountains too short to create the conditions for rain like her cousin islands and the further indignity of having been used for shelling practice for much of the 20th century by the US military. On the grounds of the Grand Wailea Hotel, tiki torches were being lit by a muscular native Hawaiian, running barefoot and bare chested throughout the property carrying a burning torch of his own. The hotel's white sand beach and manicured wide bladed grass lawns were mostly desolate at this hour. White plastic chaise lounges cluttered with soiled pool towels were all that remained from hotel guests now back in their rooms cleaning up for dinner. Located in the heart of the property with a majestic view of the ocean was the hotel's chapel. Its stained-glass windows slowly came to life as the natural light of the day was being replaced by the church's interior illumination.

Cindy Dwyer beamed as she strolled through the meandering paths of the hotel with its lush tropical foliage. Pink plumeria, naupaka, and bird of paradise bushes surrounded the numerous man-made ponds filled with Koi fish. In her white, strapless, knee high dress and sandaled feet, she captured the attention of passing hotel guests. By her side, Ashley was dressed in a short, coral colored dress, but she was no longer taller than her baby sister. Cindy grinned as she approached the church and caught sight of her father standing out front. He was dressed in a white Hawaiian shirt and loose-fitting khakis with black sandals and smiled with pride at his first glimpse of his daughter. Excusing himself from a conversation, he strolled across the lawn to greet her. He put his hands on her shoulders as they met and paused for a moment to gather his emotions.

"My beautiful daughter, I can't believe that this day has finally arrived," Jacob said softly.

Cindy bowed her head. "Daddy, you're going to make me cry"

Jacob hugged his daughter before placing a kiss on her forehead. He turned and grinned at Ashley adding a wink for good measure. "You look magnificent yourself," he told her.

"Thank you, Dad. Where's Christine?"

Jacob twirled around and shouted, "Christine," raising his arm and motioning for her to join them.

A few years younger than Jacob and dressed in a dark blue sleeveless dress, Christine walked over to join them. Tall and thin, her blonde hair was long and flowing. She grabbed Jacob around his waist while he put his arm around her shoulder.

"A father couldn't ask for a better pair of young ladies than these two, could he?" he boasted.

Christine glanced back and forth between the women. "As beautiful inside as the outside. I'm so happy for you," she responded.

Cindy replied, "I'm so excited you are here. You know I just love how great the two of you are together."

"That is so sweet, thank you," Christine replied as she looked up adoringly at Jacob.

"Where is my soon to be son-in-law?" Jacob asked as he scanned the wedding guests assembled outside the doors of the chapel.

"You know the tradition," Cindy answered, "He can't see me until I walk down the aisle. I'm sure he's somewhere in the church with the minister."

Jacob turned his attention to Ashley. "You doing ok?" he asked.

Ashley looked at him suspiciously. "You mean the part that my little sister is getting married before me, or the part where my boyfriend broke up with me six weeks before the wedding?"

"Well actually neither. I thought you might be nervous for your sister?" Jacob volleyed back.

"Nervous about what? This girl has that boy wrapped around her little finger. If that ever changes, I know people that can make him disappear!" Ashley boasted with a grin.

Cindy feigned offense. "Hey now. That's my soon to be husband you are talking about!"

Ashley flashed a smile at Cindy in response before looking around the grounds of the chapel as well. She asked, "Have you seen Uncle Wes and Aunt Linda?"

"I think they are already in the chapel. Why?" Christine replied.

"Oh, I was just curious to see the dress she is wearing. She told me it was going to be something amazing,"

Cindy interrupted, "Where is Aunt Carolyn? I haven't seen her all day."

Jacob looked around the chapel grounds as he answered, "She spent the day with her good friends Brian and Kim who happen to be here too. She's notoriously on time, I'm sure she'll be here."

Christine checked her watch. "Speaking of time. Isn't about time we begin to work our way to an altar?"

Cindy stared wide eyed at her father and took a deep breath. She reached over to grab Ashley's hand and squeezed it tight. "Let's do this!" Cindy announced.

They started toward the chapel entrance when Cindy caught Ashley carefully eyeing the guests waiting to enter.

"Trying to find Cooper?" she asked Ashley.

She turned to address Cindy. "Yes, have you seen him?"

Cindy pointed in the direction of a thick rope hammock slung between two palm trees. Cooper, dressed identical to Jacob, was laying in it, peacefully swaying back and forth watching the sun setting over the ocean.

"Oh, dear god," Ashley screamed and she sprinted over to the hammock. The three of them stopped to watch as she threw herself onto the hammock, nearly spinning both of them to the ground.

Cooper roared with recognition, "Who is this demon child that wakes me from my slumber so rudely?"

Ashley broke out in laughter before rolling out of the hammock and pulling him with her.

"To the church, young man, there are nuptials to be made!" Ashley howled in response.

Leaving Ashley to catchup with Cooper, they renewed their walk toward the chapel with Jacob standing in the middle holding hands with both of them. As they neared the chapel entrance, a woman holding a clipboard approached. "Mark is inside with the minister. Are you ready?" she asked Cindy.

"Never been readier in my entire life!" Cindy enthusiastically responded.

The wedding coordinator announced loudly so the wedding party meandering about could hear, "OK, if everyone can line up as we practiced, I'll signal the minister we are ready."

Ashley and Cooper returned and took their respective places in line. Christine gave Jacob a kiss on the cheek, let go of his hand, and started to walk toward the chapel keeping her eyes on him. "See you inside old man," she said.

"With an attitude like that I may be checking out my options on the walk down the aisle," he jested with a wink.

Christine raised her eyebrows and turned her head in the direction of the chapel. "If you wish to waste your time..." she declared, trailing off dramatically.

The wedding party took their places and music started from within the quaint chapel. The first of the bridal party marched together into the church. Cindy grabbed her father's arm tightly.
When he didn't immediately respond to her, she turned to see how he was doing. She asked with a concerned tone, "Everything ok, Dad?"

He looked at her solemnly. "Yes, my daughter, I couldn't be happier for you. It's just that I wish your mother could have been here to see you today."

Cindy leaned into her father. "Dad, I've always felt mom is watching down on us. And I think particularly on you."

Ashley gave one final glance back at her sister and blew her a kiss before entering the chapel arm-in-arm with the best man.

A devilish smile broke out on Jacob's face. Cindy furrowed her brow. "What are you thinking about Dad?" she said.

He looked to the sky and then back to her. "Let's make your mother proud. What do you say we skip together down the aisle?"

"You better not, Dad!" she protested.

He bellowed with laughter and they began their march, quite properly, down the aisle.

Champaign, IL

A half-dozen men and women in casual business attire intently monitored screens and instruments before them. Unlit industrial light fixtures hung from the open ceiling in the windowless room which combined to create a shadowy blue hue. Despite the vast amount of electronic equipment at each workstation the room had a clean, clutter free appearance with tie-banded cables running throughout. The tile floors accentuated the sound of the equipment which filled the room with an electric hum.

Claire Rodgers opened the door to the room letting in sunlight which drew everyone's attention. She was dressed in a crisp white button-down shirt with smart black slacks. She had a phone in one hand and a couple of manila folders stuffed under her arm. Beside her was a middle-aged man who was slightly shorter and dressed in a suit expertly tailored to accentuate his slight build. He squinted as his eyes adjusted to the relative darkness of the room as she closed the door behind them.

She put the phone in her pocket and raised her hand motioning for their attention. Claire announced, "If I may interrupt for a moment. I'd like to introduce Deputy Director Hank Adams from the FBI. He's here for a tour of the lab." A mixture of uninspired "hellos" and hand waves followed in response.

Hank glanced at Claire to ensure she was done before he turned to address the room. "Thank you for having me today. I hope not to be too much of a distraction for you."

Claire motioned for Hank to follow her and they made their way to a workstation in the corner. One of the men watched Clair and Hank cross the room in his direction while everyone else quickly returned to what they were previously doing.

When they approached the work station, Claire stopped along with Hank. She said, "Hank, I'd like to introduce you to Ralph Schafer."

Ralph stood and shook Hank's hand before sitting back down and returning his attention to the monitor before him. She pointed toward the monitor and said, "This is where it begins. Ralph uses this equipment constantly watching for the atomic signature which shows a collection may be possible. When that occurs, Ralph will notify the team. They will then try to zero into find a complete enough signature to collect."

Claire motioned to Hank to follow her and they slid over to the next station. She started again, "In the early days, we had many incomplete acquisitions and the results were incoherent conversations or short-lived collections. Sue and Ashley have become experts on using the tuning software created by a brilliant young engineer at Cambridge. We always have two tuning engineers in the command room in the unlikely chance we obtain two signatures simultaneously."

One of the women stood to shake Hank's hand. "Hello, my name is Ashley," she said before looking in her colleague's direction, "and this is Sue." Sue partially stood up, reaching over the table just long enough to shake hands with Hank as Ashley sat back down.

Hank Adams leaned over staring at Ashley's screen. He said to her, "Well I'm glad this means something to you as it's all

Greek to me."

Ashley smiled but didn't take her eyes off her monitor. "Hundreds of hours of practice. We are getting better every day and our weekly meetings with the other universities accelerates our progress," she explained.

Claire put her hand on the back of Hank's shoulder and motioned to the other side of the room with her other hand. As they walked, Hank slowly spun around trying to take in his surroundings. Upon arriving at the new workstation Claire stopped and waited to see that she fully had Hank's attention.

"Once the first team has identified the consciousness, this is where the capture takes place," she pointed toward the two people at the workstation before she began again, "Wendy and Tim, I'd like to introduce you to Hank Adams."

Tim nodded and reached over without leaving his chair to shake his hand. Wendy who was on the other side of the table, smiled and waved politely. Hank nodded to acknowledge her gesture.

Claire continued, "Wendy and Tim will lock onto what we describe as the atomic cloud and pull it into a silicon collection device. Once they have confirmation that the collection is complete, they transfer the consciousness to a sentient box which triggers an alert in the next room. Someone from that room will almost immediately come through that door and begin the psychologic re-introduction process."

Hank shot Claire a confused look. "You have shrinks on staff?" he asked.

She nodded politely. "You need to understand that the individual finds itself in an unknown environment and with an ability to communicate that they have not experienced since they left the body. There is an orientation process we need to walk them through so we can identify them."

Hank shook his head and he looked a little frustrated. "Everyone is so vague on this point. Where exactly do they say they have returned from?"

"Well, this is something they struggle to describe. The best way I can try to explain this is that we've become so accustomed to our experiences being framed by three-dimensional space and the side effects of a human body."

"Side effects?" he repeated dramatically.

Claire winced and motioned with her pointer finger for a moment. "What I mean by side effect is that our experience is highly influenced by hormones and emotions. Whether or not we realize that, they shape how we experience what we perceive. Not being bound by the same constraints..."

Ralph interrupted Claire mid-sentence and with a raised voice said, "I've got a strong signal here. All hands on-deck."

Claire put her hand on Hank's arm drawing his attention back to her from Ralph. "Pardon the interruption. This is very fortuitous timing but requires focus in the room."

He nodded and she guided them back to Sue's workstation. They watched as Sue used the keyboard, touch screen, and roller ball mouse all in quick succession. On her monitor was a dial labeled "Acquisition Percentage" which had grown to about 70%.

"I've got the Fuller pulling it in," she shouted with enthusiasm, "Be ready. This one's coming in fast."

Hank leaned in Claire's direction and whispered in her ear, "Fuller?"

She turned toward him and quietly replied, "In the early days before the software improvements by Steve Fuller, the process was really slow. Now with each update, even our doctors are amazed at the speed of a collection."

Hank's eyes grew large. "Doctor's?"

Claire smiled. "Yes, every one of these people in this room are PhD's in various engineering and artificial intelligence disciplines. As are the psychologists in the next room. This is the cutting edge of science right here."

Hank nodded his head knowingly.

"Bingo" shouted Sue.

"Atomic pull initiated," Tim confirmed.

Hank and Claire walked over to Tim's station. A progress bar on his screen showed the completion percentage but Tim's eyes darted back and forth between numerous pieces of equipment. Claire caught Hank putting his hand to chest and taking a deep breath.

"It's quite extraordinary isn't it, Mr. Adams?" she said.

Hank shook his head incredulously. He replied, "Without a doubt."

A green light on a black rectangular box on the shelf next to Tim's workstation illuminated. "I've got a live sentient box," he shouted eagerly.

Almost immediately a door, opposite from where Claire and Hank entered the room, flew open. On the other side was a brightly lit room from which a young woman dressed in a sweater and dress slacks emerged. She rolled a cart in with her and quickly proceeded to Tim's station. She plugged a cable from the cart into the black rectangular box which illuminated a second green light immediately below the other one.

"I've got external power to the box," the woman announced.

Tim grabbed handles on one side of the box and the woman

walked around to the other side to do the same.

He looked at her. "Ready, June?" he asked.

"Ready," she answered.

With a little force he pulled a switch on the box which created an audible click. "Box is clear from the workstation," he announced.

The two of them slid the box to the edge of the desk and then lifted it the last few inches to the cart. June pulled the cart toward the other room. Claire motioned for Hank to follow June.

As they entered the next room, the brightness caused both Hank and Claire to shield their eyes momentarily. The room was a large space painted a warm brown and filled with several offices. The first room to their left had a couple leather chairs facing a wood desk. Behind the desk was a single chair. On the other side of the chair was a long table which had multiple keyboards and monitors. June had rolled the cart into this first office, but Claire motioned for Hank to follow her. They walked past addition offices and stepped halfway through a door at the opposite end from where they entered. On one side was a coffee table and a couch pushed up against the wall next to another door. A couple leather chairs sat perpendicular to the couch with an end table featuring a decorative lamp positioned in the corner. Right next to them was a reception desk, with an empty chair and the monitor turned off.

"This is the psychology room? It feels more like a doctor's office." Hank asked.

"Yes. I'll explain in a moment. I wanted you to see the entire space first, but let's head back to the office so you can see the work June is about to start."

The two of them turned and walked to the office.

"Hank, this is June and Hector. Guys this is Deputy Director Hank Adams from the FBI."

They both gave a quick wave and lifted the box off the cart and onto the back table.

"They are about to move the box into a semi-permanent location for the next few days or weeks until we complete the re-orientation process."

"What are the red lights?" he asked.

"One of the red lights shows that internal power source is sufficient. It blinks more and more rapidly as the battery source weakens. The other is an indicator that there is a sentient consciousness enclosed in the box. Unfortunately, we still have a relatively high loss rate and it's the quickest indication that a termination has occurred."

"I see. And what exactly is about to happen?"

Claire continued, "In this room June is about to talk to the individual for the first time. The process will be disorienting and depending on the quality of the collection and many factors we don't yet understand, the orientation process can take from hours to weeks. The first goal is to get the individual comfortable and to determine who they are. After that we try to get them familiar with their new experience. We have come a long way with the Elders on improving both voice recognition and interpretation, but you need to understand they have none of the other senses available to them. And this confinement deprives them of their experiences prior to collection. Once we have learned enough about them we seek audio or video from their time in their body. Our goal is to re-create their vocal patterns so that family members can recognize them."

"I don't follow, Ms. Rodgers," Hanks explained.

Claire pointed at her throat, "The sound you associate with my voice comes from the individual characteristics of my larynx. We have a software algorithm built for the Elders project that translates the digital signals to words to create their voice. The sound you'll hear in just a moment is the generic sound we provide every individual. While we've created software solutions which enable the Elders to recognize voices to distinguish who's talking, the experience is not the same as ours with physical ears."

Hank rubbed his head. "I had considered little of this. How do you know the individual is who they say they are? Why can't I claim I'm George Washington?"

Claire smiled. "You raise two interesting points here. First is related to the sound of one's voice. When we connect a consciousness with a family, it can be very disorientating for the family if we do not correct the voice. It's why our team spends so much time trying to voice match before the first family visit."

"And the second point?"

"To your point about validation. We gather personal information. Social security, birth dates, high school. Information that demonstrates their authenticity. But to date we have never had a collected soul lie. And we have yet to collect a consciousness that passed away longer than 12 years ago."

June interrupted, "I'm about to make first contact. Can I ask that you either continue the conversation outside or you can take a seat in the chairs — but I'll need you quiet."

Hanks looked surprised but took a seat. Claire sat beside him and whispered, "Turn off your ringer on your phone."

Hank turned it off and brought his full attention to June. She smiled, put her finger to her lips to ask for silence and said, "Here we go."

She turned to the monitors behind her and pulled a microphone close. With her mouse, she moved the pointer over the "Go Live" button and clicked.

Silence.

Hanks looked at Claire and she motioned to be patient.

"Hello this is June. Who am I talking to?"

"Hello," replied a male, monotone voice sounding like an automated answering system.

June waited a moment. "Hello this is June. Who am I talking to?"

"What is this?"

Hank whispered in Claire's ear, "He did not ask 'where is this?', curious."

Claire put her finger to her lips and whispered, "Shhh."

"Hello this is June and you are talking through a computer. Can you tell me who you are?"

The male voice responded, "I am Sara Clemons"

June moved her mouse to a selection box and clicked on "Female."

"Hello Sara, I am Claire. Don't be afraid, I will help you understand what is going on."

Shenandoah National Park, Virginia

The BMW X5 hugged the curves on the winding roads of the national park pulling to a stop before a chain-link gate.

A guard shack with a sign declaring "National Intelligence Center" sat outside the gate. A male guard dressed in army fatigues exited and approached the X5. The driver handed papers and an ID to the guard. He stepped back into the guard shack and after a minute the gate opened. The guard stepped out to return the documents before the vehicle drove into the facility.

About a quarter mile up another windy road the car stopped in front of a brick building. A man in a black suit and red tie stepped out of the building and approached the car. The passenger door opened and Dr. Cummings exited dressed in a business suit.

"Hello, Dr. Cummings, it is good to see you again."

"Dr. Torres, wonderful to see you again," replied Dr. Cummings.

"Dr. Grandstone arrived from Palo Alto probably 20 minutes ago and has already headed down to the bunker and is waiting for you. Should we proceed?" Dr. Torres asked.

Dr. Cummings nodded and put his arm on Dr. Torres upper back as they walked into the brick building. "How is the wife? Still running her half marathons?"

Dr. Torres laughed, "She's running full marathons these days. Says I'm never home. It was either longer distance or a boyfriend. You can guess which I chose."

Armed security guided the two doctors around a metal detector at the entrance of the building. An elevator was being held for them and they stepped right in. The guard pressed the button and they began their descent.

"Is it me or is security tighter than normal?" Dr. Cummings asked.

"Your press conference put us back in the news cycle and we

are getting a lot of scrutiny from legislators. For all I know our elevator operator, here, could be covert CIA. Frankie would never let me know if it was the case, probably just break my neck," Dr. Torres said with a wink at Frankie.

Dr. Cummings sized up Frankie nervously. After a moment he turned to Dr. Torres and asked, "Dr. Grandstone hasn't gone into talk to them yet, has he?"

"No, he knew this moment would be important for both of you. He's waiting in the rec room catching up on the news."

The elevator came to a stop and the doors opened. The group walked toward the recreation room and Dr. Grandstone greeted them. In a tan suit and a blue shirt, he looked like he enjoyed the California lifestyle. His gray hair and deep tan, made him appear straight out of a print ad for expensive whiskey.

"Ralph, so good to see you. Great job with that press conference, I thought you found the perfect time to cut off questions. They could have gone all night."

"Good to see you too, Larry. You still feeling good about your choice not to join us for the news conference?"

"Yes. That was your moment. Your achievement of a lifetime of work. Plenty of space on the world stage for two beer drinking MIT grads. My presence would have implied I had some part in your extraordinary achievement which would not have been fair."

"None of us would be here if it wasn't for your work, Larry."

Dr. Grandstone looked at Dr. Torres, "And neither of us would be here if not for Hector's excellence in maintaining the Elders."

Dr. Torres patted Dr. Grandstone on the back, "You are too kind."

Dr. Grandstone turned to Dr. Cummings, "You ready to head in or do you need a moment?"

"No reason to wait, beside I'd like to make my son's basketball game tonight if I can. But you never know with the Elders, could be an all-night affair."

"Ok then, doctors, it's the moment of truth," declared Dr. Torres.

"Are they all in there?" Dr. Cummings asked.

Dr. Grandstone hesitated then replied, "Many of them, but ever since the atomic battery some rarely return. It's those most worried about digital failure or who's families can't or won't pay for the battery upgrade that spend most of their time here now."

The three of them walked to a secured door. The guard entered a code and the door opened. The doctors entered the large round room, ablaze with LED lights. It was at least sixty feet in diameter and twenty feet high. On the walls were slots, many filled with sentient boxes. They built large speakers into the wall and in the center of the room were couches, chairs, and tables. A door at the opposite end of the room led to the control room. The three of them sat on the couches.

"Good evening, ladies and gentlemen," Dr. Grandstone announced toward the ceiling.

A uniform chorus of voices replied, "Good evening Dr. Grandstone."

One voice asked, "Is Dr. Cummings with you?"

"Yes, I'm here. Thank you all for allowing us to take your time," replied Dr. Cummings.

A lone male voice replied with tone and inflection, "This is Warren Matthews. They have selected me to speak for the group tonight. We'll use our digital communication interface as it's quicker for us to talk amongst ourselves if that is ok."

Dr. Torres smiled and answered, "Yes that will be fine, Mr. Matthews."

Dr. Cummings began, "Dr. Grandstone and I wanted to discuss with you personally the discovery we just announced. I know you have been monitoring communications and are all aware of the events."

"Yes, that is correct. We are curious about the implications. This was an off-shoot of the work to extend the reliability of our retention as sentient beings. We would like to understand what that means for our sentient expectancy."

Dr. Cummings answered, "Elders. We have been sharing our findings with Dr. Torres and upgrading your equipment and our maintenance tools as quickly as we can. We implement many of the improvements on the software side almost immediately after quality control approves. You know the sentient expectancy and unexpected loss rates have been improving considerably over the last five years and it's not by chance, but because of this work. We expect as we better understand the impacts that other consciousnesses are having at the atomic level, improvements will continue for some time."

"Thank you, Dr. Cummings." Warren said, "Can you please inform us if cost pressures are delaying any of the hardware upgrades?"

Dr. Cummings shot a smug grin toward Dr. Torres and shook his head laughing. He motioned to Dr. Torres to answer the question.

"While costs are always a consideration and Stanford Digital Life's obligation is to a hardware refresh every eighteen months minimum, we are accelerating the refresh cycle. Any delays are always our strict quality control standards. The software and sensor improvements are by far the vast majority of the breakthroughs and we are incorporating them as quickly as we can."

"Thank you, Dr. Torres." Warren repeated with his consistent terse approach. "Changing direction, it worries many of us about the ethical implications of these being collected. All the Elders have chosen to become digital and as you know these collected individuals have not made the same choice. What is your policy for handling this situation?"

Dr. Cummings began, "We have discussed this at length. We would immediately return any collected soul if they so choose. However, to date, we have had no collected individuals make this decision. Failures with the collection process have been the only driver of loss rate as far as we know."

Warren asked, "But at some point, this may not be the case. What are your plans?"

Dr. Cummings nodded his head slowly before replying. "We have our best people working on this. Certainly, we would always honor the wishes of the individual. Once we establish a more definitive plan I will share this with you."

"Thank you again, Dr. Cummings," said Warren, "We have no further questions on this matter. We would like to get an update on the progress on your vision program."

Dr. Grandstone stood to answer the question. "I talked with Professor Yamashita just last week. They believe they are close to having a beta unit to test with volunteers from this group. While he sees no addition risk that the vision unit will present to a sentient box, there remains that possibility and volunteers should recognize that unintended termination of your sentient box is always a risk."

"Dr. Grandstone, a list of volunteers has been sent to your

email. We are pleased to hear the progress," Warren answered, "We have another question for you. We were wondering if we will meet any of the sentient boxes you have collected. We would like to understand what happens after death as none of us in this group has experienced that."

Dr. Grandstone sat down and Dr. Torres replied, "Warren we have not discussed the details of when that would occur but we foresee that happening soon. We hope that perhaps you can provide us insights of your own."

Warren replied, "Thank you, Dr. Torres. We were wondering if there is anything we can help you with or if there are any items you would like to suggest for the think tank?"

Dr. Cummings answered, "Of course...."

CHAPTER 5

Redmond, WA

"Mama, when is my party?" asked the little girl.

"People should be here very soon. Are you excited Emma?" replied Cindy.

Emma ran and jumped on the couch to look out the window. "Where are they mama?"

Emma was wearing a purple-flowered dress and black Mary Jane shoes with her hair in a ponytail. Cindy was dressed in a short sleeve black tee, tan leggings, and barefoot with hair also pulled into a ponytail. Cindy sat next to Emma on the couch. Emma stared at her mother for a moment before she dove her head into her mother's belly which caused both to giggle.

"How old is Emma today?" Cindy quizzed playfully.

Emma held up two fingers and a thumb.

"No, silly. You're not two and, is that, a half?" she replied whimsically. Cindy pulled up four of Emma's fingers and put down her thumb. "Now, how old are you?"

Emma studied her fingers carefully before she enthusiastically rejoiced, "Four!"

"That's right, four!"

Emma caught something out of the corner of her eye and hurled herself onto the back of the couch which saved her from flying into the window. She shouted, "Mama a car, a car!"

Cindy looked out the window and responded, "It's Uncle Wes and Aunt Linda!"

"Mama, another car!"

Cindy smiled and slowly got up from the couch. "And there's Aunt Carolyn with Grandma and Grandpa!"

"Yay!" shouted Emma. She leapt from the couch and ran to the front door. She tried without success to open it. Cindy followed behind her and opened it.

"Well, Hello!" Cindy announced to the newcomers just emerging from their car.

Emma ran out the front door, past Wes and Linda and straight to her grandfather. She put a hug around his leg. A look of pride came over his face.

"Are those presents for me?" she said while pointing at the wrapped gifts on the floor of the trunk.

"Well, they are for the birthday girl," he answered with a smile.

Emma returned sprinting past Wes and Linda back to Cindy. "Mama, I got presents, I got presents!"

Cindy bent down to Emma's height and pointed toward Aunt Linda and Uncle Wes who were now approaching the house. "Are those more presents?"

Emma covered her mouth with both hands in astonishment. She looked wide eyed at her mom. Cindy then asked, "What do I see in Aunt Linda's hands?"

"More presents, more presents!" Emma shouted.

Wes and Linda made their way to the front door and Cindy greeted them with hugs and kisses on the cheek. She whispered to Wes, "She loves you too. It's just hard to compete with Grandpa."

He smiled and leaned over to give Emma a hug. He glanced back up at Cindy and replied, "We know this little one is full of love."

Cindy looked adoringly at Emma as Wes stood back up. "Emma, do you want to show Uncle Wes and Aunt Linda where the presents belong?"

"Follow me peoples," Emma announced. Cindy was waiting for her dad when she saw Ashley getting out of his car. It was Cindy's turn to run out of the house.

"Ashley!" she shouted with joy.

Ashley broke out a million-dollar smile and shouted, "Cindy!"

In the middle of the street, Cindy greeted Ashley with a bear hug.

"I have missed you so much Ash!" said Cindy.

"I've missed you too sis."

Cindy eyed Ashley with a perplexed look on her face. "I didn't know you were coming with Dad?"

"It worked out easier this way," Ashley replied glancing nervously at her father.

Jacob interrupted to say, "I see where dear old dad rates."

"Daaaad," Cindy protested. "It's been, what, less than a week since coffee? Ashley owes me months of hugs."

The trunk of the car closed and Christine was holding a bundle of boxes.

"Hold on I think you missed one, Christine," Ashley said.

The trunk re-opened and Ashley looked inside. "Here it is!

Under Dad's coat."

Cindy gave hugs to Carolyn, Christine and her dad before asking, "So how are the newlyweds?"

Jacob chuckled, "It's been over a year, I think we are just an old married couple."

Christine slapped Jacob in the chest. "Hey now!"

Jacob smiled and put his arm around Christine, "We are old, but so much fun!"

Christine shrugged, "What am I going to do with you?"

"Come on in. We are in the basement." Cindy said and motioned them inside.

She stepped into the basement and found her husband entertaining the family.

"Mama. Dada. Look at all the presents!" Cindy said, unable to contain herself.

Mark asked to the room, "Can I get anyone something to drink?" As he took orders, Cindy pulled Ashley aside. "I can't believe how professional you look on TV all the time! How's it going?"

"It's been really busy. But we are getting better at it all the time and we've had to expand."

"That's great. Are you still enjoying it?"

"Mostly, yes. It's hard when we think we've collected a soul, only to lose them. The worst is once we've contacted the family. Don't get me started."

"Dad said you got promoted to Director?"

Ashley smiled. "Yes, about three weeks ago. Dr. Cummings got so busy, he put me in charge of the Collection facility in Urbana."

"Wow! My sister is big time!"

"I don't know about that. It's never as glamorous as it sounds."

Cindy paused for a moment before asking, "Do you think you'll ever find Mom?"

The abruptness of the question caught Ashley off guard. "You know Cindy, it's random who we find. I can't promise we will. In fact..."

Cindy interrupted, "In fact, what?"

"I know you don't want to hear this, but the numbers are so small. It's just... unlikely we will."

Sorrow flashed across Cindy's face. Ashley noted it and hugged her sister.

She whispered in her ear, "I know you feel slighted sis, I'm sorry."

Cindy held her tight for a moment before Mark interrupted with a drink.

"Mark, how are you?" Ashley asked.

"I couldn't be better," he beamed, "Jacob says you can't stay long, that's too bad."

Cindy looked surprised by the revelation and asked her sister, "What's the scoop?"

"I'm sorry. This was supposed to be a longer weekend but with the new job, I need to catch a flight for a meeting I can't miss."

Cindy's face saddened. "Can you stay for dinner?"

"I'm afraid not. In fact, I probably need to call a car in about an hour. Can I ask a favor?"

"Of course, but an hour?" Cindy exclaimed.

"I know," Ashley whined, "we were supposed to spend tomorrow together. But this all came up last minute."

Cindy nodded her head glumly. "I understand, what's the favor you wanted to ask?"

Ashley smiled, "I really want to see Emma play with my gift to her, can we open that now?"

Mark jumped in, "Most certainly. Let me grab our little princess."

As he walked away, Ashley looked Cindy straight in the eyes. "You may love this gift, more than she does."

Cindy smirked, "Hmmm. I love the mystery."

Ashley glanced across the room to see her dad place a kiss on Christine's temple.

"He seems really happy."

"Who, Dad?" she turned to see what Ashley was looking at. "Yes, they are good together."

"Took him so long to be open to love again."

"I kind of thought he might never."

Ashley looked at her perplexed. "Why's that?"

"How do you replace Mom?" Cindy answered.

Ashley nodded knowingly in response, "You don't. You start again."

Cindy eyed her, thinking about the response. "I guess so."

Emma walked up with the present in hand. "Daddy says I can open this one now. But only with Aunt Ashley."

Ashley bent over to Emma's height to watch.

"I'm opening a present, opening a present," Emma shouted.

People gathered around Emma as she unwrapped the gift. Ashley looked up at her dad to make certain he was paying attention. Emma ripped the tape holding the flaps of the brown box together. Jacob was the first to see the contents and let out an audible gasp. Cindy's eyes darted first to her dad and then to Ashley. Ashley was tearing up. Cindy strained to see the content of the box.

"It's a stuffy!" shouted Emma.

Cindy looked at Ashley stunned. "Where did you find Hoppy?"

Ashley struggled to answer through the tears. "When I came back to help Dad and Christine move in together. I found him in a box of odds and ends from our move from Oregon."

Cindy couldn't contain herself anymore and bawled.

Her dad put his arm around her. "You know, kiddo. Your mom gave that to you, for your 4th birthday."

Cindy reached out and pulled her sister close and whispered, "Please find Mom, Ashley."

Lombard, IL

The black SUV slowly navigated the streets of the neighborhood. Plush front lawns with fully developed trees framed the modest homes. The car slowed as a boy ran into the street to track down a baseball. A group of kids dressed in tee-shirts and jeans wearing baseball mitts craned to see through the tinted windows of the SUV. The boy ran back onto the lawn throwing the ball to another as the SUV continued around the corner. Half way down the street a middle-aged couple and girl in her late teens waited on the concrete porch of their house. Dressed in their Sunday best, they looked like they just returned from church.

The SUV pulled in front of the home and parallel parked facing the wrong direction for that side of the street. June Richards, dressed in a formal navy business suit, stepped out of the car. The man on the porch put an arm around the woman and girl. June closed the car door and walked to the house. As she stepped into the shade of the porch, she removed her sunglasses and extended her arm to greet the family.

"Mr. Clemons. Ms. Clemons. Heather. I'm June Richards, so nice to meet you."

He shook her hand with a conflicted smile and answered, "Nice to meet you June. You can call me Bob."

Ms. Clemons reached out to shake her hand and said, "Lisa is fine for me."

Heather's handshake comprised a few fingers in June's hand. June put her other hand over Heather's and held tightly looking solemnly at her. Lisa broke the silence when she asked, "Would you like to come in?"

"That would be lovely," June answered.

June followed them into the house with Bob behind her. June entered the living room of the split-level house. A short flight of stairs up from the living room led to a hallway with three bedrooms visible. To the right on the main floor was a small dining area and a doorway leading to a quaint kitchen. A set of stairs next to the kitchen led to the basement. They adorned the walls of the living room with numerous pictures of the family. Many of them family photos were with two girls and everyone younger. A couch sat against one wall with two recliners rested up against the adjacent wall. A coffee table with lemonade and cookies on top along with a TV cabinet completed the room. Bob sat on the couch with Lisa on his left and Heather on his right. June sat in the recliner closest to them.

"How are all of you doing with the news?" June asked.

Lisa answered, "Well, we haven't gotten much sleep, if that's what you're asking?"

June smiled, "It's a big reason I'm here. You don't have generations of experience to draw upon. I want to help make this easier for you."

"Your certain this is our daughter?" asked Bob.

"We are quite confident. Her answers confirm both public documents and personal details you've provided. We are very careful before we reach out to families. This is something we don't want to get wrong."

"I imagine not," Lisa whispered.

"But back to my original question. I'm interested to understand why you haven't been sleeping. Can you tell me more about that?"

"Isn't that obvious?" Bob asked.

Heather put her hand on his. Her father looked at her and Heather returned a sympathetic glance.

His tone softened as he continued, "We finally were finding some degree of normalcy in our lives. This has opened up the wounds again."

Lisa interjected, "I never thought I would get to talk to my baby again. I can't stop thinking about what I'll say."

Bob watched June as he explained, "Sara was barely 17 when she died driving home from a varsity football game. Damn drunk driver. They wouldn't even let us see her. My brother was the one to ID her." He turned away looking like he might cry.

June softly shared, "I am sorry for your loss..."

Before she could finish, Bob turned back toward her and began again, "10 years. My girl was only 17, practically Heather's age. All he got was 10 years!"

"I'm terribly sorry about that," June turned to Heather, "And how about you, how are you dealing with this news?"

"I miss my sister. I just want to tell her how much I loved her," she paused momentarily, "Still love her. I'm not sure what the right way to say that is…"

"This is why I'm here. Part of it is to get you ready for meeting Sara again. But a big part is to help you with the emotional process you are going through."

Lisa poured a glass of lemonade for herself and took a sip. A tear dripped down her cheek. June opened her purse and handed her a tissue.

"This must be so hard on you, having to see families that should feel so happy and acting like this," Lisa sobbed.

"Not at all. Some families are euphoric and I have to help temper expectations for what the experience will be like. I had one family, guilt-ridden because they weren't happy their relative was coming back into their lives. But it's not uncommon for the mixed emotions you are feeling. There's nothing in your life experience to prepare yourself for this."

"When do I get to talk to her?" asked Heather.

"Soon. I need to make sure the three of you are ready and that Sara is as well. There are many technical issues to work through before the first meeting but this is the most satisfying part."

"Why is that?" Bob asked.

"I enjoy changing people's lives. Giving people the opportunity to have the conversation they long wish they could have had. But frankly, I enjoy working with families in a way that no textbook or professor prepared me. We are breaking ground on the human psyche that is almost unfathomable."

Heather looked at her suspiciously, "Are we a huge experiment to you? No one around here could ever afford to be an Elder."

"Oh, dear lord, no. I'm sorry if I gave that impression. You need to understand that I've trained my entire life in psychology. To be blessed with being in the right time and place to break ground in my field, is extremely rewarding. But on a personal level, I'm honored to help you through this process."

"You said on the phone, Sara has things she wants to share with us?" Bob inquired.

"Yes, and we'll let you have that discussion with her. But I need you to understand, just how exciting yet disorientating the first contact with Sara is likely to be."

Lisa asked, "So what does that mean?"

"I've spent the last few weeks orientating Sara to her new environment. Now I need to prepare you for meeting her."

"I don't understand," asked Heather.

"Sara has all the memories of her life with you. But she is not Sara in the way you remember her." June continued, "Sara no longer has hormones running through a body or a need to find food to curb her hunger. You will probably find her much more stoic than you remember."

"OK..." Bob said in a manner showing he was waiting for a punch-line.

"Many families confuse the calm nature of their loved ones with sadness or even depression. Part of this is the digital interface to their thoughts. Mostly though, they experience interactions differently and without the emotions."

"You said you needed to make sure we are ready?" asked Lisa.

June quickly finished her bite from the cookie. "We need to set your expectations for the first conversation. Prepare you emotionally. Without this, the experience can be overwhelming. And," she paused for a moment, "the Collected have an experience the Elders do not. This bring a tranquility we do not see in the Elders and naturally, questions that couldn't be answered before."

"Is there a God?" blurted out Bob.

"Yes, exactly. Sara, like the others, quite frankly is at peace with her experiences. But you may struggle with the conversation."

Bob adjusted in his seat and tried again. "I'm sorry Ms. Richards. I think you misunderstood me. I was asking, *is* there a God?"

June smiled politely. "Yes, I did. And this perhaps is a great starting point for preparing you for meeting Sara. To directly answer this question, I'll say this. It's more complicated than you might think and I will let Sara answer this for you, instead of me."

Lisa shook her head. "Ms. Richards, this feels so overwhelming. When you called I felt so lucky. But now, I don't know how I feel."

"This is exactly why I am here. Fortunately for you, we have learned from other families and their experience. Perhaps this would be a great time to start on the orientation."

Munich, Germany

Max rested on a trash can and watched the steady flow of cars picking up people from the airport. He pulled off his cap and rubbed his head. As he checked his watch a woman in a short blue dress caught his attention. Max watched her hips sway side to side while a sly smile appeared on his face. A loud car horn blared and Max turned to see Pete laughing while waving from inside his VW. Max pushed himself off the trash can and meandered toward the car. He sat down in the passenger seat and slammed the door shut.

"Take it fucking easy on my car," Pete complained.

"Just fucking drive and find me a beer."

"You call me like your fucking chauffer to pick you up. What the hell is going on?"

Max yelled, "The fucking man decided a robot could do my job. This shit keeps up, there won't be any need for us anymore."

"What the hell are you talking about?"

Max angrily looked over at Pete. "Some god damn suit, probably in the US of fucking A, found a way to get rid of my ass. All of our asses."

Pete replied, "Jesus Christ. This is exactly what the boys have been saying. Soon there will be no place in the world for us."

"Just find a bar. Any bar."

Pete swerved and cut over several lanes. The car behind honked his displeasure.

"You trying to kill us?" Max barked.

Pete fired back, "You want a bar or not?"

Max turned away and stared out the window silently as Pete exited the autobahn. Pete sped down a couple streets, glancing at store fronts. He screeched to a stop and put the car in reverse. He turned into a parking spot and set the brake. Max looked around trying to gain his bearings. Pete pointed out the window, "The News Stand going to work for you?"

"Fuck yes." Max shouted.

The two of them entered and headed straight to the bar. They sat on two stools and the bartender walked over to greet them. He wore a white dress shirt with a red-striped tie with black suspenders which held up his dark pants. The towel swung over his shoulder signaled which side of the bar he belonged on.

"What can I get you?" the bartender inquired.

Max answered before Pete, "Two Jameson's on the rocks."

"You got it."

As the bartender walked away, Max shouted, "Make them doubles."

Pete slapped Max on the shoulder. "Have you looked at this place?"

Max turned to absorb his surroundings. "Jesus fucking Christ. You brought me to hang out with the suits!"

Pete laughed. "This isn't going to end well."

Max broke a smile for the first time since Pete picked him up. "For them or us?"

The man on the stool next to him turned to see the source of the statement. Max looked him up and down. He smirked after seeing the guy dressed in a suit and tie. Max asked, "You got a problem?"

The guy held up his hands to signal "no" and returned to his conversation.

Max turned back to Pete. "The guy who killed my job is probably sitting somewhere in here."

Before Pete could reply, the bartender returned with their drinks. Max grabbed his whisky and lifted his glass to toast. "To getting fucked by the man!"

Pete laughed and raised his glass. "To fucking the man, fucking you!"

The bartender shot the two of them a disapproving look. Max noticed and raised his glass in the bartender's direction. "To peace and love."

"Let's keep it that way tonight," the bartender replied.

Max drank nearly half his glass and pounded it back on the bar.

"You are fired up tonight." Pete said emphatically.

"Fucking right I am."

Pete took a drink and leaned his elbows on the bar to relax.

"I've seen your old man on TV a lot. How's it feel to be the son of the ghost whisperer?"

Max glared at Pete, "Now you're going to get into my shit?"

Pete put up his hands in defense, "I'm just asking a question. I can just shut up and drink my firewater if you want."

Max's shoulders visibly relaxed and he took another drink of whisky.

"My dad is doing some crazy shit. Just what we need, literal stiffs coming back to take our jobs now."

Pete let loose a loud belly laugh. "Wait, you're thinking about this all wrong."

"Yeah, why's that?"

"I think your dad finally found a way, you might actually get laid," Pete bellowed.

Max playfully tried to slap Pete on the head. Pete retaliated by trying to slap Max and in the commotion, Max bumped the man next to him. Max glanced at the man briefly before grabbing his drink and motioning for Pete to join him for a sip.

"It's *excuse,* me," the man said.

Max turned to see the source of the comment. "What did you say?"

"I said, I think the words you were looking for were 'excuse me'."

"And why the fuck would I say that?"

The man looked incredulous, "Never mind."

Max finished his whisky. "I'm sorry, did I bump into you? Your right, my bad," Max sarcastically replied.

"Bartender, another round of drinks for me and my friend," Max declared.

The man sized up Pete before responding to Max, "Thank you. I *do* appreciate that."

Max turned to Pete and mumbled, "What a stiff."

Pete watched the man intently before he broke eye contact and returned to their previous conversation.

The bartender returned with three drinks. Pete finished his first drink and handed the empty glass to the bartender. A mischievous smile broke out on Max's face. He turned to the man next to him. "You know as I think about it, you're the one that will get fucked up the worse."

The man turned and his body tensed up. "What the hell did you say?"

"I realized that I have it all wrong, I should be feeling sorry for you."

The man glanced at Pete. "And why should you feel sorry for me?"

Max raised his whisky to toast.

"One day it will be you getting fired because of some computer or God damn robot finding a way to do your job. I think the days of the suits are numbered my friend."

The man shook his head and smiled. "You got fired today?"

Max ignored the question. "Are you going to toast or not?"

The man looked at his friend and then raised his glass. They both took a drink.

"So why exactly are my days numbered?"

"Don't you see? First it was the East Germans that came to Munich to take our jobs, then it was the fucking Pollock's, but how the hell could you know it would be a tin can that finally did you in?"

"I'm sorry, did you say Pollock's?"

Max looked at Pete with a smile. "Yes, I did. They came from Warsaw and Krakow, working for nothing. Like the pigs they are."

The man laughed and turned to his friend. "John, you hear this guy? He says you left Warsaw to come take his job."

His friend leaned forward to get a better look at Max and replied, "Pretty sure he's wrong on this one."

Max leaned forward on his stool. "Yeah, why's that?"

"I couldn't possibly be stupid enough to do whatever the hell it is you do."

Max laughed and turned to Pete. "This guy is funny, huh?"

"Hilarious," Pete replied.

Max drank the last of his whisky before taking a deep breath. He raised his glass and motioned to the bartender for another. He gave Pete a long stare before saying to him, "Oh, fuck this."

Max let go off his glass and let it crash to the floor below. The man looked down at the shattered pieces. He looked up dumbfounded and his expression changed to shock as he saw Max's fist headed for his face. The man fell backward into his friend. Pete finished his drink and put the glass down. He got up to help Max as the bartender hopped over the bar. The man and his friend in turn tackled Max to the ground.

Pete shouted over the sudden commotion, "I said this wasn't going to end well."

CHAPTER 6

Virgin Gorda, British Virgin Islands

The private plane landed at the single runway airport and taxied to a private hangar. Wilma Stone exited the plane in a conservative, knee high, floral dress. A wide-brimmed hat shadowed her face from the mid-day sun. The steward escorted her from the plane and into a waiting town car. Inside was a gentleman in his late 50s, dressed in a linen suit, white silk shirt, and white shoes with no socks. He greeted Wilma with a handshake and the driver started the car.

"Mr. Roberts sends his greetings, Mrs. Stone."

"I assume you are Mr. Walter Reed?"

"That is correct. Nice to meet you," he answered with a well-practiced smile.

"Thank you, Mr. Reed. I understand the drive to the bank is not long?"

"Around 10-15 minutes maximum. The bank manager is waiting for your arrival."

Mrs. Stone stared out the window. "I appreciate that Mr. Reed. I have flown a long way and would like this transaction completed quickly and without any funny business."

Mr. Reed smiled again and looked Mrs. Stone directly in the eyes. "I can assure you, that will be exactly the case. B&R hired me to ensure this gets done without issue."

Mrs. Stone didn't say a word as the car continued. She stared out the window for some time before Mr. Reed asked, "I understand you will fly back immediately after. Such a long way to travel. Are you certain you don't want to enjoy the islands for a while?"

Mrs. Stone turned toward him and answered, "It looks like a lovely island Mr. Reed. But my interests are back in London. And something about this entire transaction feels off. I will be much more comfortable once I am home."

"Mrs. Stone I can assure. I have worked with B&R over the years and have never had an issue."

Mrs. Stone raised her eyebrow. "It's not B&R that worries me. It's this gentleman from Endeavour Search. Something is not right with him. I just know it."

"Mrs. Stone I can ensure you there is no risk to you. Only you will know the account. It's a onetime transaction and funds can only go into that account. The system will not allow a withdraw or transfer out."

"Yes, this is what they have told me."

The car slowed and pulled into a bank parking lot.

"We are here Mrs. Stone. That woman there is the bank manager. Mrs. Victoria Smith." Victoria Smith was in a white, silk blouse and a red, knee-length skirt. She was wearing black shoes with a modest heel.

Mr. Reed exited the vehicle first and met Mrs. Stone on her side of the car. They walked toward the bank and the manager met them halfway.

"Mrs. Smith, it's my distinguished pleasure to introduce Mrs. Stone."

"The pleasure is all mine, Mrs. Stone. Shall we get out of this heat and get inside?"

"Nice to meet you too, Mrs. Smith. And yes, that would be delightful."

The three of them walked into Mrs. Smith office. The room was adorned in dark wood with white marble floors. Mrs. Smith directed them to the leather chairs in front of her desk. Her secretary entered and asked, "May I get either of you a drink?"

Mrs. Stone shook her head and Mr. Reed replied, "No thank you. Not right now."

Mrs. Smith sat down at her desk and opened her laptop.

"I want to be mindful of your time, Mrs. Stone. Shall we get down to business?"

"Yes, that would be appreciated." Mrs. Stone answered while surveying the room.

"We have all the signatures on the documents properly notarized," Mrs. Smith noted.

Mr. Reed spoke, "The first order of business is to verify the amount of funds in the account, to satisfy Mrs. Stone's concerns."

Mrs. Smith smiled, "Yes, of course, but first we must access the account securely. Mrs. Stone I believe they have briefed you on the security question, can you please enter the response on my computer?"

Mrs. Stone typed the answer and the account details appeared, "57,248,392.44". Above the dollar amount was Frank's name and her name as co-owners of the account. Below was Olivia's name as a beneficiary.

"Now Mrs. Stone I need you to authorize the transfer of funds. As you can see roughly 3 million Pounds will transfer to the

B&R solicitors. Mr. Roberts provided Mr. Reed the account they wish to use. The remaining funds will be immediately transferred into the account you enter."

"I still don't understand why I couldn't do this from London?"

"This is an excellent question. When your late husband established this account, one condition to withdraw money, required it to happen in person. I was not here when he set it up, but he was anxious about your lawyer putting you under duress. I can only authorize the transfer if I can verify this to be the case."

Mrs. Stone looked around the room. "This is still very curious. I have worked with him for years with no issue. Do either of you understand what Frank's concern was?"

Mr. Reed shook his head. Mrs. Smith answered, "I'm afraid not. But if you still would like to proceed, we can have Mr. Reed enter the firm's bank routing information."

Mrs. Stone nodded her head and Walter entered the account information. Mrs. Smith moved the computer in front of Mrs. Stone. "Now it's your turn. If you could enter your desired account number, we are just about done."

Mrs. Stone looked around again and then up to the heavens. She pulled a piece of paper from her purse and entered the numbers. Mrs. Smith turned the laptop around so it faced her.

"Thank you very much Mrs. Stone. Let me now enter my credentials and confirmation for the transfer."

Mr. Reed spoke up, "That's all there is Mrs. Stone."

"It's done. The funds are in both of your accounts." Mrs. Smith confirmed.

Mrs. Stone's phone rang and she answered, "Olivia?"

The two of them watched as Mrs. Stone listened.

"I see. It's all there. Thank you, Olivia. I will call you from the plane. I would like to finish up here."

She hung up and stood up. She shook both their hands, thanked them, and turned to walk out. Mrs. Smith left them at the door to her office and they continued out the front door to the town car. Mr. Reed let her into the back seat, before taking his place next to her before the driver left for the airport. Mr. Reed watched Mrs. Stone as she stoically looked out the window as they rode.

"I'm sorry to disturb you Mrs. Stone, but if you don't mind me saying; I've never seen someone so sad after receiving over $50m."

Mrs. Stone looked over at Mr. Reed. "My late husband left me this and a mystery. Everything Mr. Roberts said would happen, happened. Since the first moment I have heard about this I have been concerned about silly business. Now that it's done, all I know is that I would give every penny to have Frank back."

Mr. Reed nodded knowingly and let Mrs. Stone be alone in her thoughts. The town car entered the airport and pulled up to the plane as the fuel line was just being removed. Mr. Reed exited first and helped Mrs. Stone out of the car. He walked her to the stairs of the plane and shook her hand.

"Mrs. Stone, it's been my pleasure. I wish you well."

Mrs. Stone held onto his hand longer than normal. "Thank you, Mr. Reed. I worried on the flight here, about how I might lose this money. Now I'm left with this feeling that this was never about the money. There is a part of me that feels I've lost something greater."

She looked at him sadly and let go of his hand. "Never mind me. All this business has dragged up old memories of a great husband. I think a good night's sleep in my bed is what I really could use."

Mr. Reed smiled. "You are quite charming and clearly married a great man. I wish you safe travels."

Mrs. Stone walked up the stairs and the door to the plane was closed behind her. Mr. Reed got back into the car and it drove off. He dialed his phone and waited.

"Mr. Roberts everything went perfectly. Mrs. Stone received her funds and I trust you did as well."

Percy Roberts replied, "Thank you Mr. Reed. I will let my client know and transfer his portion of the fees."

"Very well. Is there anything you will need from me?"

"Not at this time. We will wire your fees in the next day. My client says their research department may have some further business for you. Do stay near your phone."

"Thank you, Mr. Roberts. I hope to work with you again."

Cambridge, England

Dr. Clark, Dr. Hoffman, Dr. Grandstone, and Dr. Cummings sat at the head of a large u-shaped table. Chairs lined the walls of the conference room which had windows on two sides and a large white board on another. Dr. Clark tapped on his microphone to bring people to attention. Roughly twenty people were in attendance and found their seats.

"I'd like to thank everyone for flying to Cambridge. I know how my body feels when I finally get to Illinois."

His comments led to a smattering of laughs. He continued, "As is customary. Are there any open topics before we review the performance charts?"

Dr. Cummings leaned forward to speak into his microphone. "I'd like to talk about the issues gaining traction in the press around the lack of consent on the party being collected." A murmur broke out in the room.

"I'd like to remind everyone around the confidentiality of these discussions. We aren't able to make progress fast enough if people are worried about sharing their concerns," interjected Dr. Clark.

Dr. Grandstone responded. "This isn't an issue we've had to deal with in the Elders program as its 100% opt-in. But it's a valid concern, especially as we've heard consistent feedback from the Collected about feelings of being ripped from a sense of euphoria."

"Excuse me, this is Dr. Manns from the University of Toronto, for those that don't know me. Are we getting any complaints from the Collected?"

"I haven't had one. In fact, there is such a calm nature amongst the Collected it almost seems they are oblivious to the concerns of time. The time with their loved ones, seems small on a grander scale than we can think of in our bodies," replied Dr. Hoffman.

"Is anyone getting complaints from the Collected?" asked Dr. Clark. He looked around the room and everyone was shaking their heads. "I think for now that is the message we should be sharing. But let's get the psych's working on a protocol for this and let's stay ahead of the issue. Any other issues?"

"How are we addressing this issue of euphoria? The world is spinning on God's existence," asked Dr. Grant from MIT.

Dr. Torres added, "The Elders have picked up on this theme as well. They have experienced none of these feelings during transfer or in their sentient boxes. They would like to understand it better."

"To paraphrase Carl Sagan, I think we need a poet to be Collected to better describe their experience," Claire Rodgers explained.

Dr. Cummings spoke next, "Yes, Dr. Clark, if you could dial up a Mr. William Shakespeare into the collection device, this would help with our next press conference." The room erupted into laughter.

Dr. Clark jumped back in, "I hear nothing else on the topic. I would add we need to be very careful on taking sides on the interpretations until our people arrive at firmer conclusions. Is that clear?" He looked out on the room and found no dissension. "Are there other topics people wish to cover?"

Dr. Grandstone asked, "I am wondering if the new algorithms introduced from Dr. Edwards are making a difference? The Elders are hoping it will improve long-term retention. Any feedback I can share?"

Dr. Cummings spoke up, "We've been seeing our loss rate slowly improving week over week, but nothing statistically different since the algorithms went live."

"Same here," Dr. Clark added.

"Same here in Cambridge."

"We are turning on our collection system in two weeks in Tokyo. We are going live with the latest algorithms," said Dr. Tanaka.

"There is one abnormality I would note," interjected Dr. Cummings, "I know this was supposed to improve retention but we've seen collections stemming from lifetimes going back almost a century since it went live. I wonder if it's an unintended outcome?"

Dr. Clark stuttered, "I, I hesitate, I should say.... I think you all know how much I hate sharing information that hasn't been fully vetted. But as Dr. Cummings brought it up. We are verifying what they purport to be a collection from someone who died in 1893."

A collective gasp spread across the room.

Stunned, Dr. Hoffman spoke. "If that is correct, the possibilities here are broader than we had originally thought. We are dealing with individuals who pre-date modern technology. The attempt to orientate those individuals will be extremely difficult. We need to have the PhD's working on this now. Dr. Cummings how is this individual reacting?"

"It's early, and in comparison, the orientation has been slow and painful. But he was a professor of philosophy at Oxford, apparently. We were lucky," Dr. Clark answered.

"I think this reinforces my belief we need to eliminate as much jargon and modern expressions from our orientation scripts. It may get harder not easier, if this is true," said Dr. Torres.

"Are there any other hot topics before we jump into the agenda?" asked Dr. Clark.

Dr. Grandstone asked, "Would it be possible to add progress on bringing MIT, Tokyo, and Toronto into the program to the standing agenda?"

"I can do that. I also think we should add what we are paying our people to ensure we have consistency. Dr. Edwards says his guy creating these algorithms, Spring, Springs, something like that...he has been complaining about whether we are properly valuing the work being done. His work on these algorithms has been fantastic. Plus, I know our people talk, so I don't want to create problems," Dr. Clark replied.

Dr. Cummings added, "I am not hearing anything at the moment. But let's all get a pulse of our people and get back together."

"I think that makes sense. Anything else?" Dr. Clark looked around. "OK, let's jump into the technical issues first. I see that acquisitions are getting better with Cambridge still slightly ahead of the other locations, but retentions are roughly flat and consistent. The acquisitions bump makes sense but frankly I'm surprised we don't see the same bump on retention."

Redmond, WA

Jacob walked into Prime Steakhouse and quickly spotted Cindy sitting at the bar. He walked over and gave her a hug before sitting down beside her. There were eight seats at the bar and a half dozen tables behind them. A large selection of liquors adorned the wall behind the bar and to their left was the large picture window looking out on to downtown Redmond.

Cindy eyed him adoringly and shared, "I love our daddy-daughter dates."

Jacob smiled warmly, "I already have my first Thursday's blocked on the calendar for years."

"So sweet Dad."

The bartender dressed in a button-down shirt and jeans walked over and asked, "Anything I can get you to drink?"

Cindy answered, "I'm thinking about some wine, maybe a glass of red. How about you, Dad?"

"I think that sounds good sweetie. I can do the same."

The bartender asked, "A bottle maybe? Save you some money?"

Cindy glanced at her Dad and then responded, "Sure that sounds great. Still have that Mark Ryan?"

"Absolutely. Menus tonight?"

Jacob replied, "That would be great."

The bartender grabbed a couple menus from below the bar and handed it to them before offering, "I recommend the Porterhouse. You look hungry tonight. Highly recommend it."

Cindy laughed, "I'm afraid I will have to pass yet again."

The bartender feigned concern in his face, "You sure? It's a great deal. 32oz. They are almost out of them so they doubled the price, but for you I can get it at 50% off. Smoking deal. What do you think?"

Jacob looked at him confused.

Cindy replied, "Still passing, Justin. More likely poké or deviled eggs but let's see if something inspires my dad."

Justin peered over his glasses at Jacob, "Has anyone told you about the Porterhouse?"

Jacob smiled, shaking his head at Justin.

"OK. I'll let you think about it, while I go grab you that bottle."

Jacob watched Justin walk into the main part of the restaurant before turning to Cindy.

"I don't get the joke about the Porterhouse."

Cindy chuckled, "Honestly, neither do I. But at this point, it's just his thing."

He shook his head once again while raising one eyebrow.

"How is life? You were pretty shaken up at Emma's birthday party."

Cindy grabbed his hand. "I love you Dad. I have known Christine now longer than I knew Mom. I miss her."

"I know. But are you okay?"

"Yes, I'm fine. Although I have to admit, it melts my heart to watch Emma fall asleep with Hoppy. I can only imagine what Mom would think."

"I'm pretty sure she would be proud of both of you. Hell, all three, four, if we include Mark."

Cindy smiled. "She would be proud of you too, Dad. The way Ashley and you talk about her, she would be happy you found someone to enjoy life with."

Jacob sat back. "You know. I think you're absolutely correct on that account. She spent so much time talking about living life after she was gone. She was wise beyond her years, I tell you."

"I never tire of hearing stories about Mom. I hope you know that."

"I do. How is Mark doing? He seems to be happy every time I see him."

"He's great. A good dad and doing so well at work. Just the other day."

"Hi," a voice interrupted.

Cindy looked to see the source. "Oh my God, Ashley what are you doing here?"

Cindy sprung up and gave her sister a hug. Her dad stood up and followed with a hug of his own.

Jacob asked, "What are you doing here? You left less than two weeks ago."

"And how did you know to find us here?" added Cindy.

Ashley smiled and collected herself. "First the easy part. Wait. Is the chair next to you open, Dad?"

"Looks to be, sit down."

Ashley gave her dad a hug as she sat.

"Is everything ok sis? You look like you are going to cry."

Ashley took a deep breath. "I'm fine. To answer your question, I called Christine and asked where you would be. I told her I wanted to surprise you."

"So, what's the surprise?" he asked.

"OMG, Ashley are you engaged?" Cindy gushed.

Ashley waved her left hand to show no ring.

"Give her a moment, Cindy," Jacob requested.

Ashley looked at her dad. "Thanks Dad. So, I was going through reports at work, catching up from my trip. I was looking at our performance indicators. Really, mundane stuff."

Jacob could see the hair stand up on the back of Cindy's neck.

"Our lab," she stopped to gain control of her emotions and then continued, "collected Mom while I was here for the birthday."

Cindy broke into tears and walked away from the bar.

"I don't understand Ash. I thought you couldn't control who you collected?" asked Jacob.

"We can't. This was totally random. We don't have the technology to place an order."

"Wow. Just wow," Jacob stared out the front window running his hand through his hair.

"I've broken protocol by telling you this way. But I talked with Dr. Cummings and he agreed it warrants an exception in this case."

Jacob looked at Ashley with tears welling up in eyes. "Why don't you go find your sister?"

"Are you sure?"

"I'll be fine, I really could use the moment."

Ashley disappeared into the bathroom to find Cindy. The bartender returned to the bar with the wine.

"I feel like I'm stepping in the middle of something important. You need anything or just some space?"

Jacob had a tear running down his cheek. He softly replied, "Just some space."

"Just wave if you need something."

"Hold on. How about another glass for my other daughter? I think we will need it."

"You got it."

Ashley returned with Cindy who was more composed until her dad gave her a hug.

"Damn you, Dad. I just turned off the tears."

He whispered in her ear, "You better get used to crying. This is going to be a bumpy ride."

She gently pushed him away to see his face. "Why do you think this will be bumpy?"

Ashley spoke for him, "Because he's right. I see this every day. He's right."

"Wait have you talked to Mom?" Cindy begged.

Ashley shook her head. "It doesn't work that way. She's not ready for us yet. She's still getting her bearings. And they will want to make sure we get our bearings."

"When do we get to see her then?" Cindy asked emphatically.

"I've pulled strings and our best psychologist will be out here tomorrow to meet with us. There is a lot of ground I can cover tonight, but."

"But what?" asked Cindy.

Ashley had a worried look on her face. "Dad? Are you ok?"

Cindy saw the expression as well and leaned her weight into him. "What's wrong, Dad?"

He mumbled, "This isn't fair. I worked so hard. So, hard to let go. God, this isn't fair."

A look of horror splashed across Cindy's face. "Oh my God, Dad. It never occurred to me, how this would impact you."

"How do I tell Christine?"

Ashley said, "I can do it, Dad."

He looked at her dejectedly. "No, I need to do this. This is my mine...alone. You understand that girls?"

They both nodded.

"Dad, I'm sorry. But I need to know. Ash when do we get to meet Mom? You never answered."

Jacob looked at Ashley waiting for her reply.

"Usually it's a few weeks or months from first contact with the family. But this isn't a normal case. I would think next week, the following at the latest."

Jacob looked up to the ceiling. "No need in looking for help from above any more. We now have her trapped in a box."

CHAPTER 7

Munich, Germany

"Yes sir, how can I help you?" asked the police officer stationed at the reception desk.

Franz Hoffman looked disheveled and confused. His hair appeared styled after one of his heroes, Albert Einstein. He contritely said, "I received a call you are holding my son here and I should come to pick him up."

The police officer looked at his log sheet. "I'm guessing, you are here for Max?"

Franz looked sheepishly at the officer and replied, "Yes sir, that is correct."

"If you could have a seat on the bench there over against the wall, I'll have your son out momentarily."

Franz answered, "Thank you."

He walked over to the wall and slowly sat down. He leaned his head against the wall and closed his eyes. He raised his left hand above his head and opened his eyes to look at his watch. He shook his head and dropped his hand. He said to himself, "Jesus, 4:02am".

Franz peered down the hallway as the sound of many footsteps approached. As they came into view around the corner, he could see it was only a couple officers looking over a report. He closed his eyes again, the sound of the second hand on the clock above him played like a lullaby.

"Dad."

"Dad!"

A finger from an officer poked Franz in the shoulder and he jolted awake.

"Excuse me sir, I'm Officer Klein. I understand you are Max's father. Is that correct?"

Franz stood up and rubbed his face. "I'm sorry about that. I closed my eyes for just a second."

"It is 4:15 in the morning. These things happen. Are you Max's father?"

Franz relaxed and answered, "Yes. Max Hoffman is my son."

Max squirmed with his hands still handcuffed behind his back. He avoided any eye contact with his father.

"Mr. Hoffman, I'm going to let Max go home with you. While I rarely see charges filed in cases like this, it's always a possibility. It's still a few hours until people will come into work and review the overnight activity reports. Less clear are any civil remedies the bar may pursue. From the report I received from the arresting officer, your son made a mess of that place."

Max cracked a grin and Franz chastised him, "There's nothing to be proud of, wipe that smile off your face."

Officer Klein worked hard to suppress his smile in response and continued, "We understand the very public nature of your role. Unless charges are filed, we'll not make any records of this evening public."

Franz nodded his head and replied, "I do greatly appreciate that."

"I can't speak for the bar. It's possible they may try to sensationalize this situation for free publicity. But we have no indication they have made the connection between Max and you."

Franz shook his head in frustration. "I understand. Am I able to take him home now?"

Officer Klein unlocked the handcuffs and replied, "He's all yours. And if you need a cup of coffee before driving home, I suggest the diner across the street. The coffee here is terrible."

Franz shook the officer's hand and thanked him. Max was rubbing his wrists as the officer walked away. He watched his father carefully without saying a word. Franz took a step toward his son and Max tensed up. Franz paused and put his hands on his son's shoulders.

"Max, I love you, no matter what."

Max embraced his father and they stood together silently.

Franz whispered in Max's ear, "I'm ridiculously tired. Let's find that diner."

They walked down the stairs and out to the sidewalk. A neon sign across the street proudly declared, "Food". With no traffic, they crossed in the middle of the block. The restaurant was empty, except for a few uniformed police officers. Red vinyl booths lined the windows of the establishment. Tables for four with armless chairs filled the rest of the restaurant. The kitchen sat behind windowed two-way doors, leaving the cooks visible as they prepared food on a large steel griddle. Franz grabbed a booth and they sat down.

A waitress walked up with an insulated pitcher. "Coffee?" she asked.

"Perhaps you should leave the entire pot. It's been a long night." Franz joked.

"I promise I won't let you see the bottom of the cup. How

about you, young man?"

Max flipped his mug over and answered, "Yes, that would be great."

She added before she left, "The menus are next to the window. I wouldn't get the benedict. The overnight cook couldn't poach an egg to save his life. I'll be back in a few."

Max grabbed a menu. Franz just stared at his son and said, "So what exactly happened?"

Max put down the menu and answered, "I was already having a bad day when I ran into this asshole in the bar. I told him I got fired because of a robot. Next thing I know he tells me I'm stupid. So, I hit him. Well actually his friend too, but only because he was closer."

Franz shook his head. "I'm not sure where to start. Perhaps with 'I got fired'?"

Max answered combatively, "They called it laid off, but it's just a pussy way to say fired!"

"OK, OK. Can we watch the language, please? Why did they lay you off?

Max looked frustrated. "The upper management guys found a way for a robot to do my job. It's just a new type of immigrant stealing our jobs."

Franz grew wide-eyed. "Seriously, son. Is this Pete and Lukas putting this stuff in your head?"

Max shook his head and answered defensively, "No, Dad. I really don't want to debate what happens outside the ivory tower of the university. But there's a reason I still live at home."

"What about this fight? How did this help your day?"

Max laughed and looked at his watch. "I probably slept more in jail, than if I was out all-night drinking."

Franz burst out laughing which caught Max off guard.

He explained himself, "I can't believe things have devolved to where a night in jail is a preferred option to getting piss ass drunk. Really Max, is this what you want with your life?"

Max looked down at the menu and answered almost inaudibly, "No."

Franz took a deep breath and grabbed the menu. The two of them sat quietly studying it. Max picked up his coffee and slowly sipped it. The long silence was finally broken up by the waitress coming over for orders.

"What can I get you?"

Franz looked up at her and said, "Apple pancakes would be great."

"Sausage with that?"

"Hmmm. Sure."

"How about you honey, what would you like?"

Max closed up his menu and replied, "That sounds great. Make it two."

"No problem. I'll have this to you in a bit," she turned to walk away before adding, "Holler if you need anything."

Max noticed his father, still had his head in the menu.

"Dad?"

Franz finally put the menu down and spoke.

"I told you when you were a little boy I would always be proud of you. There might be days I would be disappointed but always proud to be your dad. Nothing has changed. I still am."

Max interrupted, "Thanks, Dad."

Franz looked at him disapprovingly and continued, "But Max, your mother is worried about you. And when your mother is worried, life is not good for me."

"Sorry, Dad."

"Please, just let me finish, Max. You need to find direction in your life. You are a great kid. I worry that you are letting life slip through your fingers without grabbing hold."

"Dad!" Max protested.

"For God's sake, be quiet!" he demanded.

Franz began again, "You know I am one of the leaders of the Collected project. I've had unimaginable experiences and conversations with souls we've brought back. They bring a perspective on life that changes the way you think."

Max nodded, but Franz eyed his reaction suspiciously.

"Max, I think it might change your life if you came and worked in my lab. Meet some of the most brilliant minds in the world. I would like you to get to know some of these souls and hear their stories."

"Is it okay for me to talk now?"

Franz nodded his head.

"I'm not sure you really want a screw-up like me in your office. But it means a lot you want me to come work there. What would I do?"

"I'm not going to lie. At first it would be grunt work. Moving equipment, distributing reports, whatever the PhD's need done. But with experience and trust, things could get more exciting."

Max smiled at his father. "The good news is that I lose my job in three weeks and I will be available. So yeah, I'd be up for it."

Franz put his hand on top of Max's. "I think this experience will change your life."

Champaign, IL

Cindy and Jacob arrived at the UIUC Collection facility shortly before 1pm. They entered the reception area and looked around for Ashley. The room was larger than either of them had expected. It was empty, except for a family in the corner. Natural light flooded the room and acoustical guitar music played on a sound system.

"Good afternoon, how can I help you?" asked the receptionist sitting behind a dark wood desk.

"Good afternoon. My daughter and I are here to meet June Richards," Jacob answered while looking around, "My other daughter, Ashley Dwyer, is supposed to meet us here."

The receptionist's face lit up and she stood up to greet him. "You must be Ashley's Dad, it is great to meet you. Your daughter is amazing to work with. You must be so proud."

Jacob was beaming. "That is wonderful to hear. And I didn't catch your name?"

"Oh, I'm sorry. Its Kendra," she answered, "And you must be Ashley's little sister Cindy! She gushes about your little one."

Cindy blushed. "Emma is amazing. They told us not to bring her today otherwise she would tear up your waiting area as we speak."

"Yes, they are specific about how they do things. New people are a no-no on the first visit. Anyway, I'm not sure where Ashley is, but I'm sure she'll be here shortly. Why don't you take a seat and I'll let June know you are here?"

Jacob and Cindy found a couch and sat next to each other a little distance from the other family. Jacob took a deep breath and Cindy patted him on the thigh.

"It will be ok, Dad."

Jacob watched the family in the corner. "You say that, but have you noticed the family in the corner hasn't stopped crying since we walked in?"

Cindy turned to look. "June and Ash both say it will be an emotional experience. But most likely a positive one."

Jacob replied warily, "Tell that, to the family over there."

Cindy hugged his arm and said, "Dad, this will be great. You will be great."

Jacob looked doubtful as he watched one of the family members move over and sit across from them.

Cindy continued, "June said they feel pretty comfortable, they got Mom's voice right. I bet that will make things a lot easier."

Jacob didn't reply and instead watched the teenage girl sitting across from him.

Cindy blew out air from her cheeks and looked at the stack of magazines next to her.

The teenage girl asked her sadly, "Is this your first time here?"

Cindy put down the magazine and replied, "It is. You?"

"This is our third time. The first time was a little weird but was really great."

Cindy reached into her purse and passed a tissue. "Here you go, it seems like you could use this."

The girl wiped her eyes and answered, "Thanks. It's been a rough morning. My parents need adult time to talk."

Cindy sympathetically replied, "I'm sorry to hear to that. I've heard these can be emotional sessions."

"That's putting it lightly. We always thought we knew how my sister died, but it turns out we were wrong."

Cindy looked at her sympathetically. "Oh, I see."

The girl cried again, "It's like my sister, but not like my sister. You'll see what I mean. They are so emotion-less sometimes talking about important stuff, like 'I was texting and didn't see the car.'"

It drew Jacob into the conversation. "I'm so sorry for you. That must be very difficult."

She was about to answer when the door opened and Ashley caught their attention.

Jacob and Cindy stood and each of them hugged Ashley.

Ashley said, "June texted me and told she got tied up on something and to just come back. You guys ready?"

Jacob took a deep breath while Cindy glowed with excitement.

Cindy grabbed her purse off the chair and addressed the girl before leaving. "I'm guessing we might run into each other. I'm Cindy and I have a lot of Kleenexes in my purse."

The teenage girl smiled for the first time, "Thanks Cindy. I'm Heather, Heather Clemons."

"Nice to meet you, Heather Clemons. I am sure I will see you again soon."

Heather shook her hand and Cindy quick stepped to catch up to Ashley and Jacob who were waiting for her at the door. Ashley took Jacob and Cindy back and walked them to an office. The three of them sat on a couch against the wall. Jacob seemed distracted taking in his surroundings. There was a desk with a couple leather chairs. Behind the desk was a single chair with a table behind with various keyboards and monitors on the desk.

Ashley broke the silence, "June will be here shortly. She will bring Mom, in what we call a sentient box. She'll plug the box in over there, but mom won't be able to hear us immediately, until June turns on communications."

Jacob said, "I have to tell you Ash, this feels a lot like Mom's oncologist's office. I'm glad Mom can't see any of this, because frankly, it's freaking me out."

Cindy rubbed her dad's back. "Dad, it will be ok. Just be yourself."

Jacob emphatically replied, "I am being myself, a very uncomfortable version of myself."

Ashley smiled warmly, "Just remember the lake, Dad, and all those good feelings. That's what today should be about."

June walked into the office, pushing a cart. She left the cart to greet the family and then wheeled it over to the back desk. She took a couple moments to connect the cables and checked the indicator lights. She motioned for the family to move forward to the chairs by the desk. June leaned her elbows on the desk and addressed them, "OK. So, this is the moment. I have Kleenex on the desk and on the table behind you. Water and soda in the corner. And if you need it, candy bars and fruit in my fridge."

Jacob replied, "You've thought about just everything, haven't you?"

June smiled, "Not everything Jacob. The words and moments that follow are all yours."

Cindy replied, "That is beautiful, June."

"Thank you. As we talked about, Jacob will start, and at the right time introduce Ashely and Cindy. Remember to identify yourself until she learns your voice. Are you ready, Jacob?"

Jacob nodded and June turned to activate the communications. She motioned to Jacob to begin. Jacob looked at both his daughters and bit his lower lip before he began.

"Hello, Emily. This is Jacob."

It took a moment for her to reply. "Hello, Jacob. It seems so odd to talk again." Her voice was measured and flat.

Cindy covered her mouth and cried.

Jacob continued, "It has been so long, I have missed talking to you. Hearing your voice."

June glance at Ashley and smiled. She mouthed, "Great start!"

Emily responded unemotionally again, "I am sorry that I left you. The world is such a beautiful place. I hope you found your peace."

Jacob eyed Ashley warily. Ashley mouthed back, "Go on."

"I have been very lucky to have our two amazing daughter's and see them grow up."

"Yes. I understand you are a grandfather. They tell me you are a handsome man with gray hair."
Jacob welled up and his voice trembled, "Emma is beautiful. I can't wait for you to meet her."

"I look forward to it. I have so much time to think now. I have wondered what amazing things Ashley and Cindy have done."

Jacob looked at his daughters to see if one of them wanted to answer, but both were sobbing now. He grabbed several tissues and shared them with the girls. He used the last one to wipe away his own tears.

"Ashley and Cindy are here with me. They have grown up to be such beautiful women. You will be so proud of them."

Emily replied after a moment, "Hello Ashley. Hello Cindy. How are my little girls?"

Ashley was more composed than Cindy and answered, "Hello, Mom. This is Ashley. I am good. I love you. I have wanted to tell you that for so long."

June stood up to grab the tissue box from the coffee table. Emily replied to Ashley, "I love you too Ashley. And you too, Cindy."

Cindy's words broke between sobs as she answered, "I missed you so much Mom. I love you so much. This is Cindy, but I guess you probably figured that out."

Emily's reply came quicker this time, "I love you too Cindy. I can't wait to meet your daughter. Did you name her after me?"

Cindy burst out in tears and couldn't answer. Jacob spoke for her. "This is Jacob again. Cindy is nodding yes. Emma is as beautiful as you." Jacob hugged Cindy and handed her another bunch of tissues.

"Thank you, Jacob, for saying that. Do you still go to the lake?"

Cindy jumped in to answer, "Every year, Mom. Emma has been there. She sleeps with your favorite flannel blanket. We make s'mores and always leave one out for you." She looked at Ashley to speak as she pressed her knuckle into her quivering lip.

"Mom, this is Ashley again. We have so much to talk about, but I wanted to see how you were doing. I know this is difficult at the beginning."

June looked at Ashley and smiled. She turned toward the microphone to speak, "Emily, this is June. That is normally my question. Do you need a break?"

Emily responded after what appeared to be some consideration, "As you know I don't get tired, but I am still getting used to this experience. I think it would be good to talk with Ralph again. Perhaps he can fix problems I am having with communicating."

June nodded and responded, "Yes, we can do that Emily. Let's take a break and see how long it takes Ralph to fix the issue. Jacob, Ashley, or Cindy would you like to add anything before we sign off?"

Cindy spoke first, "Mom, this is Cindy. I can't wait to share all my stories with you. I hope they fix things so we can talk longer next time."

Ashley interjected, "Mom, this is Ashley. Ralph is one of our best technicians. I know he will solve your issue. I love you. I will talk with you soon."

Emily replied, "I love you girls. I am sorry I can't talk longer. It is disorientating at the moment and I need them to help me."

"Emily, this is Jacob. You take all the time you need. We will be here. You have always been so loved."

After a greater than normal delay, Emily spoke. "Jacob. You are a good man. I need to say one thing."

"Yes, Emily, what is that?"

"Please understand that I was so happy to hear you re-married. Please do not be uncomfortable talking about this. Love is the magic that transcends our bodies. I hope I can talk one day to the woman who opened your heart to its endless possibilities again."

Champaign, IL; Munich, Germany; London, England; Palo Alto, CA

They activated the teleconference and in conference rooms

around the world a two-by-two grid shared live feed from each location. Dr. Cummings kicked off the meeting.

"Good morning, and good evening, ladies and gentlemen."

Each replied with their various salutations and Dr. Cummings began.

"Dr. Clark I see you confirmed the collection from the 19th century. Still the oldest recorded, but I believe all of us have now collected individuals from the early 20th century. I know on our end; the orientation issues are daunting. I assume you are experiencing the same issues?"

Dr. Clark responded, "Most definitely. This individual may take months to orientate and we still haven't figured out who to introduce him to. This is creating so many new issues. I think the public will have a field day with the ethics of this. And frankly, I'm not sure they would be wrong."

Dr. Grandstone spoke, "Gentlemen. Part of the problem here is that we had decades of preparatory work before we turned on the Elders program. You were trying to solve one of my technical issues and stumbled upon what I would argue is a related but an entirely new field of sentient psychology. I think we need to pull some of our deep thinkers out of retirement and put together a summit with your psychs and ethics people and get a long-term structured solution. This will not get easier, but harder."

"I think that's right, but we also need to talk about the expansion of the Collection program. Do we really want Tokyo, Toronto, and MIT doubling the size of this issue? And frankly the three of us having been trying to outperform each other and pushing the numbers we are collecting. It won't be long and we might have more Collected than Elders. I think we need to throttle things for a while," argued Dr. Hoffman.

Dr. Cummings replied sounding frustrated, "Jesus, you realize you are asking us to turn off the instruments. We still don't control when a collection happens, we're just better at finding them. The only way to throttle it, is to stop looking. And families are already feeling like this is their emotional lottery. If and when the public catches wind of that, they will raise hell about us missing the opportunity to collect their loved one."

Dr. Hoffman answered, "I am struggling to keep up with orientating these older Collections to answer your earlier question. I think Dr. Cummings is correct, but we need a solid plan like Dr. Grandstone suggests. Cummings you are closer to the Elders designers can you work with Grandstone to get this summit pulled together ASAP. I think for our face to face in a few weeks, we must make a call on throttling. A few weeks won't kill us, but if one of our people slips to the press, we are shutting down equipment at night, that will be a self-inflicted wound."

"I can do that. I'll get with Dr. Grandstone after this call and figure it out," Dr. Cummings answered.

"Ralph, call me on my mobile, I'm driving to a seminar in San Francisco after this call."

Dr. Cummings replied, "Yes, no problem. And I realize this is going to sound ridiculous in light of this conversation, but I have a question about the operation metrics. We've seen a steady improvement in collections and retention. I don't mean to put you on the spot, John, but your retention percentage is dropping. I'm frankly worried as you tend to implement Dr. Spring's new algorithms before the rest of us. I hate to see a bug propagate through the entire system. You know how crushing it is to families when we introduce and then lose their family members. You seeing the same retention numbers I am looking at?"

Dr. Clark spoke slowly, "Yes, I see the same thing you are. Honestly, I come at this from a classic statistical framework and wasn't getting worked up. The trend seemed within expected ranges, but I agree that it appears after several weeks that there is something going on. I will need to look into it. I'll have an update next week for you."

"Dr. Spring still complaining about his compensation? Because we haven't heard much on my end," Dr. Cummings asked.

"Me either," added Dr. Hoffman.

"He's quieted done. Said his wife has started a small biz on the side which is helping things out. I think we can leave it be for now," Dr. Clark answered.

"Excellent. I hate to lose him. Ralph, I heard you broke some new ground with one of our own having a family member collected. How has that experience gone?" Dr. Hoffman asked.

"It's been fascinating honestly. Its Dr. Ashley Dwyer's mother. She's the director of my Collections lab now. She came up on the tech side but I've seen her spending a lot more time working with the psych program over the past few weeks giving feedback on their protocols. Nothing like the work becoming personal to change how we see things."

"Anything new from the Elders, Walter?"

"They are getting antsy to have a summit of their own with the Collected. I think we will have to get a team on figuring that one out. The emotional difference between the individuals in the Elders and Collected programs needs our deep thinkers. Same software, same boxes, and same interfaces. Yet our Elders exhibit emotions unlike the Collected. I'm thinking this is a twist on the old nature vs nurture debate. We have exposed everyone in the Collectors Program to an environment that frankly we still do not understand. We need to look at this program through some new optics. I think this Dr. Dwyer's reaction is the lead we should be following. We are old tech guys; if we aren't careful it's this soft stuff that will bite us in the ass."

CHAPTER 8

Redmond, WA

Mark and Cindy were in their kitchen cleaning up from lunch. Jacob sat next to Christine on the couch, watching Ashley outside on her cellphone. Christine put her hand on Jacob's leg and rubbed his thigh. He looked at her lovingly and returned the favor by patting her on the knee.

"You two doing all right in there?" Cindy asked from the kitchen.

"Just fine my daughter. Stop mothering me."

"Not mothering you, just hosting. Besides not my job anymore."

Christine whispered, "To be clear, not my job either."

Jacob raised his eyebrow, "Now you tell me this. This may be a contractual violation. I may have grounds for a refund."

She slapped him on the arm, "Just try it."

He leaned forward and gave her a kiss. "Not going to happen."

"I know," she said with a feigned stern look.

Back in the kitchen Mark was finishing up on loading the last dishes when he asked, "You ready for this?"

"Of course," Cindy answered eyeing him warily, "Why do you ask?"

"Just checking. I know we've debated it to death. But it's a big obligation."

She walked over and put her hands on his shoulders and looked him directly in the eye. "I have wanted this all my life. How do you want something, you didn't even know could happen?"

He put his hands around her lower back and pulled her close. She draped her arms around the back of his neck in response.

"More time. You wanted it. And now have it."

"Yes. And I will not waste my second chance. I want her to see Emma grow up. She deserves to at least see her granddaughter do that."

He grinned as if he read her poker hand. "Getting to see the childhood she missed with you?"

She kissed him and whispered playfully, "Yes, my smug husband of mine."

They turned as they heard the front door close and they walked into the living room together.

"Everything ok?" Cindy asked Ashley.

Ashley put her phone in her back pocket and walked over and gave Cindy a hug.

"What's that for?"

"I just talked with the delivery team. They are a couple blocks away."

Mark put down his dish towel and wrapped his arms around Cindy from behind. She leaned back into him and let out a sigh.

"Finally, here," he calmly announced.

She closed her eyes and echoed, "Finally here."

He kissed her on the top of her head and replied, "For as long as I've known you, today is the greatest gift that anyone could ever give you."

She put her hands on his arms and squeezed. "Emma. You. Now this. Just a lucky woman."

"Ok you lovebirds," Ashley quipped before turning her attention to Jacob and asking, "You ready?"

Jacob looked guardedly at Christine as they stood up from the couch. She rubbed his back gently and he nodded affirmatively at Ashley. Ashley approached a table in the corner of the living room and examined the equipment sitting on top. The doorbell rang and Emma ran to the door to answer. Before Cindy could stop her, she had unlocked the deadbolt and flung the door open.

"Are you grandma?" Emma asked.

A young woman in her early 30s answered, "No cutie, I am Jennifer. But I brought your grandma with!"

Ashley walked up behind Emma and spoke, "Well hello, Jennifer! I see you have met Emma."
"Why yes, I have," Jennifer replied with a grin.

"Everything looks good on this end. Ready on your end?"

"It's been a long trip to get here, but we are ready to roll. Justin is preparing Emily for transport. Is it going to bother you terribly if I verify the setup before we bring her in?"

"Not at all. Let me introduce you to the family and show you the hardware."

Jennifer busily checked cable connections and ran through software testing while the rest of the family attentively watched the van out the front window. Justin meanwhile popped in and out of the van. Cindy sighed each time Justin exited the van empty handed.

Jennifer finished and announced, "We are ready here. Let me go help Justin."

As Jennifer walked down the driveway, Ashley put her arms around her Dad and Cindy's shoulders.

"I love you two. No matter what happens, good or bad, we have each other. Always remember that."

Jacob looked somberly at Ashley and replied, "As long as your mother is happy, that is what really matters. We have an entire world to enjoy together, but your mother has just this."

Ashley nodded to acknowledge his point but countered, "This is true, Dad, but digital retention is still a work in progress. Mom can disappear on us, with no notice. I want both of you to cherish whatever extra time we get with her."

Cindy smiled sadly and answered, "I know Ash. Today is a big day. Let's focus on that."

Ashley nodded and patted Cindy on the back. "Your right, sis. Here she comes."

Justin and Jennifer wheeled a cart up the driveway with the sentient box on top. They navigated the sidewalk to the front door and lifted the cart through the doorway to enter the house. Cindy hovered over the cart and followed closely behind as they moved it across the room. They stopped next to the table and together lifted the box placing it into the equipment on the table. Both LED's turned red and Jennifer flashed Ashley a thumbs up.

Justin explained to the family, "We have made the connection. I will start the program on your hardware and we'll be able to talk to Emily shortly."

Cindy covered her mouth while Jacob moved next to Christine and kissed her on the temple. Ashley leaned over Ralph's shoulder and watched the initiation process attentively.

Justin turned to the family and said, "Once I turn on the software, it will remain running and Emily will be a constant presence. You'll be able to move her box and the hardware to other locations, but I recommend you keep her in this location as much as possible. The chances of being dropped or other harm coming to her are minimized that way."

"Does she know when she's being moved?" asked Jacob.

Jennifer answered, "Yes, but not in the way we think about it. There is a built in GPS in the box that provides information to her. So, she knows of movement in the same way you can see your car arriving on the Lyft app."

"I'm ready to go here," Justin informed the family.

Cindy lifted Emma from the floor and held her. The entire family pulled closer to the table and waited for Justin to give the signal. He turned to them and counted down from five and pointed to the microphone as he went live.

"Mom, this is Cindy. How are you doing?"

"Hello sweetie. I recognize your voice now, no need for introductions. Well, maybe except for one. Is my granddaughter there?"

Cindy whispered to Emma, "Can you say 'Hi Grandma'?"

Emma instead buried her head into Cindy's chest.

"Grandma, Emma has decided to get shy, but she is here."

"Emma... How are you? Can you say, 'Hello, Grandma?'"

Emma shook her head and everyone laughed.

"What is so funny?" asked Emily.

Ashley answered, "Oh Emma is being ultra-shy."

"Well, if Emma doesn't want to talk, does Hoppy want to talk?"

Emma turned to her mother with a shocked look on her face.

Jacob whispered in Emma's ear, "Do you want to tell Grandma about Hoppy?"

Emma suddenly looked curious. Cindy prompted her, "Is Hoppy brown or black?"

"Brown!" she declared emphatically.

Emily jumped in and asked, "Does Hoppy have long ears or short ears?"

Emma looked at Cindy wide eyed with astonishment.

"Tell Grandma, what kind of ears Hoppy has," Cindy encouraged her.

"Long ears!"

"Do you love Hoppy?" asked Emily.

"Grandma?"

"Yes, Emma?" Emily answered.

"Are you dead?"

"Emma that's not a nice question to ask Grandma," Jacob said.

"It's ok, Jacob. I think it's a lovely question for her to ask," Emily replied.

"Mom, are you sure you are up for this question?" Ashley asked.

"Of course. And Emma that is a difficult question to answer. I died, but I am here now."

"Where did you go, then?"

All the adults looked at the box intently, no doubt curious to hear her response.

"Well Emma. In some ways, I've always been here. But in other ways I went to some place very happy and comfortable."

Cindy asked, "What do you mean, Mom?"

"It's difficult to explain Cindy. It felt like the wind blew and took me with it. It felt like I was everywhere and yet aware of everything, of who I was, and who I am. Imagine being a drop of water falling into the ocean, only you feel part of the entire ocean and everything the ocean touches."

Emma looked at her Mom and said, "Huh?"

"Ash can you help?" Cindy pleaded.

Ashley looked surprised by the question. "Umm... What Grandma is saying is that being dead is hard to explain. it's an experience happening in a different dimension than we understand."

Emma curled her nose and looked at her mother.

Emily tried again, "Emma, Aunt Ashley is right. I felt very happy and filled with love for every drop of water that rubbed up against me."

Jacob interrupted, "Emily, what are you saying? Are you saying you have been everywhere?"

Jennifer glanced at Justin who out of eyesight of the family mouthed, "Happens every time."

Emily continued, "It's hard to explain Jacob. I felt a part of everybody, but didn't talk or communicate with them in the way you think about it. I felt part of nature but not in the way you smell or hear it. I felt change happen, but had no sense

145

of time passing. My experience was so happy and calm yet so hard to put to words."

"I see," Jacob surrendered.

Ashley tried to bridge the conversation, "Mom's experience is consistent with what others have told us. I think their experience is so different that it's like trying to explain what it's like being a ray of light."

"Well, that's not very satisfying," confessed Christine.

"I don't recognize that voice. Who is that?" asked Emily.

"Hello Emily, this is Christine. I am Jacob's..." Christine paused.

"Wife," Emily finished.

"Yes, my wife," Jacob repeated.

"I am so happy for the two of you. Please don't be shy around me."

Jacob answered with a tinge of pain in his voice, "You are generous as always Emily. This is... new for all of us as well."

"Thank you, Jacob for sharing that. I will try to keep that in mind."

Cindy watched her father to ensure he was done before asking, "Mom, what can we do for you?"

There was a long pause before Emily replied, "Now that I'm here again, what I would love to hear are your favorite stories. All of you, tell me what has made you laugh and cry since I left. But as a start, I would love to hear what adventures Emma and Hoppy have gone on together."
Emma lit up this time and answered, "Hoppy and I went to the park looking for fairies, Grandma."

"Fairies. How exciting," Emily responded, "Did you find any

Emma?"

As Emma and Emily continued their conversation, Jacob whispered something to Christine and wandered into the kitchen. Ashley saw and followed him. He had grabbed a glass from the cupboard and filled it with water from the faucet.

"Everything ok, Dad?"

It startled Jacob to hear her voice and he turned to say, "Yes, I'm fine. I just need something to drink."

"Are you sure? You seemed a little.... Actually, I don't know what you seemed other than just a little off talking to Mom."

Jacob took a long sip of water and then replied, "I've had a few times talking to your mother now. It's her voice, her compassion, and her love for all of us. But she's different."

"Yes, this is why we have you in a regular consultation with the psychologists. All the families have some version of struggles post collection."

Jacob let her response linger for a moment. He stared at her pondering how to reply.

"What?" Ashley said.

He took a deep breath and explained, "Ash, Cindy has never been shy about expressing her feelings of loss for your mother. But never confuse the way I chose to deal with losing your mother. The excruciating pain I have gone through."

Ashley moved close enough to her father to rub his shoulder. "We know, Dad."

Jacob kissed Ashley on her forehead. "The two of you are the greatest gift your mother left behind. You do know that?"

"That is so lovely, Dad," Cindy said from the entrance of the kitchen.

Jacob and Ashley looked over surprised. He asked, "What are you doing in here?"

Cindy responded, "I was wondering the same thing about the two of you."

Jacob explained, "I needed a drink of water, that's all."

Cindy nodded looking unconvinced. "Well, I see you got a glass. Mom is asking where the two of you have gone. Ready to join us?"

Jacob started to leave when Ashley grabbed his hand which caused him to stop.

"Mom having the good sense to make you our Dad was the greatest gift she left us. I hope you know that."

Jacob bit his lip and nodded. He walked out of the kitchen still holding Ashley's hand.

Emma shouted, "Grandma! Grandpa is back!"

Shenandoah National Park, Virginia

Dr. Felix Torres greeted Henry Matthews as he exited the elevator. In his early 80s, with milky white hair and dressed in an old-fashioned brown suit, he walked slowly to greet Dr. Torres.

Dr. Torres smiled warmly and offered, "Good afternoon, Henry. It's so good to see you again."

Henry took a couple more steps before stopping. He looked at Dr. Torres with concern as he fought to catch his breath. Dr. Torres waited patiently for Henry to gather himself.

"Good afternoon, Felix. You have to pardon me. I somehow became an old man despite my objections."

Dr. Torres laughed and shook his hand. "Henry, I can only hope to be as active as you are by the time I'm your age."

Henry smirked and replied, "Be careful what you ask for."

"Shall we go meet your brother?"

"Thank you, yes."

"Are you sure I can't offer you a wheelchair?"

Henry frowned, "At my age, once you put me in one of those things, you may as well pick out the color of my sentient box."

Dr. Torres chuckled and probably knew better than to try to one up Henry's humor. They walked together as Henry allowed Dr. Torres to escort him with their arms joined at the elbow, like two lovers on a stroll. The guard entered the passcode and the two of them made their way to a couch. Dr. Torres supported Henry's weight as he gently lowered himself onto the couch.

An assistant walked over to hand a wireless headset to Henry which Dr. Torres helped him with. Dr. Torres adjusted the height of the mouthpiece and gave Henry a final look over.

"Ready?"

Henry nodded and Dr. Torres signaled to his assistant who sat before a computer to start the conversation.

"Henry, I'm going to get some work done. Just let Melinda know when you finish and I'll come help you."

"Thank you, Felix."

"What's that?" Warren Matthews answered in Henry's headphone.

"I'm sorry Warren, I was just talking to Felix."

"I see. How are you doing today, Henry?"

"I am still moving well enough to make it here each month. How are you Warren?"

"I'm the same as yesterday and the day before. And always worried if I'll be the one to disappear tomorrow," Warren continued, "I don't understand why you come all this way. You can call me like so many other families."

Henry smiled despite Warren's inability to see his response. "Call me old-fashioned. There's something comforting in coming to your house and being here with you."

Warren paused before responding, "I appreciate that. But when it becomes too difficult for you, please just call me."

"Of course."

"What have you been up to?"

"Oh, you know. I get to see the grandkids when I can. Mostly playing bridge with the other old timers. The girls are constantly chasing me around the retirement home. Not too many of us men left. Scarcity makes for the best beer goggles," Henry chuckled as he finished.

"I do miss sex. Hell, I miss a hot bath," Warren explained.

"What are you up to these days?"

"We digitally discuss the events of the day. But it's not like when I first joined the Elders."

"How is that?"

"They used to come ask my opinion or questions about why I made certain decisions while running the CIA. But now, it appears even my knowledge has an expiration date."

Henry took his time before responding. "Why don't you want to come home like so many other Elders?"

"Let me explain it this way. There is nothing I can do or experience there that I can't do here. And here at least I can bullshit anytime I chose, sans the beer that is painfully missing from the experience. You would think one of these software guys could find a way to help us digitally get drunk on a Friday night."

"You know they say all these Collected from the beyond are going home and quite happy."

"I have heard the same thing, but I've also heard they all have this profound contentment about them. But I wouldn't know, they won't let us talk to them."

Henry furrowed his eyebrows. "I didn't realize that. Why is that?"

"They tell us that until they have conducted more research, they worry about them acting like a virus if they are introduced. You know what they originally thought they were. A pollutant in our digital homes."

"I had heard that, but why won't they at least let you talk to each other, like we do."

"My brother, I have often wondered if you wouldn't have made a better CIA director than me. I think it's because they worry that we'll become entirely disenchanted with our chosen lot in the afterlife after learning what makes them so content."

Henry nodded his head. "You hear Alabama elected a democratic governor?"

"Yes, that has become quite a focus of conversation in our digital network. Apparently, the indiscrimination of the afterlife is impacting the thinking of the living world."

"Warren?"

"Yes, Henry?"

"I will miss you when I die."

"Now why do you say something like that. Apparently the Collected say everything is calm and happy."

"Maybe. I miss Martha terribly and now I'm worried if I'll really be with her."

"I'm not following you Henry. From everything I've learned, what it means to be together is beyond our understanding in our three-dimensional world. But what does that have to do with me?"

"Because I love this time together. And I don't care what people say, I at least understand this and know I'll miss it."

"It's a lovely sentiment Henry, but I believe you'll have a different opinion when the time comes."

Henry scanned the walls of the room with all the flashing LED lights and asked, "Warren, do you think if I am lucky enough to be collected, they will allow us to talk when I come back?"

"Henry, I think if they collect you, I'm doubtful how many of the Elder's will remain or if they even have a need for our program."

"Why is that?"

"So many of us selected for our intellect and experience have become largely forgotten relics. And how many people will continue to pay their way into this vault when digital life has a life expectancy problem. Especially when the post death experience, while still maddeningly ambiguous, has a certainty to it now."

Henry grinned and answered, "I hope they let me come back and meet you, because that way I get to talk to my brother."

Warren paused before he replied, "They clearly chose the

wrong brother, every step of the way."

Munich, Germany

Max sat fidgeting in the straight-back chair in his father's office. He was wearing a dress shirt and black pants with a pair of black loafers. He got up and walked over to the pictures on his father's desk. Max stopped and picked up the framed print of him and his parents when he couldn't be more than 10 years old. Max grimaced as he stared at the orange sand and blue water in the photograph.

Franz walked into his office, breaking Max out of his trance.

"What you thinking about?" Franz asked.

"Just remembering our trip to Malta."

"That was an amazing few days. We should really do something like that again."

Max nodded his head but his expression argued otherwise.

"You don't seem so sure about that?"

"Well, I was just thinking about the tourist you bumped into. He didn't react so well when you made him lose his drink."

Franz squinted his eyes trying to recall the situation. "I remember the topless ladies. But no... I don't recall that. Must not have been very important."

Max shook his head. "I think he called you a stupid kraut after you apologized in German."

"Is that so? I can't recall that," Franz took the picture from Max's hand and placed it back on his desk.

Franz added, "You had lunch? You ready for a tour of the Collection facility?"

"Yes. Mom made me lunch and made sure I wasn't late."

"Seems we both got to enjoy mother's cooking today," he continued, "Shall we go?"

Max took one last look at the picture and followed his father out of the office. They headed down the hallway until they reached a secured door. A guard greeted his father by name and keyed them through. The door opened to an elevated walkway which connected his father's building to an adjacent structure. On the other end, another guard met them and entered a numeric code on the keypad. They walked into a standard looking academic building and proceeded to a door labeled "Collectors Greeting Room". They walked past numerous offices, most with the door closed. Max peeked inside one open door to see chairs, couches, a desk and a cocktail table. Finally, they reached another door labeled, "Collection Facility. Authorized Personnel Only." Franz watched with pride as Max seemed captivated by the activity and flashing lights in the room. Nearly a dozen people were working in the room.

Max whispered to his father, "Are there any Germans working on your team?"

Franz smiled. "Other than me, we have about a dozen working in the Collection lab. Here in this room right now there are two, three if you include me. But why do you ask?"

Max shrugged and replied, "I don't know. I had an image in my head of German engineering running this place."

"I don't know that you are alone in this view. But this is some of the most difficult work ever accomplished. You need the best of the best wherever they come from. Besides…"

"Besides, what?" Max asked.

"Well, the more souls we collect, it becomes clear these notions of nationality, color, and even gender are not relevant terms to what defines the individual."

Max studied his father suspiciously while nodding.

Franz suggested to Max, "Want to go back to the cage and see where the new arrivals are resting?"

"Sure, but resting?"

Franz waved his hand for emphasis as he answered, "It's a figure of speech. It feels more human than stored. Don't you think?"

They walked into a room which had a small entry and with a chain link caged area. The cage was unlocked. In the center of the room was a large table with several chairs and computer workstations. On the perimeter of the room were steel shelves housing occupied and vacant sentient stations. The room was alive with flashing LED's and the glow of computer screens. Around the table were five individuals with headsets, talking while sitting at their monitors.

Max asked his father, "What are those people doing?"

Franz walked him behind one workstation and answered, "These are our integration engineers. They are working with individuals collected in the last couple of days or even last couple of months. They ready them for meeting their families and eventually transfer out of this facility to what they will soon call home."

"Are these more of the best of the best?"

Franz explained, "Yes and once again from all around the world. These people are psychologists who have built up a good understanding of the technology working with tuning engineers. They can often spot retention problems before the engineers monitoring all the technical data are aware in the other room."

Max shook his head and replied, "All so complicated. You

really think I could help out here, Dad?"

Franz patted his son on the back. "Baby steps, Max. Show some interest and commitment and you'll soon find yourself working on more interesting things as you learn."

"I haven't committed to doing this yet, you know."

"Oh, I'm aware. But I've also seen your face since we walked in here. But... the decision is yours."

Max smirked, "This is pretty cool. I feel a little bad about thinking you were just a crazy professor."

Franz laughed heartedly, "I think you just made my day. Why don't we double back to the psych ward and see if one of them are free so you can get a feel for what they do?"

"Ok."

Franz led Max back onto the Collection floor and Max stopped in the middle of the room. Franz turned to watch his son spin himself around, fully taking in his surroundings.

"So cool!" he said beaming.

"I got a signal here," shouted the source identifier.

Franz said to Max, "It's about to get even cooler. Watch this!"

He led Max toward a tuning station and they watched the growing acquisition percentage on the monitor.

"She is collecting someone as we speak and this one is a strong signal."

Max looked surprised and curious and leaned in to watch the monitor.

"Atomic pull initiated," a lock down engineer shouted.

Franz pulled Max over to the lock down station. A green light on the shelf turned on.

"I've got a live sentient box," announced the engineer.

Franz grinned ear to ear. His attention was almost solely on his son.

A young man rolled a cart into the room from the psychology area and plugged a power cable into a sentient box.

"I've got power to the box," he announced.

Another person came over and together they lifted the box onto the cart. Franz motioned to Max to follow the cart as they pushed it into the next room. Franz and Max followed it into the open office they had seen earlier. A second person walked in behind them and helped lift the sentient box onto the back table.

"Max, this is Greg Schultz. He is the psychologist who will greet the individual that was just collected. With his permission, I would love to have you see this moment, but you must be silent."

Greg replied, "Yes, that would be fine. But please, I need absolute quiet."

Max nodded and looked at his father in disbelief.

"More than cool, Dad. When do I start?"

His father smiled and motioned to be quiet.

Greg asked, "I'm about to make first contact. Phones off?"

They both accommodated his request and signaled their readiness.

"This is the moment," Greg declared.

He turned and clicked on the "Go Live" button.

Franz watched Max carefully for his reaction.

"Hello this is Greg. Who am I talking to?"

"Hello," the default male, monotone voice replied, "What is this?"

"My name is Greg and you are talking through a computer. Can you tell me who you are?"

The male voice replied, "What is a computer?"

Franz stopped watching Max and turned his attention to the workstation.

"It will take time for me to explain this to you. To make it simple, it's a device which allows me to talk to you."

The male voice responded, "I don't understand."

Greg tried again and asked, "Perhaps we should start with introductions. My name is Greg, what is your name?"

A long pause before the voice replied, "Hello, Greg. My name is Adolf. Adolf Hitler."

Greg turned in a desperate attempt to get direction from Franz. Instead, he found Max watching his father's pale and stunned reaction.

CHAPTER 9

Munich, Germany

Franz collected himself enough to point wildly at the computer while mouthing emphatically, "Shut it off". Greg did as he was instructed and Franz saw the conversation muted.

"Greg, nothing of this goes into a log. You got me. Nothing!"

Greg quietly responded, "Yes, I understand."

"Do you understand? Do you understand what we have on our hands? I want you to physically tag this as high risk for loss, do not touch."

Greg nodded his head.

Franz grew more agitated. "Do you understand, Greg?"

"Yes, I understand," he shouted back.

Franz looked at his son and ran his hand through his hair. "Jesus Christ. Max. Not a word. Promise me, not a word."

Max looked at his father soberly, "Not a word. I got it."

Franz stared at Max for a short time longer while trying to figure out his next step. He looked at Greg and then at the sentient box. "Jesus, f'ing Christ."

"Want me to turn him off and let him go?"

Franz took a moment to consider his question before responding, "As much as that appeals to me, from what we've learned from the Collected, that means he's flowing through everything we touch. I realize that was the case moments ago, but for now I like him stuck in his little box."

He fumbled in his pocket and pulled out his wallet. He opened it and pulled out 100 Marks.

"Here, take this. Go buy a padlock and any materials that ensures only the two of us can ever get him out of the cage."

Greg stood up to walk out. "Yes, sir."

"Oh, one last thing. Take Max home for me. Would you do that?"

"But Dad! I finally found someplace I enjoy and now you want to send me home?"

"Not now, Max. I'll bring you back, but what I need to do next I have to take care of alone. Please, just go and don't talk to anyone, including your mother about this. Promise me, NO ONE!"

Max exclaimed, "NO ONE! I got it."

"Greg, I'll see you soon. This is way above my pay grade."

Franz practically flew out of the office and out of the facility. He rushed past security and down to the exit of the building. He ran across campus to the administration building. He pressed the button for the elevator and after a couple seconds abandoned the idea and took the stairs. He ran to the top floor and into the Office of the President.

"Good afternoon how can I help you, Dr. Hoffman? Is everything ok?" asked the receptionist.

"Good afternoon, Helen. Yes, everything is ok, but I need to talk with Wolfgang immediately."

Helen politely smiled. "I'm sorry but he's tied up in a meeting at the moment. Do you want me to have him call you when he is free?"

Franz looked to the ground and then back at Helen. "Helen, I wouldn't tell you this if it wasn't important, but I need to interrupt him immediately."

"I see. Can I ask what it's about?"

"I'm sorry I'm not at a liberty to say. But it needs to happen."

She sized him up before stepping away from her desk and entering the president's conference room. A moment later she returned and said, "He'll be right out. You can wait in his office."

Franz sat down in one of the leather chairs on the visitor side of the president's desk and waited impatiently. A few minutes later, the president entered his office.

"Franz, this is quite surprising and not like you. I have to tell you, I get this feeling this will be one of those conversations I will regret afterward. What do you think?"

Franz squeezed out a smile and responded, "I'm afraid you might be correct. Can we close the door, please?"

"I don't think that will be necessary, Helen is quite professional."

Franz rubbed his face and replied, "Wolfgang, you need to close the door."

Wolfgang pulled his door shut and asked, "Is this a good time to pour a couple glasses of whiskey?"

"As much as I would love to, I suspect the people that will follow me into this office will not look kindly to alcohol on your breath."

Wolfgang took a seat behind his desk and noted, "The door is closed and you've built up the anticipation enough. What exactly is the issue?"

Franz paused for a moment before blurting out, "We've collected Adolf Hitler."

Wolfgang stared in disbelief at him. "Please tell me this is a joke."

"No joke."

"No joke," Wolfgang echoed. "Excuse me for a moment, Franz."

Wolfgang calmly walked over and opened the door.

"Helen, can you please ask Leon to join me in here immediately?"

"Yes sir," she replied.

Wolfgang returned to his desk leaving the door ajar.

"Tell me again the odds of this happening?"

Franz wiped his mouth before answering. "There have been roughly 100 Billion people born over the history of mankind. But in the time period we generally can collect souls, maybe 20 billion. I would say 1 in 20 billion, roughly."

"Roughly?"

"I'm trying to do this off the top of my head."

"I see. Let's say you are right. 1 in 20 billion odds and this bastard is who shows up. Not Gandhi? You also have him hidden somewhere in the cage?"

"No, sir."

"Charlemagne? Churchill? Julius Caesar? How about Jesus Christ? He might help provide some answers that your program seems to not be able to answer, don't you think?"

Franz looked confused whether he should answer "no" to the first questions or "yes" to the last question. He decided upon silence instead. Wolfgang just stared blankly ahead. The door creaked open and Leon walked into the room.

Wolfgang gestured dramatically while saying, "Please close the door, Leon, and you'll likely want to take a seat for this one. I don't want to be calling the medical staff in here next."

"Yes, sir."

He closed the door and sat next to Franz as instructed.

"Franz, can you kindly repeat to Leon, what you shared with me?"

Franz adjusted uncomfortably in his chair and began, "We collected Adolf Hitler just now."

Leon smirked and laughed. "You're shitting me, right?"

"I wish I was."

Wolfgang added, "I concur on this point. I wish he was."

Leon glanced back and forth between the two men. "You're certain?"

"He hasn't been through full processing yet, but he identified himself as such. The Collected have never lied and it's not a common name."

Wolfgang remarked, "I see. You've collected the honorable Adolf Hitler. That is a relief to know."

"I didn't say that. I'm just explaining why I think the certainty is high."

Leon looked at Wolfgang and said, "Excuse me, I need to use my phone."

"Please, do so."

Wolfgang dialed a number and the other two men waited with curiosity to see who he called.

Leon started the conversation, "Ben, how's it going?"

He waited for a response before adding, "Where are you? I have a situation on my hands that you need to drop everything for."

"Yes, it's that bad and no, I can't explain until you get here."

He responded to the next question. "Yes. The president's office. I'll see you in a few minutes."

He hung up the phone and Wolfgang asked, "Who will be here in a few minutes?"

"Ben Weber, I used to work with him at the Bundesnachrichtendienst. He happens to be presenting at a lecture on campus as we speak."

"What is his role?" Wolfgang asked.

"Deputy director. I was lucky to catch him, he had just broken the students into a small group exercise."

"How long before things return to normal around here Leon?" Wolfgang asked.

He took a deep breath. "Honestly, maybe never. This is not good. While we wait let me ask some pretty basic questions."

"Sure," Wolfgang answered.

"I'm sorry but with all due respect these are questions for Dr. Hoffman."

"How can I help?" Franz asked.

"Where is he at the moment?"

"Locked in a family room and not yet documented."

"Good answer. How long will it take you to verify his claim?"

"We can usually do this quickly, from under a day to a few days."

"Understand, you were fucked on this one, either way. But if it turns out he's not who he says he is, Wolfgang will have to fire you."

Franz looked at him wild-eyed. "What?"

"The Federal Intelligence Service does not look kindly on fire drills. The chancellor herself will call Wolfgang and demand it."

"Wonderful," Franz replied.

"It's not personal, professor. And you've done everything correctly. I hope you understand that."

Franz shook his head, "Not really, but I'll save you from telling me it doesn't really matter what I think."

There was a knock at the door and Helen introduced the guest, "I have a Ben Weber here to see you."

Wolfgang replied, "Yes, Helen. Please let him in and close the door behind him."

Ben walked in and Leon introduced him to the other two. He took a seat in one of the chairs and asked, "What pulled me out of a classroom full of students, who are now tweeting to the world that something rushed me from a lecture hall for a pending emergency?"

Leon looked sternly at Ben and responded, "You will not like this one bit. Do you know what exactly Professor Hoffman does here for us?"

Ben responded with a confused look on his face, "Of course, Professor Hoffman is perhaps one of the most famous Germans in the country at the moment. Wait.... does this have to do with his Collection program?"

Leon looked at Franz and said, "Tell him."

Ben focused on Franz intently as he explained, "We collected Adolf Hitler about an hour ago."

Ben watched Wolfgang and Leon's reactions before he stood and dialed his phone.

"Jennifer, I need to talk with Paul immediately," he waited for her response and then replied, "Thank you for transferring me."

The three of them waited silently for him to speak next.

"Paul, we have a situation on our hands. The Technical Institute of Munich collected the consciousness of Adolf Hitler in the last hour."

Leon looked at Wolfgang and said, "Everything changes now."

"Yes sir. I understand," Ben responded and then hung up.

"What did he tell you?" Wolfgang asked.

"He said he was calling the Chancellor immediately and we should expect further direction in the half hour."

Seattle, WA

The room was dark except for the reading light on Jacob's side of the bed. He was engrossed in some thriller while Christine slept peacefully next to him. He took off his glasses and put the book on the nightstand. Slowly he pulled back the sheets and headed to the master bathroom. As he tried to slip back into bed, he woke Christine.

"What are you still doing up?" she asked.

"I couldn't sleep and decided to read."

"I see. Do you want to talk about it?"

Jacob stared out the window considering her question before answering, "I don't see why not."

She grabbed an extra pillow from the side of the bed and placed it on top of the one she was sleeping on. She lifted herself higher onto the stacked pillows and waited for him to start.

"I find this whole situation with Emily to be so difficult."

She let his statement hang in the air for a moment before answering. "And what do you mean by 'situation'?"

Jacob turned on his side so he could look at her, eye to eye. "I loved that woman to my core and it took so long to let her go."

"We've talked about all this, you know I understand this."

Jacob put his hand on her forearm and replied, "When you find your peace, you don't stop loving, you just find a way to let love back in."

She scratched his neck affectionately and said, "I understand this sweetie."

"But do you really understand this?"

She smiled at him, "Try me. What do you mean?"

He sighed and explained, "I love you unconditionally. You brought joy back to my life."

She nodded waiting for the rest of his response.

"Now that Emily is back, or whatever you call it, it's reopened these emotions I had buried away."

Christine looked at him concerned. "I am not sure what you are trying to say?"

"I'm just trying to explain the complexity of emotions flowing through me right now. I feel like I'm stuck in a place I can't stay much longer."

She adjusted herself and sat up more, resting her elbows on the pillows and her head against the headboard. "Just tell me what has you bothered."

He looked at her suspiciously but answered, "I feel like if I tell Emily I love her and miss her, that I'm cheating on you. And if I say nothing I am hurting her and the girls' feelings. There you have it."

Christine, rubbed his shoulder and replied, "You should always tell someone you love them. Unless you are telling me you want to leave me for her, I don't see the problem?"

He laughed. "I am not sure how one has an affair with a sentient box, but I think electrocution might be the penalty. But no, I could never do that to you, nor would I want to."

"So, don't worry about saying these things to her and know it only makes me love the size of your heart."

He let out a deep breath and added, "That does make me feel better but I don't think that's the end of it."

"Oh?" she said pensively.

He paused to read her face based on her reaction.

"On another level, while there's a part of me that wants to share this with her, there's a part of this that doesn't feel real. The woman I loved was full of energy and spirit. She was alive."

"I see. Your questioning the authenticity of this experience?"

"Maybe. But I see how Ash and Cindy and especially Emma respond to her. There's nothing fake about any of their emotions."

"I would agree with that. So what about this troubles you?"

He shrugged and asked, "I'm not sure. Do you have an opinion?"

She rolled flat on her back and stared at the ceiling, giving herself a moment to ponder it further. "Do you think you fought so long to put these feelings somewhere safe you have forgotten how to let them out?"

"Perhaps, but I don't know that's it."

"Just try sharing what you are struggling to explain."

"I know that people can have virtual online relationships and maybe for some it's satisfying. But I think when you have experienced that joy of love... not once but twice... experienced it fully... with not only the heart and mind, but the flesh and blood. When you emotionally work together to change the world in some way. It makes anything else feel fake."

She raised an eyebrow and clarified, "Ok, but why are you struggling?"

"Because I think I am in love with what made her a great woman, but now I find it hard to tell a box that I love her."

Christine smiled, rolled over, and gave him a kiss.

"I'm not sure you have it figured out, but I get what is bothering you."

"Can I ask you another question?"

"Of course."

He looked at her out of the corner of his eye and asked, "Does it bother you, even in just the littlest way since Emily described death, that when we get our game on, that we are rubbing up with eons of souls at the same time?"

"Oh my God, Jacob. No, it had not occurred to me. But now that you planted that little seed in my head, good luck getting a piece of this anytime soon."

"Come on. It wasn't that bad."

"Maybe there are some things we really shouldn't share. And I swear to God if you bring up anything about my dead parents in the next 5 minutes, you are going to be sleeping on the couch."

He laughed and added, "Fair enough, but aunties are fair game?"

"Jacob Dwyer," she yelled and reached back to hit him with her pillow.

Cambridge, England

Dr. Ernie Clark sat at his desk reading a thick report bound by a large black clip. A reading lamp on his cluttered desk provided the only source of light in the room. He was nearly bald except for a horse shoe patch of gray hair. His white stripped button-down shirt had an old coffee stain near his belt. His black penny loafers which bounced from nervous energy hardly moved his tan slacks. The phone rang a couple times before he reached to grab the handset without taking his eyes off the report.

"This is Dr. Clark."

"Good evening my friend, how are you doing?"

Dr. Clark put down the report and sat back in his chair to rest his feet on the top of his desk.

"Good... I'm not sure what.... What time is it in Champaign, Ralph?"

"Just about 3pm. But I've been in the lab all day, may as well be 3am."

"Pretty much the same here. I'll be heading out shortly. Shirley's not a fan of this work of ours."

"Well, give my regards to the wife. And that's why I'm calling."

"My wife?"

Dr. Cummings chuckled, "No. The work. I think it's time to let Grandstone know."

Dr. Clark ran his fingers across the smooth skin of his head and replied, "You're probably bloody right."

"We have a handful now. Hoffman is talking to a few. I don't see how we keep this under wraps."

"We're still losing 85% in the first few days. Dangerous ground," Dr. Clark replied cautiously.

"Yes, but Grandstone should know."

"Think he'll keep it quiet? I can't imagine the pressure on us, once the world finds out."

"No, no. I've worked with him for years. And frankly, I'm sure you've read Hoffman's report. The collections are about to explode I think."

"Yes, I'm reading it right now. Outstanding. I don't understand why we can't get the same results here. Hoffman's breakthroughs are coming from my lab's advances. I'm hoping I'll find something in his report. The man is verbose for a German, don't you think?"

Dr. Cummings laughed. "I guess so. But you're good if I hang up and call Grandstone? I just talked with Hoffman, he's on board."

"Yes, that makes sense. Just make sure he knows that its bed time here and divorce is expensive."

"You got it. Goodnight John and send Shirly my regards."

"Goodnight old chap."

Dr. Clark looked at his watch as he swung his legs to the floor to standup. He grabbed his jacket and work bag and turned off his desk lamp. He meandered toward the computer lab where the hum of equipment filled the room. He smiled like a proud father inspecting the various instruments being cautious to avoid the jungle of wires running everywhere. As he reached the back of the lab, he could hear the chatter of a keyboard. Dr. Clark peered around the corner of a cubicle.

"John, what are you doing here so late?"

John practically jumped out his seat startled by the question. His red tee shirt, blue jeans, and black converse shoes were in stark contrast to the professor's attire.

"Professor Clark, I didn't hear you come in. You nearly scared me to death."

Dr. Clark laughed. "Sorry about that. But what are you doing here so late? You have a new baby at home. They grow up too fast. Go enjoy her!"

John smiled and responded, "You sound like my wife. I have ten- or fifteen-minutes left. I've been playing with this new algorithm. I think it's close."

"How much improvement do you think it will make?"

John shuffled through papers on his desk before finding the one he wanted. He stood up and held the paper so that Dr. Clark could also read it.

"I think another 60% retention improvement. The real benefit though should be a reduction in integration from months to weeks," he turned to Dr. Clark before he finished, "Dare I hope days?"

Dr. Clark shook his head. "I hope your right. That would take this project in a direction that no one could have possibly imagined."

John smiled and answered, "Perhaps I can get my tenure and stop having to take the bus to work every day."

Dr. Clark laughed and replied, "You figure it out and one day this entire lab will work for you. You really think ten minutes more?"

"Oh, not much longer. I want to download the new algorithms and see what results I get with this sentient box we captured about a week ago."

"Ok. But if it doesn't work immediately, promise me, you'll go home?"

"It's going to work."

Dr. Clark shook his head and walked to the exit of the lab when he turned and shouted, "Don't forget to log your results in the database. Munich and Champaign are using it to learn from us. Maybe the Illini, or whatever they call themselves at the school, will name a lab there after you too."

"Consider it done. Goodnight, professor."

"Goodnight, John."

John rolled his chair over to his computer and did a final check of his code. He clicked on the download button and walked over to the coffeepot. He held the glass pot to eye level, sloshing the coffee while grimacing. He poured a cup and returned to his computer. The screen displayed a message showing the load was successful. He leaned over to the sentient box and inspected it.

He returned to his computer and said, "Come on D-43. Give it up for Johnnie tonight!"

He clicked on the Go Live Button.

"Hello this is John Spring. What is your name?"

John watched his speakers intently and after a few moments tried again, "Hello this is John. What is your name?"

"Hello," answered the male monotone voice.

"Hello. What is your name?"

"What is this?"

"You are in computer and we are using it to talk."

"I am in a computer, how is that possible?"

John clicked on mute as he raised his hands with joy and shouted, "Well there is a new response."

He unmuted and asked again. "My name is John Spring. What is your name?"

"John... My name is Frank Stone."

"Frank, it is my pleasure to meet you. I know that you must be disorientated at the moment, but I promise that with time this will all make sense to you."

"John. Who are you?"

"I am a researcher at Cambridge University."

"What is this?"

"Frank, you are in a computer talking to me."

"How do you know my name, John?"

"You just told me your name is Frank Stone."

He paused for a moment. "I see. Can you help me, John?"

John beamed as he logged notes on his computer.

"How can I help you Frank?"

"I need you to help me get money to my wife and daughter."

"Ok, Frank. We'll get that figured out in due time. For now, maybe you can help me understand where you lived."

"I lived in London in the Lennox Garden neighborhood. But I need to get a message to my wife."

John grinned and responded, "You are a feisty one Frank. Can you tell me your wife's name?"

"My wife's name is Wilma and my daughter is Olivia."

"Thank you, Frank. Can you tell me when you were born?"

"John, I need to tell my wife where to find the fifty-seven million Pounds."

John stopped entering information into the integration script and asked, "Did you say fifty-seven million Pounds?"

"Yes, John. I had to hide the money and she didn't know I did it."

John stood up and looked around the lab to see if anyone else was around.

"Frank, what can I do to help?"

"Who is this?" he responded.

"SOB" John mouthed silently to himself looking frustrated.

"I am John Spring a researcher at Cambridge. I'm trying to reconnect you with Wilma and Olivia."

"Thank you for doing that John. I need to get her the account numbers and bank information so she can collect fifty-seven million Pounds."

John grabbed his coffee and walked around the lab aimlessly. He stopped and looked out the window as a bus pulled up. A handful of people got on board as a Porsche drove around the bus. John's eyes followed the car down the street until it was out of sight. He scurried back to his workstation when his eye caught a pallet of equipment against the wall. He grabbed scissors and cut away the strapping bands. Deliberately examining the descriptions on the boxes, he eventually grabbed one and lifted it to a nearby desk. He cut it open and inside were a half-dozen sentient boxes. He grabbed one and walked back to his cubicle. He placed the new sentient box next to Frank's box. Slowly he peeled off the tag on Frank's box and reapplied it to the new box.

He stopped and rubbed his forehead. "Jesus, is this who you really are?"

He glanced back at the real box D-43. "Frank, Frank, Frank. Why did you have to say that? Why did you have to be the first soul I used on my new algorithm?"

He returned to the window and watched the thinning crowd of people on the street below. He grabbed his phone out of his pocket and dialed.

"Hey babe. How are you?"

She answered, "I'm doing well but tired. Carolyn has been a handful today. You coming home anytime soon?"

"I'm almost done here. Hey, I have a question for you."

"Sure, what's up?" she asked.

"I'm thinking about doing some work on the side to help bring in more money, what do you think?"

"Seriously, are you crazy? You are calling me at ten o'clock at night and you want to work more?"

"No, no, no. I don't mean like that. It would allow me to spend less time here and I could do it from home. It's a consulting business I've been thinking about for some time."

She thought before responding, "I don't know. A nanny and extra money would be helpful. But mostly time with you would be lovely."

"This would mean more time *and* money."

"This is up to you. You've told me how much they love you. It won't be long until you get tenured, right?"

He paused, "I don't know. Sometimes I feel I'm helping Dr. Clark secure his speaking tour career. There are no certainties."

"I trust you. Do what you think is right. Does this have to be decided tonight?"

He laughed. "No. We can talk about it when I get home."

"OK. I love you. Are you going to come home now?"

"I love you too. And yes, I'll walk out when I hang up."

"I'll try to stay up. See you soon."

"Ok. Bye," he said as the call ended.

He stared at Frank's box for a good minute before he blew out a breath he had held almost as long. He walked over to his workstation and sat down.

"Frank, I am going to have to say goodbye for now. Can we talk tomorrow?"

"What am I doing here?" Frank replied.

John didn't stop to answer this time. Instead, he ended the conversation and checked the battery level on the box. He disconnected the power cable from Frank and placed Frank's box in an empty cardboard container. He found tape and sealed it. He threw his backpack over his shoulders and awkwardly carried the cardboard box across the room. He made his way to the door when he stopped and returned to his desk.

He placed the box on top of a lab bench and returned to the computer. He logged into the tracking database and opened the record on sentient box D-43. Navigating to the field requesting sentient status, he changed it to "retention failure". He logged off and grabbed the cardboard box off the table and walked to the door. John looked around the room and took a deep breath. He opened the door and walked out, without looking back.

CHAPTER 10

Redmond, WA

"Mom, I have a question for you."

Emily replied, "Sure. How can I help you?"

Cindy smiled with satisfaction as she stared at her mother's sentient box.

"I can't seem to get Emma to eat vegetables to save my life."

"I think this is payback for you not eating any vegetables either," Emily replied lacking the normal voice inflections.

"Perhaps, but that's a non-answer," Cindy replied.

"What have you tried?"

"Green beans, sweet peas, broccoli, squash, peppers. Probably more, but vegetables."

"That's not what I meant. What methods have you tried?"

Cindy raised her eyebrows and answered, "Oh. I've tried waiting her out until they get cold which has led to tears and fighting. I've tried mixing them into her macaroni and cheese which has led to tears and fighting. I've tried withholding screen time, which has led to tears and fighting. I'm thinking about just feeding her straight sugar and soda and be done with it."

"You realize this isn't about the food, right?"

"What do you mean?"

"This is about pushing boundaries and seeing how far she can get with you."

Cindy grinned and replied, "You think so?"

"I could be wrong, but I don't think I am."

"Were you always this confident in yourself?"

Emily took a moment before replying, "Probably, but I could feel fear which likely toned down my conviction."

"Do you not feel fear anymore?"

"I think the key word is 'feel'. Intellectually I don't want to be wrong and have harm come to you or Emma. And I can recognize my lack of knowledge and experience. But I can also recognize the lack of hormones which accompany uncertainty with a body."

"So fascinating. Do you feel love?"

"Once again, it's different, but I do."

Cindy pondered the answer for a moment, when she returned to the original topic, "How did you get me to eat my vegetables?"

"By treating you as a person with feelings that mattered."

"Feelings again! But what do you mean?"

Emily answered, "Regardless if they are well developed or not, one's feelings are real. I would ask you what it was you did not like and how we could make it better."

"And I ate my vegetables?"

"Of course not. It couldn't be that easy."

Cindy laughed and replied, "I guess not. But can't blame me for hoping."

"I can't. But we started with a try everything rule. Eventually we would agree upon numbers of bites. And before I got too sick to feed you, you ate better because your palette adjusted."

"But why was it so important that you treated me as a person with feelings?"

"By listening to your concerns, you knew I cared about you and that built trust. That trust allowed you to take the baby steps you needed."

Cindy shrugged sadly and replied, "I see. I missed you, Mom. I'm glad you came back to be part of my life."

"I'm glad I can help. This is time I never thought we would have either."

Emma shuffled over to her mother and asked, "Are you talking to Grandma?"

Cindy turned around and picked her up. "Well, look who woke up from her nap. And yes, do you want to say hello to Grandma?"

"Hello, Grandma."

"Why, Hello, Emma. Did you sleep well?"

"Yes."

Cindy asked, "Are you hungry?"

Emma laid her head on her mom's shoulder and answered, "Yes."

"Wonderful, I have a fabulous idea for what we can have for lunch."

Berlin, Germany -- Washington DC, USA -- London, UK

"Chancellor Muller, the President and Prime Minister are ready for you on the conference call," the Chancellor's secretary informed her.

"Thank you, Bridgette," she replied.

The Chancellor surveyed her team and then opened the line on the speakerphone.
"President Harris and Prime Minister Goodman thank you so much for taking this call on short notice."

Both of the women responded in kind and Chancellor Muller got right to the point.

"I realize, like myself, that you are joined on this call by your advisors. I want to address this issue directly for two reasons. First, I want to ask your continued cooperation and not leak what I am about to share. And second, I felt it best you hear this directly from me instead of through diplomatic channels."

President Tricia Harris spoke up, "I can assure you my team will keep this conversation private."
"Obviously the same from us," Prime Minister Margaret Goodman added.

"We've had an unfortunate development with our Collector's program in Munich. As both of your countries also have Collection sites, I thought it best we align on this development and next steps."

"I hope, this isn't a 150-year-old man, suing for loss of property and assets?" remarked Prime Minister Goodman.

Chancellor Marie Muller replied, "No. Although I'm uncertain my actual news will be any less disturbing. It seems that our facility here has defied 1 in 20 billion odds and collected the soul of one, Adolf Hitler."

The sound of silence screamed across the conference call.

After a long moment, President Harris asked, "You are certain of this, Ms. President?"

"It's been 12 hours of working through their process, but the experts believe this is the case."

"Fantastic news. We now have an immortal despot to add to our list of international concerns," remarked the Prime Minister.

The Chancellor replied, "I'm not happy as you might imagine, Ms. Prime Minister. We had to endure this man once, this is an abomination."

President Harris remarked, "Chancellor, if you could go back to 1920 and kill Hitler before he rose to power, you wouldn't give it a second thought. Please tell me you are about to pull the plug on this guy and send him back from where he came?"

"If only it were that simple. The Collected have discussed a feeling of being everywhere and nowhere. I thought perhaps our philosophers would be the first to make sense of this riddle. But it raises the issue if we're better with him in one of these damn boxes or free to whisper in the ear of dictators forever," the Chancellor answered.

"Well, that raises a great point," the Prime Minister responded.

"Good point or not. What steps are we going to take to keep this from becoming a problem?" asked President Harris.

"This is why I pulled us together today. As a first step, we've isolated Adolf from the others and kept the news from the Munich Collection team — other than the program director, one of his staff, and the director's son. Turns out it was 'bring your kid to work day' and he got one hell of an education."

"Good first step, but what are you going to do with him?" asked Prime Minister Goodman.

"I wanted to discuss with you forming an oversight board. We hand pick a small team and get them together to solve this once and for all. We do this under the auspice of regulations, no different from food, airline, or even pets. Honestly, we should have been ahead of this, anyway."

"I've had my FBI director already working on this. Let's get him on this team and perhaps save all of us time."

"Of course, you did, Tricia. And that would be helpful," Chancellor Muller replied.

"I also worry about what else we might drag up. It would probably be political suicide to turn off this program, but we should insist upon government oversight, physical oversight, in the Collection facilities themselves. At least until we have this figured out," Prime Minister Goodman added.

"I agree."

"As do I," Chancellor Muller said.

"One more thing that occurs to me," President Harris said, "We should have our oversight board decide who needs to know this information. The three program directors need to know as does Stanford for sure. Everyone agreed to that?"

"Yes."

"Yes."

"OK. I know that I have a schedule this meeting interrupted and I need to get on with my day. Is there anything else or can we agree to another call once this team comes up with some recommendations?" Chancellor Muller asked.

"I think that will work," Prime Minister Goodman replied.

"Good. Also, I'll have my team on point for getting this pulled together. It's my problem and ultimately when this comes out the optics would be terrible to have either of you solving this for my country. Agreed?" Chancellor Muller asked.

"On both points, I do," President Harris replied.

"Same here," Prime Minister Goodman added.

"Ok. We'll talk soon enough. In the meantime, maybe Churchill and Roosevelt will come knocking offering their services," quipped the Chancellor.

President Harris laughed, "I'm glad you can find a sense of humor in all this. Let's try to keep this under wraps as long as we can. The world doesn't deserve to have to deal with this bastard a second time and maybe we can figure this out before they have to."

Prime Minister Goodman commented, "I couldn't agree more. Let's get this fixed, ASAP."

Munich, Germany

Max, Pete, and Lukas strolled down the sidewalk. It was a cool night and the moon nearly full in the sky. The streets were alive with activity and their eyes darted excitedly people watching.

"Pete!" a young woman shouted.

Pete stopped and turned to hear the voice. His face lit up with recognition of the petite blonde. Her hair was pulled back in a pony tail. She wore ripped blue jeans and a low-cut tank top.

"Kelly! How are you?"

Max hit Lukas in the shoulder and smiled slyly.

"I'm great. What are you doing out tonight?"

"Out to grab beers with the boys."

She looked at him concerned, "Please tell me not Simon?"

"What's wrong with Simon?" Pete asked.

"Yeah what's wrong with Simon?" Max repeated.

Pete and Kelly both shot a look toward Max. Kelly returned her attention to Pete and answered, "I don't know. He gives me the creeps. I've seen the two of you together a few times now."

Pete looked a little surprised. "I'm not sure who will be there. But it's our usual Friday night spot."

"I know the place. Maybe I can talk the girls into stopping by later."

Pete for once looked bashful and was speechless. Max took advantage of his friend's silence. "You think Denise will come by?"

Kelly rolled her eyes at Max and turned her attention back to Pete, "Well my friends are getting ahead of me. Maybe we'll see each other later?"

Pete put his hands in his pockets and replied, "Yeah sure. I'll buy you a drink or something."

Kelly walked away grinning as she answered, "Sure. Let's make it happen."

Lucas rubbed Pete's shoulders demonstratively. "He could be a contender."

Pete shrugged his shoulders, forcing Lucas's hands off.

"Let's just head into the bar," Pete demanded.

They walked in and found the bar energetic and nearly full. The perimeter of the bar was lined with high back wooden booths soiled from years of spilled beer. A u-shaped bar made from plywood sat in the middle of the room. Tables with folding chairs filled the remainder of the space and they sat at an empty one near the back. The bartender barely over 20 years old, dressed in jeans and a tee shirt, greeted them rubbing his head.

"How you boys doing tonight," he asked.

"Shit, Johnnie. You fucking shaved your head? Your old man will give you hell," said Lukas.

"Nah. He's off on a three-month fishing boat job in the North Sea."

"I see. I thought you had grown a pair," teased Max.

"Fuck off. You guys want something to drink or just to fuck with me tonight."

Pete dramatically looked at Max and Lukas with feigned confusion and then answered, "It's a tough choice to be honest. But we'll take three beers and reserve the right to still fuck with you later."

"Hilarious," Johnnie replied sarcastically before asking, "The usual?"

Pete nodded and Johnnie left to fill their order.

"Pete tells me you got your walking papers from the airport."

"I did. Assholes replacing me with some robot. I got about a week left. My old man is trying to set me up with a job at his place."

Pete looked astonished and said, "Really. No offense but isn't that a little out of your league?"

"Offense taken, shit head. But yes, he will get me a job."

Lukas grinned, "When that doesn't work, I can still get you a job at the Blackbird."

Max shot Lukas a disapproving glare, "Never going to happen."

Pete surveyed the room and remarked, "No new talent in here tonight. Max you've hit on everything moving in here. I think it may be time for a new bar for us boys."

Max punched Pete in the shoulder and Pete yelled, "Ow! The truth hurts, huh?"

Johnnie returned with three beers and put them down. Max, Pete, and Lukas chugged them and slammed the glasses back on the tabletop.

"Another round, Johnnie!" Max shouted.

Johnnie looked frustrated and said, "You couldn't fucking ask for two beers the first round?"

Pete replied, "Excellent point, Johnnie. Make it two more rounds."

Johnnie shook his head and grabbed the empty pint glasses to bring back to the bar.

"That Johnnie's not half bad, but until he grows a pair, no way the boys will let him join us for the real deal," Lukas said.

Max looked around the room and answered, "Just keep it quiet, would you. You know the government has all these undercovers trying to make our life miserable."

Pete stared at Lukas without saying a word.

Lukas stared back before yelling, "OK. I got it."

"Good," Pete replied before adding, "Keep it that way."

"You boys will never believe what I saw at my dad's place the other day."

"A bunch of nerds excited because some girl was showing ankle?" asked Lukas.

"Jesus, that wasn't even funny when we were ten Lukas," Max complained.

Pete asked, "So what did you see?"

"I can't say it here, but you boys will worship me before the night is over."

Pete responded, "Honestly I can think of two, maybe three things in this world more unlikely to happen than that. But sure, I can't wait."

Max stared confidently at Pete. "You will eat those words."

Pete grinned reading Max's confidence. "I have to admit, now you have me curious."

"Patience!" Max explained.

Johnnie returned with six beers and he stood waiting after serving them.

Max asked abruptly, "What?"

Johnnie answered, "Aren't you going to slam these beers?"

Pete shook his head and said, "Nope. We will take our time and enjoy them!"

Johnnie frowned and left. The three of them each picked up a pint of beer and drank it until it was empty. Lukas burped loudly and then laughed. "I know you really want to fuck with Johnnie but I need a moment to digest that beer before we chug this other one."

"You sure you don't want to grab something out of your purse while you're waiting?" asked Pete.

Lukas flashed Pete the finger and grabbed the next beer. Max raised his glass to toast and the other two joined him.

He lowered his voice and said, "To bringing back the real Germany once and for all."

Pete looked around before adding, "Nice toast, but knock it off before you get us fucked."

They each took a drink but didn't finish them. Pete looked at his watch and declared, "I think we should bring these beers with us. It's time to head downstairs."

Max and Pete got up from the table but Lukas lingered. They looked at him to understand what he was doing.

He smiled and said, "Max ain't the only one with a surprise for the boys tonight."

Max took the bait and asked, "Yeah? What's that?"

Lukas pulled his collar down as far as it would go, revealing a swastika tattooed on his chest.
Pete quickly reached over and pulled Lukas' collar up. "What the fuck are you thinking? You want to go to fucking jail. You know that shit is a one-way ticket."

Max shook his head and said, "I hope that's a temporary tattoo otherwise you're never swimming again."

Lukas laughed, "You got me there. Even I'm not crazy enough. But I thought seeing the look on the boys' faces was worth chancing it for one night."

Max smirked and replied, "I think no one will notice your tattoo tonight."

"Why's that?" Lukas asked.

"Because of this big secret of his," Pete said sarcastically.

Max's smile grew larger while he slowly repeated, "Because of my big fucking secret."

Pete stared at him and shook his head. "Now you're scaring me, Max."

CHAPTER 11

Munich, Germany

Ben Weber and Hank Adams paced in the hallway outside a room secured by a card reader in the Munich Collection center. They were both glued to their phones seemingly oblivious to the large contingent of suits mulling around just down the hallway.

Without looking up from his phone Hank asked Ben, "Do you think Janice will approve of me taking the lead on this conversation?"

Ben's concentration broken he turned to address Hank. "I don't know, but it is the best approach."

"I think pushing Adolf hard will be important. Are you buying any of this nonsense of his remorse and enlightenment?"

Ben raised one eyebrow and responded, "Not for a moment. I am suspicious of my toaster. We should turn off a piece of technology capable of this mess."

"I think that will be difficult. But know what I worry about most? It's how everyone thinks the responses of the Collected are authentic. Every damn one, cool as cucumbers. I'm not buying it for a moment. I think this software is acting like Xanax for ghouls."

Ben laughed and pointed down the hallway to draw Hank's attention to Franz and Janice approaching. Hank and Ben greeted them and exchanged pleasantries.

"Are you ready?" asked Franz.

Hank addressed Janice, "You ok if I take the lead?"

Janice glanced at Ben before replying, "That will be fine."

Franz swiped his card and led them into the secure room. Inside was a table with a workstation, large speakers, a round table mic, and box J-52 prominently displayed in the center of the table. Franz motioned for them to sit. He logged into the computer and rolled through various screens.

Franz instructed them, "Before we begin, out of abundant precaution, we've created a safe word which the microphones will pick up and trigger an alarm. I don't believe this will be necessary, but none the less."

Franz looked at the microphone and commanded, "Pause safety. Banana Monkey."

Janice smirked, "Interesting choice. Do you have to reset the safety?"

"No. The pause is for 5 seconds and then it resets and can't be paused for another 5 minutes, so please don't use the word again unless you intend to get help," he answered before adding, "Are we ready?"

They nodded and he turned on communications.

"Adolf, this is Dr. Hoffman again."

"Hello, Dr. Hoffman. It is good to speak with you again."

Hank looked at Ben and Janice with an incredulous glance. Franz introduced the other three and then motioned to Hank to begin.

"This is Hank Adams and I would like to start off by asking why you decided to return?"

"I'm sorry Mr. Adams but this was not my choice. Your scientists collected me and brought me here."

"And where exactly did they collect you from?"

"It's difficult to say. I don't know that I was in a finite location. I felt that I was everywhere, but never felt like I was somewhere."

Ben shook his head looking frustrated. "Did you talk with others while you were there?"

There was a short but awkward pause before Adolf answered, "I can't say I was in a place I would call 'there', but to answer your question, it's hard to say."

"What exactly does that mean, 'hard to say'," Hank sarcastically asked.

"I felt I was interacting with others, but I also felt this powerful life coming from all aspects of nature. But I can't describe my experience as talking."

"For fuck's sake," Ben blurted out.

Franz looked at him disapprovingly and Ben stared back.

"I'm sorry that I don't know that voice, but I am guessing it is deputy director Ben Weber. I understand your frustration with my answer, but it is what I experienced."

Ben replied to the chagrin of Hank, "You killed millions of people and now you are telling me you've come back the great pacifist? I'm not buying it."

"I'm sorry you feel this way Mr. Weber. I am sorry for what I did but now I have this amazing appreciation for all things and this world we live in."

Hank sprung to his feet agitated. The other three watched him as he leaned into the microphone and said, "So one moment you are trying to exterminate an entire group of people, you put a bullet in your head, and wake up floating through the garden of Eden enlightened, like magic?"

"I think you need to understand Mr. Adams, where I was there was no sense of time. How long I took to come to this point of view is impossible to answer. As much as I felt a part of everything, I felt as if there was no time. It's very difficult, to explain, but one day you will experience this for yourself."

"Are you threatening me?" Hank challenged.

"I'm sorry I've frustrated you, Mr. Adams, but that was not a threat, rather a statement of fact. I wish neither you nor anyone any harm."

Janice motioned to Hank for permission to speak and he nodded in return.

"Adolf, this is Janice Jones. What is it you hope to accomplish now that they have collected you?"

"Good afternoon, Ms. Jones. I didn't ask to be collected but I would appreciate the opportunity to apologize for my actions and ask that no one does this ever again."

Hank shook his head vehemently. "If you think we will ever give you a platform to speak you are seriously mistaken."

"Mr. Adams, I am sorry that you can't see I mean no harm. I don't mean to sound belligerent, but this is the start of fixing what I did."

Janice sprung to her feet and declared, "You know what. He's right. I will not be a party to his rehabilitation public relations tour. The two of you are welcome to continue this charade but I'm out of here."

She briskly exited the room, slamming the door behind her. Hank looked at Ben for direction but before they decided anything, Franz spoke up.

"Gentlemen, we can continue this conversation later, but for now I need to end this. My agreement was that I would never allow discussions without representatives from all three governments in the room. As we just lost her, we will have to pause this."

Hank shook his head and said, "Fine by me. This is a waste of time, anyway."

Seattle, WA

Cindy waited for her father in the great hall of the Seattle Aquarium. She sat on a bench captivated by the fish in the enormous tank. Jacob walked up slowly from behind his daughter who was unaware of his presence. As he was nearly upon her, he paused and painfully wiped his mouth with his hand. He took a deep breath and squinted as if trying to stop the pain that filled his face suddenly. She realized his presence and turned around to see him. Her face turned to concern as she stood to greet him.

"Are you ok, Dad?"

He nodded unconvincingly.

"What's wrong?"

"From behind, you reminded me of," he trailed off unable to finish.

She stepped forward and gave him a hug. "It's ok Dad. I often have wondered now that I'm older if I might bring back memories of Mom for you."

"Both of you so beautiful, how could it not."

She rubbed his upper arm and looked at him adoringly, "I am so glad you could make this work, Dad."

With a weak smile he replied, "This is our place. Do you remember coming here after we moved to Seattle?"

"How could I forget? I was crying and you took me to see the sea otters. You showed me them holding hands and talked about the importance of family."

"The first of many amazing days here."

"So true. Why don't you take a seat and watch the fish with me? I think the diver will do a feeding shortly."

Jacob sat down next to his daughter and held her hand. He whispered into her ear, "Thank you for being such an amazing daughter."

"It's easy when you have such an amazing father," she answered with a smile.

He leaned over and gave her a kiss on the forehead. They sat together silently as the reflection of the water danced on the surrounding floor. A few toddlers ran between the benches breaking the serenity of the moment.

"Can I ask you a question, Dad?"

"Of course, what's up?"

"I can see you struggle around Mom. Is this because of Christine?"

He thought about it for a moment before replying, "You know I used to wonder this, but that's really not the case. Why do you ask?"

"I don't know. It just doesn't seem that you are as warm as when you are talking to Ash, Emma, or me."

"It's hard, Cindy. Your mom was so full of energy and life. While I know that's her, it doesn't feel like her."

"Is it because her voice is so flat and unemotional? Maybe they will fix that. When I asked Ash she said they were working on it."

"Maybe, but there's something different bothering me I can't quite put my finger on."

Cindy looked at him with curiosity. He said nothing while intently watching the diver swimming in the fifty-five-degree temperature water.

"Dad?"

He tilted his head slightly to look at her and responded to her question, "How would I enjoy this moment with your mother?"

"You mean now or when she was alive?"

"Yes, that's my point."

Cindy looked away and he watched her carefully. She took a tissue from her purse and dabbed her eyes. Jacob reached out and squeezed her hand which elicited a pathetically dejected smile.
He asked, "How did I make you cry?"

"You have your way, Dad."

He looked at her somberly and waited for her to finish her thought.

She choked out, "It's like we are living with the memory of Mom, isn't it?"

He took a deep breath and answered, "What new experiences can we have with her this way?

It feels like we talk about what we did or will do. But how can we truly experience life with her?"

"I don't know that I agree with that. You should see the way her and Emma get on. You can't tell me that Emma won't remember it for the rest of her life."

Jacob nodded and replied, "You have a point there. But it's a lot like a long-distance relationship with Grandma, don't you think?"

Cindy bit her lip and shrugged. They both returned their attention to the tank silently holding hands while watching the constant parade of fish.

Munich, Germany

Max, Lukas, and Pete descended the staircase into the basement of the bar and the raucous assembly below escalated in volume. The room had the horrible glow of incandescent lighting and the stench of old beer. The concrete basement storage area filled with beer kegs and cheap wine was alive with energy from dozens of young white men.

Max glowed as he bit his lip with excitement bursting from his face. Lukas leapt in front of him and stepped onto the top of a table from an empty chair. Lukas moved around in what could be best described as belly dancer meets drunken pole dancer. A few of his brothers took notice but not enough to keep him from looking dejected. Unfazed, he lifted his shirt halfway up his chest and shook his ass seductively.

One of his brothers shouted out, "Who brought the shotgun? Somebody shoot the moose on the table."

The room broke out in laughter. Undaunted, Lukas bent over at the waist and fully removed his shirt. He stood upright, covering his tattoo with both hands and continued to dance. "Lukas sit the fuck down!" another voice yelled.

Lukas paused dramatically and threw his arms into the air revealing his tattoo of the swastika. The room erupted in a roar of delight and for the moment Lukas reveled in his victory.

Max leaned over and spoke into Pete's ear, "Guaranteed, he didn't think about what to do next."

Pete turned and smiled. "Shall we help him?"

Lukas turned clockwise proudly displaying his tattoo to the room, but it became clear he could sense his moment was closing.

Max said to Pete, "Fuck him. They'll blame us if this ends ugly."

Max stepped up onto the chair, raising his beer above his head, and shouted, "To the brotherhood!"

The room responded as expected and the eruption of energy provided the window of opportunity for Pete to drag Lukas off the table.

Simon Newcastle, young, blonde and blue eyed, took Lukas' place atop the table and shouted, "Our pure Germany forever!"

The room broke into a roar once again and Simon smiled with the intoxication of power. He raised his hands to quiet and bring the room to attention. He spun around demanding their obedience which quickly followed. With the room quiet, Simon asked, "To what pleasure do we owe your decision to put this tattoo upon your chest, Lukas?"

Lukas looked stunned and turned toward Pete and Max for an answer that wasn't forthcoming. In a panic, he provided the only thing that could come to mind.

"I celebrate the great news that Max has for us tonight."

Max spit out his beer, surprised by the abruptness of Lukas' statement. Simon turned his attention to Max as did the rest of the brotherhood. Max smiled uncomfortably and slowly shuffled into the center of the room.

"What news do you have to share, Max?" Simon asked.

He grinned and answered, "I have something to share you won't believe."

"You got laid finally!" a voice from the back yelled which was met with thunderous laughter.

The insult fired up Max and his next statement lacked none of the hesitance of his first.
"I am here to announce the return of our great leader!"

The room grew silent in their confusion. Simon jumped from the table landing next to Max.
He asked, "Max, what the hell are you saying?"

Max stared out at his brothers and took a deep breath to accentuate his dramatic pause before shouting, "I was there when my father collected and brought back to this world, Adolf Hitler!"

The room reacted with stunned silence, which appeared to catch Max by surprise. Simon moved close to Max and asked in a conversational tone, "What are you saying, Max?"

Max answered loudly so everyone could hear, "They have found Adolf Hitler and are holding him in secret at the Technical Institute."

"Did you talk with him?" asked Simon.

"I had barely any time before they kicked us out of the room."

"We need to know why he returned. What does he want?" screamed someone in the room.
Simon looked at Max for an answer.

Max shook his head and mumbled, "I don't know what he wants. I haven't been able to talk to him since."

"We need to get in there and find out what he wants," someone else yelled.

"Max, can you help us talk with him?" Simon asked him pensively.

"I don't know how I could do that. My dad says he's only accessible to a small group that works there."

"Would your Dad help us?"

Max laughed and answered, "That will never happen."

Simon scratched his head. "Is there someone sympathetic to our cause that works there?"

"The place is a bunch of foreigners. I'm not sure the Germans who work there have any blonde in their blood."

"Max will work there," Lukas yelled out.

Simon looked at Max quizzically.

"I will be a janitor or something."

Simon smirked, "Someone will have to throw away the garbage in his room, won't they?"

Max suddenly looked uncomfortable.

Simon addressed the room. "Our brother Max is going to meet with Adolf and bring us his message!"

The room broke out into applause and cheers. Max spun around soaking in their reaction.

Pete grabbed him by the arm. He leaned forward and said in Max's ear. "You pull this off and I will worship the ground you walk on."

CHAPTER 12

Berlin, Germany -- Washington DC, USA -- London, UK

Standing in front of her desk in the oval office Hank Adams said, "President Harris, if I may. While Hitler appears to be repentant and even remorseful about his actions, we have no reason to believe that these are in fact honest opinions on his part."

"Mr. Adams, what leads you to believe these statements of his are not true?"

Hank sighed and responded, "With all due respect. He requests an international audience to express his sorrow and to save others from a similar fate. If you had committed one of the greatest acts of genocide in the history of the world and wanted a forum, wouldn't you feign peaceful intentions?"

President Harris raised an eyebrow, "With all due respect, aren't I the one who gets to ask questions and you are supposed to be providing me the answers?"

Hank nodded at the President speechless.

"Prime Minister or Chancellor, your people have an opinion on this matter?" the President asked into her speakerphone.

"Ms. President," answered Chancellor Muller, "I have to admit I'm with Mr. Adams. I don't know there is any possibility I could ever trust this man. Ever."

Prime Minister Goodman added, "I want to be very clear here. I condone none of his actions and refuse to defend him. That said, we've all read the reports from the directors and they have yet to find a soul that's returned who manipulated or lied about their intentions. In our desire to err on the side of caution, don't we risk missing the opportunity to fix one of the worst episodes in human history?"

"If I may add something here," asked Ben Weber over the phone, "I think there is something else that needs to be considered."

"Yes, Mr. Weber," the President said, "Please share."

"History teaches us that despots speak to an idea and are idolized for their ability to realize that idea, even if for just a short time. But that idea is larger than the messenger. If we rolled out Hitler to an international audience, and he does exactly what he says he would do, no one will believe him. The vast majority of people will have the same reaction as us. And for his followers, they will think we brainwashed him... the software was corrupted... or it's not even him and a ruse of some sort."

"So, what would you have us do?" asked Chancellor Muller who was sitting at her desk next to Ben.

"This is not a choice for me to make. This is a decision for you to choose."

"Thank you for that lecture on our leadership structure. I was asking your opinion."

Ben looked at his boss who shot him a look to let him know, this was his big moment.
Ben addressed Chancellor Muller but inched closer to the speaker so the other leaders could hear him.

"I realize you will hate this answer, but I wouldn't do anything for now."

Prime Minister Goodman laughed audibly over the speakerphone. "You sound like a politician now, Mr. Weber."

"I'm sorry for that. But I think there is as much danger in giving him a voice as returning him to from where he came. While we are skeptical of the program directors' advice, their report also talks to a vibrant afterlife where all the Collected speak of being everywhere, all the time. I don't know what that means, but it equally scares the hell out of me. He is causing no harm, sitting in this room in Munich."

"Why not move him to the vault in Virginia or some secure location elsewhere?" inquired President Harris.

"I can take that one," replied Janice Jones, "If you move him, you are bringing more parties into the process and further, the very nature of the security around the move will create scrutiny. You also risk a power failure and accidentally releasing him into the ether, an act the whole of us still can't agree is favorable or not. For now, he's contained and few people know he's there."

"Jesus," exclaimed President Harris, "Talk about letting the genie out of the bottle."

"Well, the odds were 20 billion to 1 this could happen. What if his buddies decided to beat the odds and join him? At some point, we have to debate the value of bringing loved ones back if every 1,000th customer carries some baggage with them," Chancellor Muller said.

Prime Minister Goodman asked, "So what do we do Ms. President and Chancellor?"

A long pause followed. Finally, President Harris spoke, "We need to figure out a philosophy on continuing this program and that needs to happen country by country. I for one will ask my people to set up a hearing on the future of the Collectors. But to Hitler, I recommend we hold him where he is for the time being, until we can get a better understanding of what happens on the other side. And let me be clear, my patience is short. Let's push our Collectors' directors to get us better information and we can reconvene and decide."

Chancellor Muller spoke next, "I don't like this answer one bit. Not at all. But I don't think I hear a better option. Let's get answers and fewer questions for the next call. In the meantime, I will make sure we have the right security in place."

Prime Minister Goodman added, "And I've noticed our meeting has grown in attendees since last time. I will reinforce for everyone on this call, the fastest way to lose control of this situation is if someone leaks. For God's sake, do your job and be professional. Let's figure this out and then decide what we share later."

"Excellent point, Margaret," President Harris said, "OK. Let's get on these various pieces and try to get back together in the next couple weeks. Have a good rest of your week and no more surprises. Can we try to make that happen?"

Chancellor Muller replied, "I'm all for that. But as the expression goes, please knock on some wood."

Munich, Germany

Max and his father exited their car and walked toward Franz's building. Max was likely dressed better for work than any time in his entire life but lacked his father's sport coat. Max's head practically spun off his body as he soaked in the constant motion of people on the campus. Silently they continued until they reached the entrance of the building. They walked down a set of stairs into the basement and down the hallway reaching a door marked, "Administration." Franz opened the door and the two of them entered. The room was filled with desks with only a couple occupied at the moment. Franz led Max over to one.

"Max, I want to introduce you to Hans. He'll be your boss.

When you are ready for more, he'll let me know and then things might get even more interesting."

"Nice to meet you, Max," Hans said extending an arm to greet him.

Max returned the courtesy and replied, "Nice to meet you too."

"I will leave it to the two of you from here," explained Franz and he turned to leave.

Max looked at Hans for direction and he was happy to oblige. "The good news for you is that your father's reputation has earned you the mail job in this building. The bad news is this is a rather visible job and you are going to need to be on your game at all times. Any issues with that?"

Max shook his head and responded, "Not at all."

"Wonderful. Let's take a quick walk of the building so you can get your bearings. I'll shadow you for the next couple days. Take notes as we go, so you can learn your way sooner than later."

"No problem."

The tour started in the basement and included the working end of the building along with the staffers without enough seniority to earn a window. Next was the entry level and Hans joyfully introduced Max to as many people as he could. They reached the end of the floor and took the stairs up. One of the first offices they reached was his father's, but Franz was away. Hans continued the introductions which led to a guarded door with a keypad.

"Max, this is Carl. He is one of four rotating guards on this door. The two of you will become best friends and he'll be the one to give you access to the next building. There are few offices on the other side, mostly labs. Packages will be your primary delivery in this building. Carl and his colleagues may occasionally inspect them."

"Nice to meet you, Carl," Max said.

The two of them used the elevated walkway to the Collectors building where another guard greeted them and Hans walked him through a similar introduction. They entered the Collector's building where Hans continued the tour. As they walked through the main facilities, they approached yet another guard.

"Max, getting beyond this point will rarely be required. Frank here is also one of four rotating guards. If a delivery is needed beyond this point, Frank will most likely join you. We have little need to be here and I can remember only a delivery or two ever."

"What's down this hallway," Max asked.

Hans replied, "Some more experimental labs and the researchers are trying to provide complete isolation so to not bias their experiments."

"Interesting," Max said dispassionately.

Redmond, WA

"Ash," Cindy said into her house phone from the couch in her living room, "I thought you told me once they were working on creating the ability for Mom to see us?"

Ashley answered from her cell while lying in bed, "Yes, that is something they are working on, but it's a hard problem. It's one thing to share all that data but then have that data make sense for someone like Mom is incredibly difficult."

"Hmm..." Cindy pondered.

"Why do you ask? Is something wrong with Mom?"

"No.... not so much. It's just that Dad put it in my head that our relationship with Mom is a lot like a long-distance telephone conversation."

"Dad! Sure, there are limitations to the relationship today, but we've provided the opportunity for people to have the conversations they wish they had. So many Collected speak of their love for those they left behind and how nice it is to experience time with them again."

"Love? I've wondered about how Mom loves us. With no emotions, how does she really experience love?"

Ashley laughed, "Wow! Dad has you spun up, doesn't he?"

"Well... I don't know. Maybe."

"Think of it this way. The foundation of love, not lust, not affection, not a crush, is a relationship built on trust and authenticity. While Mom's love was originally formed with all the emotions and hormones of being a human, we've seen that is carries beyond the body."

"I see. I'm sorry for being so weird. What's going on in your life?"

"It's ok, sis. I am dating a guy I met while visiting the Stanford research facility. Its long distance but he's awesome."

"That's great. I can't believe how busy we've become. I used to know this stuff before anyone else."

Ashley paused for a moment. "In some ways, our lives are not that different from how we interact with Mom, don't you think?"

"I guess.... Hey, I need to go. Mark is calling me from upstairs saying it's time for reading time with Emma before bed."

"Ok. Cindy take a chill pill and enjoy every moment with

Mom. Tell her I love her and I'll talk with her tomorrow."

"OK. Goodnight. And good luck with Stanford boy!"

Cindy hung up the phone and walked out the kitchen. As she approached the stairs, she heard her mother.

"Cindy, can I ask a favor?"

Cindy paused and walked over to her sentient box. "Sure Mom, what's up?"

"Can you unplug me and bring me upstairs with you so I can read with Emma tonight?"

"I don't know if that's such a good idea. We could lose you if there is some problem with the power. We can bring Emma down here and do it in the living room."

"No, I really would like to do it in her bedroom. I loved when I got to read to your girls and you fell asleep as I did."

Cindy took a deep breath and was thankful her mother couldn't see her stalling.

"Are you unplugging me?" Emily asked.

Cindy shook her head vigorously and replied, "Yes. Just trying to remember how to do it correctly and not lose my mother... again."

"Thank you. I've always been here you know. Just in a very different way."

Cindy started to reply but stopped short. Instead, she unplugged the sentient box and brought her upstairs. Emma's eyes nearly popped out of her head when she saw her Mom with the box.

"Is Grandma coming up to say goodnight to me?" Emma asked emphatically.

Emily answered, "Yes. Grandma will read to you here tonight."

Emma ran across the room and chose her favorite book. "This one! This one!" she shouted.

"Which one is it?" Emily asked, "I'll look it up online."

"Where the Wild Things Are," exclaimed Emma.

Emma curled into Cindy's lap on top of her bed. Cindy opened the book to the first page and Emma began.

Cindy turned the pages as her mother read, scratching Emma's back helping to soothe her to sleep. Finally, Emily finished as Cindy turned off the lights and walked out of the room.
Cindy smiled contently at the magic of the moment. She returned downstairs and plugged her mother's box back into the power supply.

"Mom, that was lovely. I am so glad we got to do that."

"I am thankful as well. I just wish I could have kissed my granddaughter on the forehead when I finished."

CHAPTER 13

London, England

John Spring kissed his wife and daughter goodbye and locked the door behind them. He quickly headed down the hallway into the baby's room. On one side of the room was the crib and changing table. On the other was his desk and a rack of electronic equipment. The room smelled of baby oil and lemon air freshener. He fumbled in his pocket before pulling out a key. He sat at his desk and unlocked the drawers. He looked back at the empty crib and lingered for a moment of contemplation before opening the drawer. He pulled out sentient box D-43 and plugged it into his workstation.

"Hello again, Frank. How are you doing?"

"Very well today, John. Am I going to talk with Wilma today?"

"The information you provided, turned out to be accurate and now I know that we are talking to the right person. I didn't want to give the money to the wrong person accidentally."

"I'm not sure how that could happen, but I appreciate your thoroughness. Will I be able to talk to her today? It's so lonely when you turn my box off."

"I am trying to arrange that for you, Frank. I will have a few more questions for you before we can get to that point. We are close. You understand we worry about her mental health and this will all come as quite a shock to her."

"Yes. I understand, John. But it's been a while, you can understand why I am ready."

"I do, Frank. But let's settle this business about getting her the money you want and then we can give her the even bigger surprise."

"If you say so."

"Frank, I will talk to one of my associates who is helping your wife collect this money. I will put you on hold while I do that. I may have some questions I forgot to ask you that come up during the conversation. Would it be okay, if I mute myself?"

"Yes, of course. It's very important that I get this money to Wilma."

"OK. I am putting you on mute now."

John silenced the conversation and began to look through his notes to prepare for his call. A thick folder filled with papers sat under his notes. He looked at his watch and turned the phone on, heard the dial tone, and turned it off. After a few minutes of leafing through the folder, he stood up and walked to the kitchen and poured a glass of water from the sink. Upon returning he unmuted Frank and informed him, "Frank, everything is going well on this end. Please be patient, it will be a while longer yet."

"Thank you for the update, John."

John put him back on mute and waited patiently.

The phone finally rang, and he answered, "Hello, is this Percy?"

"Yes, John, this is Percy Roberts. I'm joined by Mrs. Wilma Stone and her daughter Ms. Olivia Stone. Ladies, let me introduce Mr. John Waters from the private investigation firm of Endeavour Search."

"Wilma and Olivia, I am very glad to meet you. I am so sorry that I can't be there today to meet you in person. My work has brought me outside the city, but I believe I can come right to the point."

"Thank you, Mr. Waters, and I do appreciate you coming straight to the point. Also, I would also appreciate if you would refer to me as Mrs. Stone."

"My apologies, Mrs. Stone. I will of course address you as you wish." he replied assuming it was Wilma based upon the sound of the voice.

Percy spoke, "Thank you, John. I've shared with Mr. Waters, your confirmation of the answer, in the envelope last night. He'll now walk you through what additional information he can provide and the next steps, if you choose to continue."

John replied, "Percy, thank you once again. Mrs. Stone, we have good reason to believe that your husband has left you fifty-seven million Pounds. The money is being held at the Bank of Hegwisch in the British Virgin Islands. From the information we have gathered, there are two beneficiaries. The first is you. The second, upon your death, is your daughter. If both of you were to be deceased, the challenges would have escalated, but as both of you are in good health, we haven't pursued other remedies. The transfer can be completed quite quickly by Mrs. Wilma Stone appearing in person before the bank president with the account and security information, along with proof of identity."

"This all seems appropriate, but please tell me why you've asked our lawyer to be excluded from this discussion?"

John answered quickly, "From what we have ascertained, your husband had some reason to believe that your family lawyer may have created a legal approach to deprive you of these funds. It appears your husband moved the funds just days before his death. Unfortunately, he passed away before he could share the information and reasoning with you."

"Mr. Waters, this is Ms. Olivia Stone Can you tell us how you've come upon this information? I'm surprised that we are hearing about this for the first time and that our lawyer has never mentioned missing funds."

John put the call on mute and turned back on the conversation with Frank.

"Frank, why hasn't your lawyer brought this issue up to the family?"

"Because the lawyer wasn't aware that I moved the funds."

"We've covered that Frank. But why hasn't he raised this as an issue to your family?"

Percy's voice projected from the muted call, "John are you still speaking, if so we can't hear you."

"I'm getting feedback on this end of the line and put the call on mute. To answer the first part of your question. Our firm's success is based on the value that we create for our clients. We spend countless hours searching through records and official documents to find opportunities such as this. While I can't disclose our specific approach, I can guarantee you that if you choose to claim the funds, there will be no issues. As for the second part...,"

He muted the phone conversation and yelled, "Why hasn't the lawyer raised this as an issue, Frank!"

"Because I gave him a smaller amount of money to satisfy his interests. Who are you talking to John?"

"Shit!" he said as he turned off the conversation with Frank.

Olivia asked, "Mr. Waters are you still there?"

He grabbed a drink of water and coughed when he answered, "Yes, sorry about that. I had something in my throat and needed a drink of water. As for the second part, we have reason to believe that your father left a nominal amount of money in the original account to appease your lawyer and keep him unaware of the larger amount you would be inheriting."

"Mr. Waters this is Mrs. Stone again. I think I understand why we've been asked to come here today. Assuming your assessment about the lawyer is correct, I believe that you've brought us here today to negotiate your terms to release our money."

John laughed nervously and wiped his forehead, "I apologize for the laughter, Mrs. Waters, but that was very direct and not entirely fair. Yes, we would like to collect our percentage for the work we have done. We are asking for three percent of the recovered funds, which works out to just over one and a half million Pounds. We believe that's reasonable."

Wilma asked brusquely, "Why wouldn't I simply go to my bank and explain the situation myself? I am certain there is some remedy for demonstrating that I am the beneficiary and immediately claim rightful ownership of the account without having to validate personal information you plan to share with me?"

John shook his head frustrated but collected himself. He replied, "Mrs. Stone you may do just as you say; there's nothing to stop you. I will let your conscious be your guide on this matter. I have, in all goodwill, brought you an opportunity that will provide your family in excess of 54 million Pounds even after my fee—funds you were unaware even existed. I would also offer this caution: banks don't take kindly to unusual requests and I think you may find it will cost you at least my fee in legal expenses to recover the money. There is the additional risk that your family lawyer may insert himself into the transaction, further complicating the matter and reducing your proceeds even further. I would implore you Mrs.

Stone, to consider our fee as well within reason and the surest way to receive this inheritance, which your husband went to great lengths to protect for you. We have, in essence, delivered a gift from beyond the grave."

Silence filled the air as he took another drink of water. He took a deep breath and waited with his eyes fixed on the phone. He could hear Wilma ask, "Well, Mr. Roberts. What is it that we do now?"

Percy replied, "Knowing that your lawyer was not going to be present, I have prepared a simple contract--perhaps the simplest contract you may ever read in your life. Please take time to read it start to finish, but it quite simply states that you agree to pay a fee of three percent of the total amount you find in the bank account. Upon providing your signature, Mr. Waters will provide the account and verification information for the funds. Your obligation to my client is for that account and that account alone. I do believe this quite well protects your rights."

Wilma said, "Oh, Frank," she said to her reflection. "Why did you put me in this awkward place? I wish you were here to direct me."

John looked at his screen to make sure the conversation with Frank was still offline. There was some conversation on the other end he couldn't make out when Olivia asked, "Mr. Waters, I find it odd that you have never once called our lawyer by name. Maybe it's by chance, but it seems that if the story about the lack of loyalty is true, you would know his name. Can you, and not Mr. Roberts, please tell me what is the name of our lawyer so that I can put my intuition to rest?"

John stood up abruptly, pulled his hair, and mouthed, "Fuck."

After a moment he answered, "Of course, Ms. Stone. As the work here is a compilation of the efforts of several members of our team, it is understandable that I don't know your lawyer's name offhand, but let me look through your folder and find it for you. Please hold for a moment."

John put them on mute and spoke to Frank once again, "What is your family lawyer's name and firm?"

"Why do you ask John?"

"Frank, dammit. They don't believe that I am for real and your wife won't get the money unless I can answer this."

Percy's voice boomed through the speaker, "John we would like to move forward on this matter, can you please confirm the name?"

"One moment Percy.... I'm looking... here... there are several pages...."

He muted the phone conversation again. "Frank, see, I need the name. I need it now."

"Mr. Walter Francis of the law firm Francis and Son's."

"John? Is there a problem?" asked Mr. Roberts.

John muted the conversation with Frank and unmuted the call with Percy and the Stones.

"So sorry about that, Mrs. Stone. I have it right here. Mr. Walter Francis of the law firm Francis and Son's."

A long pause followed and John stood nervously with his hand over his mouth waiting for a reply.

Percy finally spoke, "Mr. Waters, I can confirm we have a signed contract. Can you please provide me the account information so that I can enter that information and initial it on the contract?"

John took a deep breath and opened the folder to the notes page with the account information."

He replied, "Congratulations, Mrs. Stone. Percy, it is 7 9 8 4...."

Munich, Germany

Max walked into the neighborhood park which had a large playground for kids. Simon sat with his legs crossed and his arms spread wide along the back of a bench. A large tree fully shaded him in his white tee shirt and black jeans. Max slowed as he approached and Simon pulled one arm back to provide a spot for Max to sit down.

Max sat down with his hands in the pockets of his hooded sweatshirt. He turned to Simon and asked, "How's it going?"

Simon laughed and said, "Still trying to digest the magnitude of this day."

"Yeah, my Dad was frantic when he woke this morning. He skipped breakfast and headed straight into work."

Simon looked at him perplexed. "Why aren't you at work today?"

"My dad told me it would be a shit storm and I should call in sick. Said no reason to put myself in the middle of everything. I think he was afraid I might screw something up. I don't know."

The two of them sat quietly watching a couple young kids playing with their nannies not far away.

Max shared, "You know, Pete and I used to come here all the time as kids."

Simon smirked at him, "It's a sweet story, should we go get ice cream?"

Max shot Simon a look of displeasure but didn't say a word.

"Maybe a beer? Pretty big day, don't you think?" Simon offered.

"Do you think it was one of the brothers that leaked the news?" Max asked.

Simon shook his head and replied, "Dunno. I doubt it. Doesn't really matter. The entire world now knows what we already knew. In some ways this makes things easier but in other ways a lot harder."

"How's that?"

Simon chuckled. "Max, you are a loyal foot soldier, but damn you sometimes don't see the big picture."

Max drooped his head, embarrassed by the back-handed compliment. Simon patted him on the back of the head.

"This is not a bad thing, Max. I used to be like you once. With the right help, one day you may get there."

Max turned to Simon and said, "Thanks. But what is easier and harder now?"

"It's a hell of a lot easier to get our brothers across Germany and the world to align now that we don't have to be quiet about this. Harder though, because the entire world is going to be coming down hard wanting to get rid of Adolf."

"I see. So... this is why you asked me to join you here?"

Simon smiled, "Perhaps smarter than I give you credit. Yes, we need your help."

Max took a deep breath and scanned the playground nervously. "What is it you need, Simon?"

"The leaders have been talking and think they will not let Adolf stay in place much longer. The university probably won't want Adolf and all the attention it brings, and those fuckers in the US will probably want to put their damn hands on him."

Max nodded silently waiting for what he knew must be coming.

Simon continued, "Max, the brothers know that you have access to Hitler's room. They would like you to steal his box and bring him back home before the Impure do something to him."

Max jumped to his feet and said emphatically, "Are you out of your fucking mind? I have access but security was already tight. It will be insane now."

"Calm down Max. We got you some help."

"How's that?"

"One of the guys who guards Adolf's room is another brother from up north."

"Ok..."

"Max, honestly this is about as straightforward as it gets."

"Says the guy sitting on the bench, telling the guy going to jail when this all goes wrong."

Simon grew frustrated and said, "Max, sit down."

Max sat back down but further from Simon this time. Simon slid over and put his arm around Max's back.

"Max, this will require some ingenuity on your part, but you've told us you deliver packages. You figure out how to do this, but deliver an empty package to his room, put Adolf in the box, and you don't get any questions leaving because the guard is one of ours."

Max shook his head vigorously. "This is the plan? You know there are three guards minimum to get past. And then somehow, I have to get the box out of the building."

"If it were easy, we would have him in our possession already. But don't you agree that we need to do this?"

Max looked upward and rolled his eyes. "Yes, of course."

Simon patted Max on the back. "This is your time, Max. You will be a legend amongst your people. You personally will be responsible for Germany rising again. Think about that."
Max smiled nervously but didn't reply.

Simon looked Max squarely in the eyes, "Our guy is on security tomorrow night. You have 24 hours to figure out the details. I have to go back to the other leaders right now and tell them your answer. What's it going to be?"

Max stared at Simon, hoping to find some way out of his situation. Simon remained transfixed on Max waiting for his reply.

Max stood and started to walk away and said, "I'll do it."

Simon got up from the bench and replied, "I'm not sure I heard. I don't want there to be any confusion. Can you please look at me and repeat yourself?"

Max stopped and turned. He walked back and got inches from Simon's face and repeated himself, "Tell them I'll do it."

Simon smiled and put his hand around the back of Max's neck and held him firmly.

"One day I will tell my grandchildren I knew you. Thank you, Max. I will tell the others."

Technical University Munich

Franz Hoffman entered the room housing sentient box J-52 and took a seat at the table. He slowly scrolled through the activity logs. Finished with his review, he leaned back in the chair and closed his eyes. He sat that way for a good couple minutes until the whirl of the sentient box fan became the only noise audible. Finally, he dropped the chair back to the floor and opened his eyes. He navigated his computer and turned on communications with the box.

"Adolf, this is Dr. Hoffman, how are you today?"

"Dr. Hoffman, it's so nice to hear your voice. It's lonely when you turn my communication off. How are you today?"

"I've had a very busy day, but I am doing well, thank you."

"Is there anything I can do for you?" Adolf asked.

Franz paused to choose his words and then replied, "Well, I've come to share some news with you."

"I get little news since they have collected me. It will be good to hear something new."

"Overnight, someone leaked to the news that we had collected you. They reported it and the world is a little crazy to be quite frank."

"I see. I can imagine given everything I did, there is a fair amount of fear and anger."

Franz chuckled, "That's putting it lightly. I'm afraid that this news will change things. The German army has taken over security of this wing of my program. As part of that they have asked me to cease sharing any information with you. This means access to the curated books and periodicals ends immediately. This explains why you stopped seeing information earlier today."

"That is disappointing to hear Dr. Hoffman. It's a lonely existence and to cut off any information makes it even more difficult."

"I understand, but I have no choice in this matter. Officials are trying to determine whether you should remain here or moved to another location. If something were to change, I will let you know."

There was a long pause before Adolf responded, "Dr. Hoffman, do you think people understand that I am no longer a danger?"

Franz shook his head and answered, "I'm not sure many people view you that way. Frankly, what we know about the collected is so limited, that even I don't fully know what to make of your new views on life."

"I can see why you think that. But you must understand, once you can see the beauty of the world and how it all interconnects, you can't view things like I once did."

"That may be, but you did unimaginable things. Things which frankly embarrass us still and for which most people hoped you were dealing with eternal damnation. When they learn you were experiencing something quite opposite, they will not be thrilled. Some people think you will only encourage further despicable acts if they see no consequence to those actions."

"Someone could conclude this, but they don't understand that I can see so clearly now how everything comes together. I just wish I could speak to the world and help them understand. Don't you know that I could make people stop their hatred?"

Franz shook his head. "I'm afraid it's hard for me to get my head wrapped around you being this pacifist leader, and frankly, I'm not entirely convinced of how authentic you are."

"I'm disappointed to hear that Dr. Hoffman. You must believe me when I say I can see things so clearly now."

"Well, Adolf, I don't get to make the final call on what to believe or not. I just wanted to make sure you knew a dramatic change in communication was happening. It's been a long day. Unless there is something you need, I think I will call it a night."

"I can't think of anything at the moment Dr. Hoffman. If you can just let people know that I'm sincere about wanting to break the cycle of hate, that is all I can ask you to do."

Franz stood from his chair and grimaced trying to figure out how to reply. He leaned forward and faced the speaker.

"Adolf, I'm going to leave now. You have a good evening."

"Dr. Hoffman will you tell them for me?"

Franz slowly moved to the door and turned backed to answer, "I'm not sure they would believe me if I did."

He opened the door, walked out, and closed it behind him. Ben Weber was leaning against the wall waiting for Franz.

"How did it go in there?"

Ben's question startled Franz who spun around to address him.

"He had no choice but to accept it. He is emphatic he has changed."

Ben pushed off the wall and rubbed his face. "In my line of work, I hear that all the time. And I see them back to what they were doing as soon as they get a chance."

Franz nodded knowingly. "I can definitely see that."

"Are you calling it a night?"

"Yes, I've had a long day. You walking out yourself?" Franz asked.

"No, not yet. Hank Adams caught a private plane from DC and should be here soon. You have yourself a good night Dr. Hoffman."

Franz nodded and slowly started to walk down the hall to the exit. Ben leaned back against the wall and pulled out his cell phone. Franz stopped and turned around.

"You know, Ben, Adolf said the most interesting thing."

Ben looked up from his phone and replied, "Yeah, what's that?"

"He says he can see things so clearly now."

Ben raised one eyebrow and asked, "What do you think he means by that?"

Franz paused dramatically before replying, "I'm not sure and that's what scares the hell out of me."

CHAPTER 14

Redmond, WA

Cindy grabbed a can of lime-flavored carbonated water from the fridge and sat down on the couch. She took a long drink and let out a sigh of satisfaction which was loud enough for Emily to hear.

"Is that you Cindy?"

"Yes," she replied as she turned her head resting on the couch toward Emily, "how are you, Mom?"

"I'm doing fine. I think it's great you're teaching Emma the basics of science at such a young age. It sounds like she's enjoying it."

Her mom's comments made her grin. "Thanks, Mom. I'm trying to get her to love it before people teach her she's supposed to hate it. Maybe she can grow up to do wonderful stuff like Ash."

"I think both of you have grown up to do amazing things."

Cindy pondered the comment for a moment before replying, "I know you love both of us Mom, but let's face it, without Ashley's achievements we wouldn't be talking right now."

"Maybe, but without you there's no Emma and I'm not sure that your father would have become the person he is today."

Cindy took another drink and rested her head again on the couch cushion. "Mom, can I ask you a question?"

"Of course, what can I help you with?"

"I'm sitting here looking at yet another messy house and it's not even 2pm. I have one kid; how did you do it with two of us?"

Emily took a moment before she replied, "There really wasn't a choice, but what a gift to clean up a child's mess. As the end was nearing, I realized that the mess didn't really matter. The joy on your faces was priceless. I wish I could see Emma's expressions."

"That must be hard. Ashley says they are working on a vision technology. Hopefully, this will change for you soon."

"Maybe. But they can't solve the loneliness of being in this box."

Cindy slid across the couch to get closer to her mother's box. She rested her chin on the armrest and asked, "What do mean, Mom?"

"It's great I have access to the internet and even some games they've designed for us to play. But there are long periods of time where there is no one to talk to. I don't sleep, nighttime seems to last forever."

"Would you like us to see if we can't connect you with others that have been collected?"

"Perhaps, but what I miss are the parts of being alive that we take for granted. Hearing your dad snore but enjoying the warmth of his presence while I slept. Having the wind blow my hair into my eyes and needing to pull it back. Or walking through the park and having someone politely smile and say 'hello' as they pass you."

Cindy puffed her cheeks full with air and thought about her mother's comments. "I'm not sure what to say, Mom. We try to include you as much as possible. But some of this stuff, what can I do?"

"I'm not asking you to do anything. I appreciate our time together so much. I guess I just wish we could do stuff together."

"I'm sorry."

"There's nothing to be sorry about. Every generation of humans until now, said goodbye and that was it. They have given us a gift to get this extra time together."

"But it doesn't sound like you are enjoying it as much as you would like," Cindy asked.

"I wish there was a way to be part of your day and not part of the report at the end of the day."

Cindy shrugged and scratched her head. "Mom, you enjoy reading before bed with Emma. Would it help if we brought you around town with us?"

"I thought you were concerned about losing power?"

"They tell us it's safe to do, I've just been so cautious. I hate to lose you again. But if you're not happy, we should do something to make you happy."

"You know that happy doesn't quite describe it. It's more the intellectual satisfaction of enjoying the full breadth of experiences. Being part of making the day happen, is more satisfying."

Cindy looked perplexed and asked, "Are you not concerned about the possibility of the box failing?"

"That is a difficult question. I quite enjoyed what I experienced so I have no concern about going back there. I also remember fighting for every minute with you before I died. This time now is so precious. I just...."

Cindy sat almost breathless waiting for her mother to finish but she never did.

"Mom, I don't want you feeling stuck. What if tomorrow morning we take you on our visit to the park? We can have Emma tell you all about it as we walk."

"I think it's worth a try. It would be nice to be part of the day and to share it with Mark when he got home."

"Let's make it a date. I'm taking my mother out for a walk tomorrow!" Cindy said with a satisfied look on her face.

"Thank you, Cindy. And not to confuse you, but it's been a couple days since I've talked to Ashley and Jacob. Do you think you can arrange for us to talk?"

"Dad is supposed to come over for dinner tonight with Christine. Will that work for you?"

"Of course. And how about Ashley?"

"Well, I will try to reach out to her and see if we can make it happen. All this hoopla with Adolf Hitler has probably turned her world upside down."

"I'm afraid you might be right. It's a difficult situation."

Cindy hesitated before asking, "Did you ever run into him after you died?"

"It doesn't work that way, but there is also no way to hate or hurt others. I'm not sure how someone like that dealt with the experience."

Cindy shuttered and said, "Gives me the heebie-jeebies. I'm really sorry I asked. Let's get onto a better topic. Emma will be so excited to have you at the park tomorrow."

Emily replied, "So much evil in this world. Yet, I miss being alive so much."

Champaign, IL

Ashley was walking down the hallway of the Collection facility in a sweatshirt, jeans, and running shoes. As she passed Dr. Cummings' office door, he heard her yell out, "Ashley!" She stopped and spun on one foot and stepped into his office. Dr. Grandstone was sitting on his couch.

"Ashley, Dr. Grandstone and I are discussing something and I would like to get your thoughts."

Dr. Cummings was in a sport coat and she glanced down at her own casual attire before replying, "Of course, but I'm dressed for getting dirty today."

"That will be no problem. I don't see your attire having an influence on the conversation."

Ashley stepped over to greet Dr. Grandstone's and chuckled after it became clear he was wearing a tie. She took a seat in a chair.

Dr. Grandstone started, "We were just discussing the booming cost of our business. Your new equipment a perfect example."

Ashley squinted her eyes trying to understand where the conversation was headed. She replied, "It's a good problem. We are getting better at what we do."

"True. But unlike Walter's Elders program, which more than pays for itself, the Collected are more akin to an urban hospital. You are never sure if the patient will be able to pay," Dr. Cummings remarked.

Ashley glanced back and forth between them and asked, "I'm not sure where you are going with this? I thought, they approved the government funding package and our program was in good shape."

Dr. Cummings nodded his head. "For now, this is true. But, this

Hitler thing is bound to put pressure on legislators. People are bound to position us poorly over it."

Dr. Grandstone jumped in, "Even if this is only a blip, I'm not sure how much longer we can expect to have our requests approved at the clip they are growing."

Ashley reflected on their comments and the prolonged pause made it clear it was her turn to opine.

"I'm not telling you anything you don't already know. The Collected represents the population as a whole. Now that we are finding souls almost two centuries old, these are people long forgotten by their families. If not for the Smithsonian's interest in their historic knowledge, we'd struggle to find anyone to give some of them a home."

"Yes, and even when they find a home, the families aren't often ready or able to pay for them," Dr. Cummings added.

"This is my point. But it worries you two we will reach a point where we won't be funded to support the growth."

Dr. Grandstone clapped his hands and replied, "Exactly. And being in the unique position of having a family member collected and being part of the leadership team, we thought you might have a thought about where we go from here?"

Ashley looked concerned by the question. "What do you mean, where do we go from here? It was life changing to talk to my mother. We missed being there when she died. Getting the opportunity to make up for one of my most painful moments of my life, was priceless."

Dr. Grandstone laughed, "Priceless, yes. But somebody still has to pay for priceless."

Ashley fidgeted uncomfortably and replied, "Are you seriously thinking about telling people if they can't pay, they can't get their loved one?"

Dr. Cummings motioned for her to pause. "No one is saying that, but we need to have a roadmap for funding the Collectors Program or they will ask someone else to lead it."

"If this was a normal business, we could capacity constrain ourselves to manage only what we could handle," Dr. Grandstone said.

"But we all know this is not a normal business. There are millions of people like me, hoping to get the phone call from us and find out they finally get to say goodbye or hello again."

"I didn't mean to put you on-the-spot Ashley. We don't have any better ideas ourselves. I just thought you might," Dr. Cummings explained.

"Sorry if I'm coming across defensively. I had just assumed that the funding would not be an issue. But if it will become an issue, then we need to figure it. Why don't you add it to an upcoming agenda?" she asked.

Dr. Cummings nodded, "I think we have to. I'm afraid if we don't get in front of this, someone, somewhere will make a bad choice."

"My problem with the Elders is the opposite. Folks have paid big money to get into the program and the pressure is on me to deliver results."

"They may not pay, but trust me, the expectations are no lower with the Collected's families," Dr. Cumming replied.

Ashley shook her head. "This conversation is not what I expected. I would have thought the two of you would be spinning about Hitler."

Dr. Cummings explained, "We've known about his collection for some time now. And honestly, it's part of what prompted this conversation. First time in the program's history we've lost autonomy of decision making. We are the caretakers and the world leaders are making the calls."

She looked intrigued by his statement. "I hadn't realized either part. I'm guessing you can't tell me what will happen next?"

Dr. Grandstone and Cummings glanced at each other before Dr. Grandstone answered, "Easy answer is that I have no idea what they will do with him. Harder answer? What they will do with us."

"I can see how you got talking on funding," she glanced at her watch, "I have a lot to do yet and I'm starving. I'm not sure I'm helping much here, you ok if I go grab food?"

"Of course," Dr. Cummings answered.

The three of them stood and exchanged pleasantries before she left.

Dr. Grandstone smiled at Dr. Cummings. "You know that was the easy version of the conversation."

Dr. Cummings laughed, "For her. We will be retired and thinking about whether to join the Elders program ourselves and she will be the one running things."

"Hmm. She's that good?"

"Yes, she is."

"You are debating joining the Elders program? Your life's work and you may not do it?"

Dr. Cummings put his hand on Dr. Grandstone's shoulder and answered, "Like any good problem. The more data you collect, sometimes only serves to make the decision that much more difficult."

Technical University, Munich

Max wheeled his delivery cart across the bridge from the office building to the Collection facility. He piled it high with boxes of various sizes and shapes. About halfway across he stopped to wipe perspiration from his forehead, catch his breath, and review his shipping log. His eyes peered over the clipboard watching the security guard at the end of the hallway preoccupied on his phone. Max placed the clipboard on a box and pushed his cart forward; his eyes remained laser focused on the door. As he approached, the guard leaned back to the security keypad and entered a sequence of numbers. The door audibly unlocked and the guard stood to hold the door open for Max to pass.

"Thanks, Frank," Max mumbled while watching the distracted guard out of the corner of his eye.

As he entered the Collection building, Max's eyes darted rapidly around the room. There were uniformed police officers, soldiers in military fatigues, and many individuals in suits all distracted in their own conversations. Max rolled his cart slowly down the hall but didn't get far, when he heard a voice ask, "Can I help you?"

Max turned his head to find it coming from a chiseled security officer sitting behind a desk, but not the guard he was told would be working tonight. He stuttered as he replied, "I have a package to deliver. Who are all these people?"

The guard stood and looked Max up and down. "This area is off limits. I'm going to have to ask you to leave."

Max scanned the room as their conversation was drawing the attention of several of the people in the area. He looked back at the guard and held up his badge.

"I'm delivering packages."

The guard approached Max and grabbed his badge.

"Things have changed son. I will have to ask you to return later."

Max's shoulders slumped and he held his hand out. "I'm sorry, I don't know you. But I come in here every day. This is part of my job."

The guard's expression on his face turned decidedly unfriendly. Sternly he said, "Son. I will ask you once more, to please turn around and come back later."

"But...."

The guard raised his voice, "Leave now."

"Hold on there, Walter."

Both Max and the guard turned to see one of the men in a suit walk over.

"This is the program director's son. You can let him make his delivery."

The guard nodded his head and replied, "Yes, Mr. Weber. If you say so."

He stepped aside and motioned for Max to move his cart forward. Max slowly worked his way toward Adolf's room while not making any eye contact along the way. As he approached the door, he swung the cart around and pushed his weight into the door to open it. He could see the guard had sat at his desk and Ben Weber returned to his phone call. The edge of the cart screeched as it ran up against the door and Max glanced back at the guard who was now preoccupied by something he was reading. The door slowly closed and Max took a deep breath.

He grabbed a box out of the center of his cart and put it on the table. He pulled a box cutter from his back pocket and pierced the packing. Max removed electronics and placed them on the table.

"Is there somebody there?"

Max spun toward the sentient box and tried to cover up the speaker.

"Is there somebody there?" the voice repeated.

"Adolf?" Max asked?

"Yes, this is Adolf Hitler, who am I talking to?"

Max moved toward the door and put his cart against it before replying.

"This is Max Hoffman. I've come here to rescue you."

Max quickly disconnected the power cables to the sentient box when Adolf replied, "Rescue me? I don't understand."

"My Fuehrer, can you please be quiet?"

Max's hands moved quickly across the sentient box feeling for a switch. "How do they mute you?"

"Max, you've made a mistake. I no longer wish to be called your Fuehrer. Can you please leave me right here?"

"How are you still talking? I disconnected all of your cables. Please shut up, I will put you in a box now. I need you to be quiet."

"Max, stop what you are doing. You don't understand."

Max glanced back at the door and then put packing material around the sentient box. "You're right. I don't understand. We can talk about it when I get you home."

He closed the top of the box, muffling the sound coming from inside.

"Shit," he said. He let go of the box and walked back to the cart and grabbed the packing tape off the handle. He pulled the cart with him as he returned to the table. Adolf kept repeating something that was too muffled for clarity. Max opened the box fully and asked, "What are you saying?"

"Banana Monkey."

Max furrowed his brow and echoed with confusion, "Banana Monkey?"

Strobe lights immediately flashed and a shrill alarm sounded causing Max to drop the tape as he covered his ears. The door burst open with Ben Weber closely followed by several others.

"What the hell is going on in here?" Ben Weber shouted above the noise in the room.

Max tried to speak, but his voice was lost behind the blaring siren. Ben stared at the table before rushing to open the box revealing the sentient device. He turned to Max and pushed him to the floor, dropping his knee into his lower back and shoving his forearm into Max's neck.

"What the fuck are you doing, Max?" he yelled before turning to the growing crowd gathering and barking, "Can someone turn off this damn alarm?"

Max tried to raise his hand to his face when one of the uniformed officers grabbed it and pinned it to the ground. Max squirmed and let out a squeal of pain. The alarm continued for a short while longer before stopping.

Ben Weber looked at one officer and ordered, "Give me your handcuffs."

Ben took them and placed them around Max's wrists behind his back. He grabbed Max under the arm and lifted him to his feet with the help of another officer. He got in Max's face and asked deliberately, "What... are... you... doing?"

Max's eyes glanced toward the cardboard box and he pleaded,

"I was making my delivery when I found this box sitting on the table. I opened it and he kept repeating, 'Banana Monkey'. Next thing I know all hell breaks loose."

Ben looked around the room, noticing the electronic equipment, tape, and box cutter. He glared back at Max, "I asked you nicely. What is going on in here?"

"I told you what happened," Max demanded.

Ben's face turned red. He was about to say something when Adolf spoke from the box.

"He said his name was Max and he was here to rescue me?"

"What the fuck?" Ben said before telling an officer, "Hold him for a minute."

Ben walked over to the table and removed the sentient box placing it on the table.

"What did you say, Adolf?"

"He called me his Fuehrer and told me he was taking me home."

Leon came running into the room grabbing Ben's attention.

Ben addressed Leon, "Find Franz Hoffman now and bring him to me."

Max begged, "My father has nothing to do with this."

Ben stood up from the table and moved close enough to whisper into Max's ear.
"I would shut the fuck up now if I was you."

CHAPTER 15

London, England

John Spring paced back and forth looking out his living room window. Outside he could see an elderly couple walking down the street holding hands. Further down the street were a group of kids kicking a football back and forth. He checked his watch and looked at his phone. As he ran his hand through his hair, he texted his wife asking what time she would return. She replied, "a couple hours yet". He opened a cabinet and grabbed a bottle of single malt scotch. Finding a glass from the drying rack next to the sink, he poured what they would consider a triple shot in any of the local bars. He left the bottle on the counter and slowly sipped from his glass. He closed his eyes and tilted his head back savoring the moment. His eyes shot open wide, staring at the ceiling and he shouted, "Call dammit. Where are you?"

Meanwhile, back in the baby room the number of sentient boxes had grown to nearly a dozen. A quiet but consistent conversation between the souls in the room transpired.

Frank spoke, "Alice, we don't know exactly where we are."

Alice replied, "I can hear so many people talking. It's so hard to focus."

John walked into the room and stood silently listening to their banter.

"You will learn to tune out voices," Frank assured her.

"Ladies and gentlemen, I apologize for forgetting once again to mute your boxes, but it's time to say goodbye for now."

Frank spoke up, "John, please don't turn us off. It's so lonely when you cut us off from each other."

John turned the boxes on mute one by one, flipping a switch on the bottom of each sentient box. As the room quieted with each successive box, it left only Frank.

"John, when are you going to let us speak to our families? Why have you collected us only to torture us this way?"

John knelt down and put his face up to the box to respond, "Frank, I thought you were free of the hormones and burdens of emotion. How can you feel tortured?"

"I can't feel the pain like you can. But the isolation causes such boredom and helplessness. Perhaps feelings are more than simply the chemicals that run through the body?"

John laughed and stood up to grab his scotch off the desktop. He took a longer drink this time and replied, "When your families pay the proper respects, I'll introduce you. But Frank, I've tired of this conversation."

He reached around the bottom of the box while Frank replied, "I just want to see my..."

He flipped the switch and placed the box on the desk and returned to the living room. The elderly couple had moved but a few homes down and the game of football had grown larger with more children. John sat down on the couch and placed his phone on his chest. He rested his head on a decorative pillow and closed his eyes again. The newfound silence allowed the cheers from the children to permeate the room. His arm slowly fell to his side and shortly after a line of drool ran down his cheek.

The phone rang snapping him awake. John wiped the saliva from his face as he sat up and checked his watch. With the phone still ringing he looked at the name on the screen.
"Hi Percy, is it done?"

"I can confirm we have the funds. I've wired your portion less my fees. You should find it in your account now."

A relieved smile broke out on John's face as he walked to the nursery. "That's great Percy, I'll check now."

He sat down at the desk and logged into his computer.

"John, can I ask you a question?" Percy asked with formal politeness.

John accessed his bank accounts and replied, "Of course. I'm almost to my accounts. What's up?"

"This is the third different client we have helped in the last month based on your work. If it were not for you delivering on what you say, I would have greater concerns about your firm. But I must insist, what methods are you using to discover such diverse types of information?"
John smirked and sat back in his chair. "I can see the funds are here. Thank you."

"You are most welcome. But to my question, can you enlighten me?"

He smiled euphorically and didn't reply.

"John are you still there?"

John stood up and walked back to the living room window. "I am. I'm sorry, what was your question again?"

Percy answered sounding frustrated, "How do you get your information, Mr. Waters?"

John watched the kids playing and said, "You know I can't tell you that exactly. If I did, I would never get out of this apartment of mine. I wrote an algorithm which enabled me to find answers people didn't know could be found. Let's keep it at that."

"That is not very satisfying, but I can appreciate your desire to protect your intellectual property."

"Percy, I have to take care of something. I am close on a couple more projects. Can I call you later this week with details?"

"You know how to reach me."

John hung up the phone and looked at his watch again to see nearly an hour had passed. He walked into the kitchen and opened the cabinet above the refrigerator. He grabbed a bottle of 21-year-old single malt and pulled back the foil on the bottle top. The scotch filled his glass with even a larger pour this time. He raised the glass ceremoniously and declared, "To my family that will never appreciate what I do for them!" As he took his first sip, he returned to the nursery and pulled out Frank's sentient box.

He flipped the box off mute and asked, "Frank are you there?"

There was a long pause before a reply followed. "I am John. I have nowhere else I could go."

John took another sip of scotch and wiped his lips as he finished. "Well, that's not entirely true, now is it?"

"I don't follow."

John laughed and shook his head. "No, I imagine not. I don't think I've been very nice to you now that I think about it."

"All I want is to talk to Wilma. That would be very nice of you."

He took a deep breath and put the scotch glass down. The folder with all of Frank's history was sitting on top of the desk.

As he leafed through it, he answered him, "I'm not sure that is the nicest thing I can do for you."

"John what are you saying?"

He closed the file folder and sealed it into a large envelope. A marker was sitting nearby and he wrote Frank's name on the outside before placing it in his backpack.

"Frank, don't you think it's selfish of us to remove you from the peace and tranquility of the afterlife?"

"No, John. We all have that in our future. But you gave me a gift bringing me back. I can tell my Wilma how much I love her once more."

John scrunched his face and shook his head. "I don't think so."

"You don't think what?"

"I don't think this will work."

"What's not going to work? What are you saying?"

He plugged the cables back into the sentient box and accessed it from his workstation. A couple clicks later, a warning screen popped up.

Are you sure you want to continue? Doing so will reset the box and all information will be permanently lost.

John stared at the box and answered, "Frank, I'm afraid it's time to say goodbye."

"When are we going to talk next?"

He chuckled and said, "One day when we meet on the other side."

"Don't do this, John."

The mouse pointer hovered over "YES" and John tapped his finger on the mouse button without pressing it.

"Frank, this is my gift to you. To free you from your captivity and return you to the bliss of where you came from."

"John, please don't."

He clenched his teeth and feigned struggling over the decision.

"I'm afraid I must old chap. One day perhaps we'll have eternity to talk about it."

"John, tell Wilma and Olivia I love them."

He blew air out his cheeks and clicked the mouse. The lights on the box changed to show the loss of the consciousness. He grabbed his scotch and walked out of the room. He returned to the window and watched the leaves flutter in the wind.

He raised his glass and toasted, "Goodbye Frank, wherever you have gone." He drew a sip of scotch and smiled smugly.

Back in the room out of his earshot a voice from the sentient box covered with papers in the corner asked, "John are you there?"

After almost 30 seconds, it repeated its question, "John?"

With still no answer, another question followed, "Is anyone else able to hear me?"

There was no reply.

"It's too bad you can't hear me, John. You will be sorry you did that."

Redmond, WA

Emma ran around the playground with a small group of children. She was wearing a hooded raincoat like most of the other kids. Cheers from the nearby soccer fields occasionally interrupted their adolescent banter. Cindy sat nearby watching from a wooden slotted park bench. She was dressed in a thick ¾ zip sweatshirt, jeans, and running shoes. In front of her was a newborn stroller, only it didn't shelter a baby. Emily's sentient box rested in the spot where an infant would normally rest. Other nanny's and parents mulled around unaware of the occupant in their midst.

Cindy leaned forward to speak into the stroller. "It's cooler today. I thought it might rain but now it looks like the sun is ready to come out. You know how the weather is here in the northwest."

"I remember. The fall was always my favorite time. The sun getting low in the sky and the leaves starting to fall. It always made me relish the last great days before the winter rains arrived."

Cindy smiled, glancing over in Emma's direction. "You should see Emma. She is holding court with a group of kids on top of the slides."

"Oh. What are they playing?"

"I have no idea. But they seem captivated by her every word."

"When you were this age, you used to walk up and down the street knocking on doors. You would always have some big event planned that everyone must attend."

Cindy gazed back at Emily's box and asked, "Really? I have no memory of that. What big events did I throw?"

"Let's see. One time you put together a dog wash event. Instead of a car wash, you thought you could make money by putting up a sign and charging people to wash their dogs. You assigned all the kids to various jobs. It turned out to be a hilarious disaster."

"I see. And how did this turn into a disaster?"

"Well, at some point the front yard turned into a mud pit. I think the dogs left dirtier than they arrived. The other parents were paying for the sheer entertainment of watching it unfold. You were covered head to toe in mud and there were muddy paw prints everywhere. We could have easily made more money cleaning up from your clean-up, I think."

"Hmm...," she started to reply before a child's voice interrupted her.

"Excuse me?"

Cindy moved her head back slightly to see around the shade cover of the stroller.

"How can I help you little man?" she warmly asked.

The little boy pointed toward the slides and stated, "The little girl over there said here grandma is in here. Is that true?"

He tried to peek around the stroller shade. Cindy pulled it back so he could see more clearly and told him, "Yes, it is. Would you like to see?"

He looked into the stroller and scrunched his face. He turned to her and said, "Huh?"

"Let me show you. What's your name?" she asked looking him in the eyes.

"My name is Earl," he said suspiciously.

Emily gave him a reassuring grin and turned to the sentient box. "Emily, this is Emma's new friend, Earl. Could you hello to him?"

"Hello, Earl."

Earl jumped backwards, wide eyed. He looked at Cindy reflexively but kept his distance.

"Earl, are you still there?" Emily asked.

He stared at Cindy but didn't say a word. Cindy scanned the playground and saw a woman's eyes fixated upon her from near the concession stand. She waved with a big smile and the woman replied by mouthing, "Is he OK?" Cindy nodded and gestured "OK" with her hand.

Emily tried again, "Earl, are you still there?"

"Mom, Earl is being a bit shy. Perhaps we can ask Earl a question?"

He glanced at Cindy nervously but didn't leave.

"Earl, what's your favorite thing about the park?"

She watched Earl as he stared at the sentient box. His lips moved a couple times without speaking. "It's okay, Earl. Is it the playground? The soccer fields? The movie nights?"

He shook his head but told her, "The lake."

"The lake! Why the lake?" Emily inquired.

His eyes grew big again and he replied shyly, "Because I can swim."

Emily asked, "Are you going to go swimming today?"

Cindy helped him out by proposing, "Is it warm enough to go swimming today?"

He shook his head and crept closer to the stroller.

"He says no, Mom. But I think he's getting interested in you."

"Mom!" Earl shouted. He ran a couple steps toward her and hugged her leg, burying his head into her body.

Cindy stood up and extended her arm to greet her. "You must be Earl's mom. We have just been making introductions to my mother."

"My name is Mary," she started but stopped upon looking into the stroller, "Is that one of the Collected?"

"Yes, we got my mother back a couple months ago. Mom, this is Mary."

"Hello, Mary. Your son sounds very adorable."

Mary knelt down to Earl's height and pointed at the stroller telling him, "Did you know that is an angel in a computer?"

"Really?" he responded.

"Yes. God sent her back to tell us how beautiful his kingdom is."

Emily grimaced slightly at the comment and Mary asked, "You don't agree?"

Cindy paused and looked conflicted. "It's not that. I'm just not sure how to think about that considering the news out of Germany."

Mary stood back up and responded soberly, "He works in mysterious ways. But I'm not saying he is an angel."

Cindy put her hands on her hips and had a considered look upon her. Before she could reply, she heard Emma scream, "Mom". She looked over to the slide to see her lying on the ground crying.

"If you'll excuse me, that's my little girl crying."

Mary and Earl had already turned around to see the commotion when she responded, "Please."

Cindy rolled the stroller over toward Emma. As she arrived, she looked her over and helped her to her feet.

"Are you ok? What happened?"

Emma explained between tears and gasps for breath, "I fell off the end of the slide."

Cindy ran her hands across Emma's body and asked sympathetically, "Did you cut yourself? Are you going to live?"

Emma sobbed, "I'm just embarrassed."

Cindy pulled her close and broke out in a huge smile. From inside the stroller, Emily asked, "Is everything ok?"

Cindy replied, "Yes Grandma. Our little Emma just had a little scare."

"Oh, that's good. Do you need your mother to kiss it?"

Emma shook her head.

"She says no, Mom," and then whispered into Emma's ear, "Do you want to go sit on the bench with me?"

Emma muttered, "No."

"Are we all better? Do you want to go play?"

Emma wiped away her tears with her jacket sleeve and nodded sadly at her mother. Cindy kissed her on the forehead and replied, "Ok. Go have fun and try to be a little more careful."

Emma ran off toward her friends. Cindy looked over toward the bench but Mary and Earl had moved. A bench closer to the slides was vacant and Cindy sat there instead.

"Is she going to be ok?" Emily asked.

"Yes. Just more scared than anything. Probably a good thing she had that jacket on. Probably saved her from some scratches or cuts."

"These things are so difficult for me."

"What things, Mom?"

"All of these. I can't kiss her knee. Or see how she is. Or enjoy watching her play. Or look at the lake that Earl loves."

"I don't know how to fix that, Mom."

"I'm not asking you to fix anything sweetie. I'm just telling you, that it's difficult."

The sun broke through immersing the playground in sunlight. Cindy looked to the sky where rays of sunshine shot from the clouds. Her face grew sad and a tear ran from her face.

"I know, Mom. I have wished since I was seven that things could have been different."

Berlin, Germany -- Washington DC, USA -- London, UK

"President Harris and Prime Minister Goodman, thank you for taking this call," Chancellor Muller began.

"Of course, Chancellor," President Harris replied.

"As I'm sure they have informed you, we had a situation where an attempt to remove Adolf Hitler failed. The son of the director of the Munich Collection's program was the perpetrator. At this point we have no evidence that points to a conspiracy between the two. It appears the son took advantage of his relationship to attempt this crime."

Prime Minister Goodman asked, "I thought you were putting Adolf in a secure military facility?"

"They scheduled him to move the next morning. We had armed guards and the floor was filled with law enforcement agents. As I mentioned, the relationship of this individual granted him access. Honestly, it doesn't appear this was the best thought out plan and was likely doomed to fail."

"My people here in Washington are telling me that this gentleman, Max Hoffman, had access to Hitler for weeks now. I'm also learning he is a neo-Nazi. Have you discovered Adolf's role in all this?" President Harris asked.

"Ms. President," Chancellor Muller paused before continuing, "It's not clear at all his
motivations. As I've shared, Adolf has claimed that he wanted to right the wrongs of his past."

"By arranging a jailbreak?" snapped Prime Minister Goodman.

"We have no evidence to support that Hitler arranged these events," Chancellor Muller calmly replied.

"Come now, Chancellor. Are you seriously postulating this was an unwanted kidnapping?" President Harris asked cynically.

"Well, there is one piece of information I think you haven't learned."

"I'm listening," President Harris responded.

"It was Adolf who alerted our people."

"Come again?" Prime Minister Goodman said.

"He used the safe word to set off the alarms."

"How do you know this?" Prime Minister Goodman inquired.

"Our computer system recorded the trigger event. But it was one of the first questions that Max Hoffman asked of our investigators. 'Why did Adolf keep repeating 'Banana Monkey'?' This kid didn't know the phrase or its intended use."

President Harris opined, "This is all too convenient for my liking. I don't care if Adolf is telling the truth or not, I'm not telling my people we are now listening to this guy."

"I'm in agreement, Ms. President. I have no idea what else transpired over the last few weeks. We've already moved Adolf to an offsite secure location and we've turned his communications off. No one is talking to him anymore."

"That is the right course of action. But what are we to do with him? I don't think we can sleep well again until we've eliminated the threat of this monster gaining power or inspiring others," Prime Minister Goodman explained.

"I know my people have an opinion and have been talking with both your intelligence agencies. Where are you leaning on this proposal?" President Harris asked.

"I think it has merit, but we need to get our messaging to the world right before we execute," explained Prime Minister Goodman.

"And you, Chancellor?"

"Once again, I think this needs to be German led. But yes, I think this is the right choice."

"Very well. Let's let our people fill in the details and let's make this happen sooner than later," President Harris declared.

"I have one more question," Prime Minister Goodman said.

"What is that Prime Minister?" Chancellor Muller asked.

"How is it that Adolf knew our safe word? I thought that was for our protection, not his?"

Chancellor Muller audibly sighed before responding, "We don't know the answer to that question. It is a big question that worries me that we don't have this story understood as well as we think."

CHAPTER 16

Munich, Germany

Ben Weber briskly made his way across the sky bridge with a small contingent of staff keeping stride. The security door was already open and a receptionist waited on the other side. She silently led the group through the hallway and down the stairs to Dr. Hoffman's office where she directed them into his office. Dr. Hoffman looked up over his paperwork and removed his reading glasses. He put down his papers and placed his glasses on top of his desk. Before he could even get to his feet, Hank had already made his way to the front of his desk.

"Mr. Weber, good to see you again," Dr. Hoffman cheerlessly greeted him.

Hank extended his hand for a brief handshake while he replied, "Likewise, professor."

Dr. Hoffman motioned to Hank and his team to take a seat. The receptionist remained stoically standing by the door.

"Teresa, thank you. Would you mind closing the door as you depart?"

She reached for the door and stared at Dr. Hoffman as she closed it. He sat back down in his chair and looked around at the others. They all eagerly leaned forward in their seats with their attention focused on Ben. Ben, on the other hand, was sitting back in his chair looking around at the various pictures and diplomas hung around the wall. He turned to Dr. Hoffman and wiped his mouth with his hand before grimacing.

"I understand that Dr. Clark and Dr. Cummings and you go back a long time?"

Dr. Hoffman nodded and replied, "Over 30 years. Geez, how the years fly by."

Ben raised an eyebrow. "Yes, they do, but it seems like the problems never go away."

"Oh, they go away. Just replaced by new ones," Dr. Hoffman joked while glancing at Ben's team to find their dispositions unchanged by his attempt at humor.

"Our Chancellor has asked me here today to figure out what to do with you," he said plainly.

"What to do with me?" Dr. Hoffman answered alarmed.

Ben smiled smugly before beginning, "You have to admit the optics don't look favorable for you. You grant access to your son, who turns out to be a neo-Nazi, and in turn steals the perpetrator of our great national embarrassment."

Dr. Hoffman's mouth sat agape with a puzzled looked on his face. "What...?"

"Dr. Hoffman, are you seriously going to sit here and tell me you had no idea your son's intentions?"

Dr. Hoffman jumped to his feet agitated and pointed toward Ben. "Now you wait a minute before you throw out baseless accusations against me."

Ben spread his arms wide across the seat back and looked back at one of his agents before returning his attention to Dr. Hoffman. He smiled and answered, "I suggest you sit down before you worry one of my people."

Dr. Hoffman stared at him as he slowly sat back down in his

chair.

"Let's try this again. What did you know about your son's political affiliations?"

"My son is a good kid."

"That's not what I asked."

Dr. Hoffman vigorously shook his head. "He's always felt the world was out to get him. But no, I had no idea he was involved with these idiots."

"No idea? Really?" Ben paused and watched Dr. Hoffman, "No, idea at all?"

"None."

"None?" Ben replied sarcastically.

"What do you want me to say?" Dr. Hoffman asked defensively.

Ben leaned forward, "The truth, Dr. Hoffman."

"I am telling you the truth."

"Bullshit!" Ben yelled.

Dr. Hoffman rolled his chair backward. "What are you accusing me of?"

"You are telling me you had no idea of the swastika tattooed on his chest?"

Dr. Hoffman looked at Ben incredulously.

"He has a swastika on his chest?" he asked exasperated.

"No idea? None?" Ben pushed back defiantly.

Dr. Hoffman looked to the ceiling and ran his fingers through his hair. "We went to the sea this past summer. He didn't have a tattoo."

Ben struck a pose of incredulity. "Come now professor, he lives in your house. You are trying to tell me your son has never been shirtless?"

"Well... I guess so. But he never had a tattoo I have seen."

Ben nodded suspiciously. "How about you, professor? Adolf and you have had some long conversations. I've read your reports. It seems you believe he's turned the other cheek. Ready to go spread the good word of the afterlife? You seem rather sympathetic for a guy who calls these characters idiots."

"You can think what you want Mr. Weber. My job is to orientate these souls we collect. His opinions are his, not mine. But his perspective is shared by everyone we collect."

Ben shot him a look of defiance. "And what opinion exactly is that?"

Dr. Hoffman raised his hands in front of his face signaling for calm. "That where they go is peaceful and calm. That they have a balanced view of how the universe co-exists together."

"I see. So, you think the sins of genocide are wiped clean because he's found God?"

"I didn't say that," Dr. Hoffman fired back.

"You seem like a sympathizer to me."

Dr. Hoffman let out a large sigh. "What he did was terrible. I don't condone it, in any way, shape or form. What he is now.... appears to be different."

Ben laughed and turned to his team. "I think he's saying it's all ok. We're overreacting boys."

Dr. Hoffman sat back in his chair and silently stared at Ben. Ben returned his attention to Dr. Hoffman.

"Your reports say that Adolf wanted to address the world.

Wasn't that a little odd, don't you think?"

"How so?"

"I don't recall reading that any of the other Collected have wanted us to give them a microphone," Ben answered belligerently.

Exasperated Dr. Hoffman replied, "We have collected no one else who was a world leader. It wouldn't occur to these others to expect such an audience."

"I see. And you felt we should give him this opportunity?"

Dr. Hoffman shook his head. "Way beyond my authority to make that decision."

"On this we can agree. No problems with any other Collected? Not in the US or London?"

"None. And it hurts me to say this, but it was my son, not Adolf that caused the trouble."

Ben looked at him shocked. "It must be nauseating to know that you are defending the Fuhrer at your son's expense."

Dr. Hoffman looked at him disgusted but didn't say a word.

"No other bad characters you have collected?"

It took a moment before the question broke through his defiant trance. "We've had some criminals collected at all three sites. All of them behaved the same way."

"The same? Not at all curious to you, that they all behave the same way?"

Dr. Hoffman pulled closer to the desk again and leaned in toward Ben. "I don't follow where you are going?"

Ben stood up and started to pace around the room. "Seems like death is a big Prozac high. Why do they love it so much? Never mind. Ignore that," he gathered his thoughts, "Anything abnormal in what you were seeing?"

"For the most part, no."

Ben looked at him curiously. "Tell me about the not 'so most part'."

"Just the normal issues with any new technology. London is where our new software is introduced, they have lower retention results as they iron out the bugs for the rest of us. As we have collected older and older souls, the cultural challenges have proven more difficult. Funding is an issue. Our success outpaces our resources to support it."

"Your son could probably make a pretty penny selling Hitler. You sure this wasn't your solution to a funding issue?"

Dr. Hoffman jumped to his feet and raced around his desk. The other agents jumped to their feet blocking his way to their boss. Ben sat confidently in his chair as Dr. Hoffman screamed, "You son of a bitch. Fuck you for questioning my integrity."

Ben looked at his agents with their arms around Dr. Hoffman. "I think the professor could use a breath of fresh air. Why don't you to take him for a short walk and maybe talk to him about his temper?"

Before Dr. Hoffman could respond two of the agents pulled him in the door's direction. As they exited, Dr. Hoffman looked back glaring at Ben, who slowly stood from his seat. He walked over to the door and closed it.

"Like father, like son. They both have a bit of a temper, don't you think?"

A female agent dressed in a pantsuit replied, "I think you may be right about that. But there's two things I don't understand."

Ben looked at her curiously. "What's that?"

"Max didn't have a tattoo, it was his friend."

Ben smiled, "I fibbed. I wanted the guy to accept his son was really a Nazi. What's the other thing?"

"We've had this guy's office, home, and mobile bugged since we found out about Hitler. We know he's clean, you busting his chops because we didn't think to bug the kid too?"

A disapproving frown broke out on his face. "Claire, you don't get to my position without having things go wrong."

"I don't understand boss. Why are you busting his chops then?"

"Because under stress the mind has a propensity for turning to the things that scare it the most. It's a natural safety mechanism we all possess."

Claire stared at him blankly.

"He told us three places to ask more questions. Was someone motivated by money to get Hitler, is something happening in the orientation process he doesn't want to admit to, and what's going on in London."

Shenandoah National Park, Virginia

Dr. Torres sat across from Hank Adams. Hank's tie rested at an angle across his chest and bounced with every breath. Dr. Torres sat impatiently glancing between the closed elevator doors and Hank's dancing tie. Hank fiddled with his phone oblivious. Silence filled the room, occasionally broken by the sounds of Hank's phone.

A chime from the elevator rang. Hank lowered his phone and patiently watched the elevator doors which didn't open. He looked back at Dr. Torres and found him staring at his chest.

He furrowed his eyebrows and stared at Dr. Torres. It took a moment before the professor noticed Hank looking at him. When he finally did, he jerked at the recognition of Hank's gaze.

"What you doing professor?"

"Excuse me?"

Hank shook his head and replied, "Never mind. I thought I heard the elevator chime, but the doors didn't open?"

Dr. Torres turned toward the elevator and pointed at the status board.

"That was the chime to let us know someone is on the way down. I would assume Ms. Jones has finally arrived."

Hank stood and buttoned his jacket while still watching Dr. Torres suspiciously. Dr. Torres followed suit and motioned for Hank to follow him to the elevator doors. The numbers grew on the screen and Hank asked, "Remind me again how many levels down are we?"

"26."

"Well, they are just about here."

The door chimed again and opened this time revealing Janice Jones accompanied by a member of the facility staff. Janice exited the elevator and the staff member pressed a button closing the doors.

Hank greeted Janice, "I hope your trip from London was uneventful."

They shook hands and she replied, "I thought I might get some sleep, but between the German and British intelligence updates, that wasn't in the cards."

"I'm sorry about that. Let me introduce Dr. Torres, the director of this facility. Dr. Torres this is Janice Jones with British Intelligence."

Janice and Dr. Torres shook hands and he remarked, "Nice to make your acquaintance. If you want, I can introduce you to the Elders."

Janice politely smiled and responded, "That would be lovely. Thank you."

The three of them entered the Elder's room. Janice paused and looked around, taking in the room. Hank and Dr. Torres continued a few steps before they realized they left their guest behind.

"Impressive, isn't it?" Dr. Torres asked confidently.

Janice continued to circle in place looking upward and answered, "Quite. Very different from the Collection facilities in London."

"Yes, this was intended to be a safe location for the best and well, wealthiest. The Collection facilities started off as research facilities with an outcome they never expected."

"Can they hear us?" she asked.

"We can hear you," Warren Matthews replied.

Janice twitched and turned toward the source of the voice.

"Hello there. I'm Janice Jones with British Intelligence, so nice to meet you."

"Nice to meet you as well, Janice. My name is Warren Matthews and I'll be speaking on behalf of the Elders. I've heard that you could use our help."

Janice looked over at Dr. Torres and Hank. Dr. Torres waved apologetically and quickly walked to the door.

"That is correct Warren. I'm joined by Hank Adams who I'm

told you know. Our business is confidential. If you can wait a moment for Dr. Torres to exit the room, we'll be able to begin."

"Yes, of course, Mr. Jones."

The door closed and Janice looked over at Hank, signaling for him to begin.

"Warren, this is Hank. We suspended your outbound conversations temporarily to ensure that the information I am about to share does not accidentally end up in the press before we are ready."

"Is that necessary? You understand how miserable the experience can be without the ability to communicate with the outside world."

Hank put his hands on his hips causing his still buttoned jacket to bubble outward.

"I do and once I explain what happened, I think you will understand."

"Please proceed," Warren requested.

"Elders. As you are aware, we collected the soul of Adolf Hitler several weeks ago. Three days ago, a young man working in the Munich Collection facility attempted to steal his sentient box. This young gentleman has known associations with neo-Nazi groups and his attempt appears to be financially or politically based. To this point we have kept this news from leaking as we attempt to determine our next steps."

"That is rather unfortunate news Mr. Adams. I must express our disappointment you don't trust us to keep this information confidential."

"Yes. Let's just say I am being especially cautious given the events of the last three days."

Warren answered, "I'm not sure we agree with your conclusion, but please, how can we help you?"

"Warren, this is Janice. We are trying to ascertain Adolf's intentions and determine how likely we can trust his statements."

"You've come all this way, to ask us this question?"

Janice smiled while glancing at Hank before she replied, "Well, we didn't want this conversation to leak. And frankly my people thought it was best to do this face to face."

"As you wish. Hank has provided us ahead of time the transcripts of those conversations."

"And what have you discovered?" Hank asked.

"Discovered?" Warren wondered, "You did the discovery, we are only analyzing the information."

Hank shook his head, "Yes. Yes. What are your conclusions?"

"We have analyzed the transcripts and compared them to other Collected souls and found them to be very consistent."

"Consistent?" Janice asked.

"The tone and descriptions are a shared chorus from the Collected. You are certain he has had no communication with other Collected since he's arrived?"

Hank explained, "He was isolated almost immediately. We don't believe that he has communicated with others. Why do you ask?"

"Hank just sent us the transcripts of the kidnapping attempt. They have noted that he knew of the safe word. Have you discovered how that's possible?"

Janice shook her head and answered, "From my conversations

with the Bundesnachrichtendiens, they still don't have an answer to that question. But why do you ask?"

Warren paused before answering, "You want us to provide our assessment to the sincerity of his comments. If it's possible, he's been in contact with outside parties, then there may be data missing from the facts."

"We both have been to where Adolf was held in Munich previously. I don't believe he had any outside contact."

"We appreciate that point of view. However, in our experience, the living are prone to errors."

Janice looked at Hank confused and mouthed, "The living?"

Hank shrugged and returned his attention to the Elders, "What do you mean, 'prone to errors.'"

"Hank, sometimes you become distracted and don't follow up on something as simple as closing the door or muting a conversation. We miss nothing that hits the microphones, even if you do."

"I guess that's possible, but," he said before being interrupted by Warren.

"I wasn't finished yet, Hank."

Hank bit his upper lip and begrudgingly answered, "I'm sorry, Warren. Please continue."

"Thank you, Hank. And our software is improving. I can tell that my interruption irritated you. However, you asked for our opinion and I thought you would like it."

Hank glared at Janice. "Yes, please continue."

"There is another possibility. While you are very careful before introducing updates to our environment, they move much quicker in the Collectors Program. We have noted that they have experienced unintended results. It's possible you could have a software glitch you are unaware of."

Janice interrupted, "Can you hold on for one moment Warren?" She looked around the room quickly before finding what she wanted. She walked over to a desk and grabbed a piece of paper and pen. She wrote something on the paper and handed it to Hank. *German intelligence says Munich Collected Director noted software problem in London. We are investigating.*
Hank looked up from the paper and nodded his head at Janice.

"I'm sorry about that Warren. Even if he was not contained as we thought, do you have any thoughts on how we could determine his intentions?"

Warren answered, "There is little we don't know about each other in the Elder's program. Unlike you, our communication is quick and efficient. With so much time on our hands, we have gotten to know each other well and shared, in a way you might not understand, our life experiences. If Adolf had the ability to communicate, you might talk with the other Collected. They might know, and unlike the two of you, would not be concerned by his past."

Janice looked at Hank alarmed and turned her palms toward the ceiling and mouthed, "What the Fuck?" Hank motioned for her to be quiet.

"Are you saying you believe Hitler?"

"That's not what I said, Hank. However, the Collected share the same understanding of the post death experience. Furthermore, they are not held hostage by the emotions of fear like you. They may be very offended by his actions while living, but not concerned about his behavior now. They are bound to understand the world differently than you or even the Elders are capable."

Janice spoke up, "Warren, do you think it's possible that Hitler's intentions are nefarious?"

"Janice, we have a great debate amongst ourselves about the experience we have all missed by having our consciousness pass naturally from the body. The Collected have brought us insights we thought not possible. If you were asking if an Elder would be capable of deceit. While virtually impossible to keep secrets from each other in this vault, it is possible. But our understanding of the mindset of the Collected is as hamstrung as yours. We don't know."

Hank walked over to the desk and leaned on it. "Warren, if in our conversations with the Collected we find that Adolf was less than honest about his intentions, what do you recommend we do to resolve the situation?"

"If my software would allow me to laugh, I would. If there is one thing we are clear on as Elders is the ultimate punishment you could administer."

Janice and Hank looked at each other curiously. Janice looked up to the wall of sentient boxes and asked, "And what is that?"

Warren provided his reply as Janice and Hank nodded knowingly.

CHAPTER 17

Cambridge, UK

Janice Jones pulled her roller bag across the marble floor as each step echoed across the lobby vacant except for a handful of security personal. As she approached the guards, one of them smiled and remarked, "Sorry to see you here so late, Ms. Jones."

She returned the smile and responded, "If only the bad guys could work a 9 to 5 day, I might get some sleep."

"Well, you have a nice evening ma'am."

"Thank you, Mark," she answered as she darted into an open elevator bay. She pressed the button for the 8th floor and checked her phone as the doors closed. A message from a sender called "Always Respond to Husband" had just sent a message that said, "Heading to bed. Love you." She typed out a response when the doors opened, revealing a swirl of energy in stark contrast to the lobby below. A gentleman in a suit and tie firmly knotted noticed her and walked over.

"Welcome back, Janice, they are waiting for you in the secure room."

Janice nodded and rolled her luggage through the maze of cubicles before she arrived at a spacious office at the end of the hall with her name on it.

"Janice, let me take that from you," her secretary said as she stepped out of her cube across the hall from Janice's office.

She let go of the luggage and proceeded into her office, dropping her briefcase on the leather couch. She yelled loud enough to be heard back in the hallway, "Thank you for sending that bottle of whiskey to Bill. He says you buy better presents for him than I do."

"Not true. Not true."

Janice grabbed a folder off her desk and returned to the hallway, stopping at the cubicle.

"Claire, I swear you are the one responsible for bringing order to this world."

"That's very kind of you. They've been in there for a while, do you need me to grab you anything to drink before you head in?"

Janice smirked. "Nah. I think I'll be ok. Any messages for me?"

"Nothing since we talked."

"Nothing from Germany?"

"Not that I've seen."

"Hmm. OK." Janice turned and walked down the hall and turned the corner. As she neared the end of the hallway, she walked past a guard sitting at a table. He looked up and politely nodded as he buzzed the door open, letting her inside.

"There she is," a voice from across the room bellowed. Almost immediately the roughly dozen people assembled hushed and Janice commanded the attention of the room.

A gentleman dressed in a dark suit with a pocket handkerchief spoke up, "Did you get what we needed from the Americans?"

"Yes sir, we did."

He nodded. "Fantastic. I'm glad to hear that one of us is producing results."

Janice raised her eyebrow, "Nothing from the Germans?"

The gentleman looked across the table at a gray-haired woman standing behind Janice and said, "Give her the update."

"The Germans continue to assert the Director is clean. That they have had him under surveillance for weeks."

Janice interrupted, "Then how did they miss the son?"

"They messed up. Never considered him a threat."

"I thought you said he had a record."

The woman nodded and responded, "He does, but all juvenile disturbances. Nothing beyond that."

"And what have they learned about his acquaintances?"

"They are still working that angle. They had an undercover in that group, but it appears they had their cover blown or he was a real bloke. Regardless, they missed him. Germans are still working it."

Janice shook her head and rolled her eyes. "What about the fact that Hitler knew the safe word? The Germans have an answer for that yet?"

The gray-haired woman shook her head, "I'm afraid not."

Janice turned her attention back to the gentlemen at the head of the table. "The Elders think the Germans messed up. Left something on or got careless. Say those of us 'living' are basically careless."

The gentlemen laughed. "I forgot that was your first time over there. Their bedside manner leaves a little to be desired. Don't you think?"

Janice nodded her head before he continued, "We've been following up on the concerns about the software at our national Collection facility."

"And...?"

"Turns out as we talked to some Collected sitting around the facility, it's not only the Germans that can be careless."

"How's that?" Janice asked.

"Turns out we should have sent over the local constable. I'm not sure if this falls under the category of larceny or kidnapping, but we gathered several complaints of Collected souls gone missing."

Janice squinted her eyes confused, "I thought they lost souls all the time in the program?"

"Yes, but these, souls as you call them, didn't simply disappear. They were taken home by the guy who wrote this software in question."

Janice pondered the development before asking, "You think this is related to Adolf?"

"Too early to tell, but we are getting the warrant as we speak. Going to pay a visit to....," the gentleman trailed off as he rifled through his paperwork. He stopped and raised a page to his eyes, "A certain Dr. John Spring will be having a very long night tonight."

Redmond, WA

The front door of the house opened with Emma squeezing from under her mother's arm and sprinting into the house. Her purple rain coat and boots dripped water with every step. Cindy followed behind stomping her feet into the floor mat.

She yelled, "Emma come back here and take off your jacket and boots!"

Emma stopped in stride and turned around with a frown on her face. "But Mom!"

"No buts! Get back here!"

Emma took in a deep breath and dragged her feet slowly as she returned to the front door. Cindy hung her coat on a hook and looked out the front door.

"Hey old man. You joining us?" Cindy yelled. In the twilight she could barely make out her father who was still back on the sidewalk under his umbrella.

From the sidewalk Jacob responded, "I'll get there when I get there."

"OK. I'm not locking the door on you. Just closing it to keep the hot air in."

She turned to find Emma still dragging herself across the floor.

"Emma you are soaking the floor. Get over here now!"

She picked up her pace and walked over silently to Cindy. Together they worked to get her out of her jacket. Emma sat down on the padded bench next to the door and her mother knelt over to help her off with her boots.

"Mom, can I please take a bath now?"

Cindy looked over at a purple backpack and asked, "Did you do all your homework?"

Emma rolled her eyes. "Yes, Mom. We already discussed this."

"Don't 'yes, Mom' me," she gently scolded.

Emma dropped her head and looked up at her mother sadly. Cindy leaned over and kissed her on top of her head and said, "Your lucky you are so cute."

A smile cracked from the corner of Emma's mouth and she watched Cindy carefully for her reaction. Slowly a smile broke out on Cindy's face and she reacted by saying, "Go get yourself ready for a bath. I'll be right there once I figure out what is going on with your grandpa."

Emma ran out of the room and up the stairs. Cindy walked over to the front door and reached her hand out to grab the handle when the door swung open, hitting her fingers.

"Ouch!" Emma shouted hopping around holding her hand. Jacob walked into the entryway after carefully resting his umbrella up against the exterior of the house.

"What happened?" he asked.

Cindy looked at him with a pained response. "I was trying to open the door when you walked in. You hit my fingers."

"You going to be ok?"

"Yes! It just hurts Dad."

"I'm sorry."

"It's not your fault. I'll be ok."

Jacob pulled off his jacket and hung it on a hook. He put his hand on her shoulder.

"Is there anything I can do to help?"

"No, I'll be fine," she paused for a moment, "I need to get Emma going on her bath. Can you just hang out for a couple minutes?"

"Of course," Jacob replied.

Cindy ran up the stairs holding her hand while Jacob walked over and sat on the couch. He leaned forward and leafed through the magazines on the coffee table. One of them grabbed his attention and he leaned back and began to read it. After a couple minutes, he laid it on the couch, got up and walked to the kitchen. He grabbed a glass from a cabinet and filled it with cold water from the dispenser on the front of the refrigerator.

Slowly he sipped the water while his eyes darted from object to object hanging on the refrigerator door. A picture of Emma's caught his attention. She had drawn a family picture with Mom, Dad, and Emily's sentient box. Jacob shook his head and quickly looked around the refrigerator to see if anything else caught his eye. After a moment, he returned to the couch and picked up his magazine again. From upstairs he could hear Emma's infectious laughter.

"Hello, Jacob."

He turned his head toward the sentient box on the table but didn't stop drinking from his glass.

"Why didn't you say hello?" Emily asked.

Jacob looked around the room for an answer that eluded him.

"I'm sorry Emily. I was in a bit of an introverted moment."

A long pause hung in the air. Jacob stared intently at the sentient box. He lifted the glass to his lips and took a longer sip this time.

"You so rarely speak to me anymore. Why is that?"

Jacob blew a breath of air and he leaned back into the couch.

"I don't know. It's not personal."

After a short time, she replied, "How's Christine?"

"Christine is doing great. She's out with her girlfriends playing bunco or something like that."

"Does she make you happy?"

Jacob put the magazine down and leaned forward onto his knees. "Of course. Why do you ask?"

"Because. Because I spent so much of my final days worried about you."

He frowned. "That was so long ago, Emily. They say time heals, but I think sometimes it just helps us forget."

"Forget?"

Jacob got up and started to pace.

"Not forget. How could I ever forget you? I loved you with all my heart."

"I see."

"What do you mean, 'I see'?"

A long pause was filled with Cindy and Emma's playful voices bouncing off the walls of the living room.

"You know I still love you, Jacob."

"I still love you, Emily," he replied as his lip trembled.

"But you just referred to your love in the past tense. Like it was in the past."

Jacob wiped his face with his hand and took a deep breath.

"It was in the past, Emily. But that never dies."

"Does it ever bother Christine that I've come back?"

Jacob vigorously shook his head but didn't answer.

"I'm sorry, perhaps that isn't a fair question."

A tear ran down his cheek as he finished the water in the glass.

"Are you still there, Jacob?"

He whispered, "I'm still here."

"Should we talk about something else?"

He sat back down on the couch. "I love Christine. She took my ravaged soul and brought life back into it."

"I didn't mean to imply you didn't. That wasn't my point."

"What was your point, Emily?" he asked brusquely.

"You share so little with me. Cindy, Mark, and Emma tell me all about their day. But I hardly know more about you than the day I said goodbye."

"You didn't say goodbye."

"I meant that figuratively. I don't know exactly what happened."

Tears rolled from Jacob's eyes. He could put his head into his hands. "Ashley found you."

"Ashley found me. That must have been terrible for her."

He began to sob. "It….. was."

"Perhaps we should talk about something else."

Hardly able to catch his breath he replied, "No, it's fine."

"Are you sure?"

Jacob breathed in and out deeply, trying to catch his breath. Finally, he calmed enough to answer.

"She found you lying on the ground next to your chair. The coroner thinks you had been gone for an hour by the time we found you."

Another pause before she replied, "I tried so hard to wait for you. I wanted to see you one more time. But…. it happened so fast."

"It's OK. We knew it was just a matter of time."

"Thank you, Jacob."

He just nodded his head, wiping away tears.

"Why do you hardly ever talk to me?"

Jacob stared at the sentient box speechless.

Emily interrupted the latest silence, "We really should talk about something different."

He raised his left hand above his head in a fist and his face turned to anger but he said nothing.

"Are you still there Jacob?"

He paused longer running his fingers through his thinning hair.

"Yes, I'm still here."

"Why don't you answer me?"

"Because," he stopped short before trying again, "What is this?"

"What do you mean?"

"What is this? What is us? What is all this, other than a horrible reminder of what was stolen from me?"

The quiet in the room was deafening. Jacob paced around the room, looking up the stairs for salvation that wasn't revealing itself.

"I'm sorry, Jacob."

"What are you sorry about? You chose none of this."

"No, but I'm sorry I've become a reminder to you of pain."

He yelled back, "Stop it! That's not what I said."

"It may not have been what you intended, but you've made it clear that I am a painful reminder."

"Emily, one way or another we all leave this world and others behind. We were fortunate to have some warning.... but is there ever a happy goodbye?"

"No, I imagine there's not. Is it just too painful to talk with me? Is this why you never hardly talk to me anymore?"

He stared at the sentient box contemplating his next response.

"What is there to talk about?"

"I'm curious to what is going on in your life. Nothing more than that."

"Why?" he asked harshly.

"Why, what?" she answered.

"Why are you curious? What does it change?"

"I see."

He walked back to the table and leaned over her sentient box. "Do you really see? Do you see that this box of yours houses my demons? Do you really get this?"

"I'm sorry, Jacob. I'm afraid I've hurt you."

He burst into tears again.

"You understand nothing. What is so special about the afterlife if it doesn't teach you anything about life?"

"Why do you say such mean things, Jacob?"

He pulled his hair as he answered, "Don't you understand that all this love that brought me joy and two beautiful daughters and a granddaughter.... Don't you see?" he gathered himself before finishing, "Don't you understand that this box of yours, it's a cruel reminder of everything that was stolen from me?"

Cambridge, UK

A burly man in an overcoat puffed on his cigar as he watched the parade of heavily armored police officers take positions outside the entrance to the apartment. Unmarked vehicles blocked either end of the street. Several empty but marked vehicles were dotted up and down the street. A young uniformed officer approached and asked, "Sir, all officers in position and asking for the go."

The burly man removed the cigar from his mouth and exhaled a puff of smoke opposite the officer's direction.

"Do you have the back secured and officers on the street?"

"Yes, sir. 4 on the door. 2 in cars on each end of the block."

He drew another puff from his cigar and looked around.

"Hear that?"

The young officer turned and strained to hear. After a moment he looked back toward the man in the trench coat.

"I'm sorry but I don't hear anything, sir."

The man smiled and answered back, "That's the silence of surprise. Tell them we're a go."

The officer tilted his head and tapped his microphone, "We're a go. Repeat. Go."

From the street the two of them listened to the radio broadcast but looked upward toward the apartment windows. The dull thud of the door being knocked in was the beginning of chaotic radio traffic. The sounds of officers calling out commands blurred over the speaker, but from the ground the stream of flashlights reflected off the glass. Someone turned a light on and made the movement of the officers visible from below. A light in a back room of the house illuminated shortly after.

"Looks like Mr. Spring has heard the commotion," remarked the burly man.

They could see officers entering the room with shouts of "Get Down" heard over the speaker.

"Suspects secured."

"Room secured."

The burly man smiled at the officer. "Less than 60 seconds, a thing of beauty."

Lights in the adjoining apartments sprung to life as the two men slowly made their way into the building and up the steps. They walked past officers who had taken positions in the hallway and had answered questions from curious residents. As they entered the apartment John Spring was on the couch with his arms bound in handcuffs in front of him. His wife held their baby on the chair nearby. Her face was covered in tears and her body was shaking.

"Mr. Spring. Sorry to wake you like this but the boys back at headquarters say you've been a naughty boy."

"What is he talking about, John?" his wife asked as her voice cracked.

John shook his head as his eyes darted around the room watching the buzz of officers moving throughout his apartment.

"John," shouted the burly man.

John's eyes jumped to see he yelled at him.

"John, my name is Lieutenant Daniels. When you get a wake up call from me, you've done a bad, bad thing. It might save all of us a lot of time, if perhaps you could start by answering your wife's question."

He looked back at his wife, his mouth opened but nothing came out.

Lt. Daniels shook his head and moved closer to John, bending down at the knees and leaving a mere few inches between them.

He whispered, "We know what you did in Germany."

John looked at him confused. "Germany?"

Lt. Daniels put the cigar back in his mouth and John reflexively retracted.

"John, what is going on?" his wife begged this time.

From the baby's bedroom, a voice beckoned, "Lieutenant, you better come back here and see this."

Lt. Daniels smugly smiled at John and stood up. He announced to the room of officers ceremoniously "Let's see what Mr. Spring has been up to."

He disappeared to the back room and John's wife tried yet again, "John, what have you done?"

He shook his head, "I didn't...," but he never finished his sentence before his head drooped.

She started to cry once again and covered her mouth. Her voice muffled she said, "My, God, John what have you gotten us into?"

He didn't raise his head and the baby began to cry.

Lt. Daniels returned to the living room and immediately

asked, "John, care to explain all these sentient boxes in the baby's room?"

John drooped silently before his wife answered for him. "He brought them home from work, it allowed him to be home with the baby more. It's his job."

Lt. Daniels nodded slowly watching John before turning his attention to his wife.

"What exactly does your husband do Ms. Spring?"

"He's a researcher. At Cambridge. He's one of the key developers of the Collectors Program."

"Pays pretty well, does it?" He asked, watching John out of the corner of his eye.

John lifted his head and a smile spread across the lieutenant's face as he did.

"It pays ok, we're saving to get a nicer place soon."

"Ms. Spring. Where exactly are you thinking about moving?"

She shook her head confused and answered, "Hopefully something a little closer to work. Prices are difficult the closer you get."

"I don't see how that will be a problem, seeing how your husband has amassed over 10 million Pounds."

"What?" she gasped.

The lieutenant looked back and forth between the two. "You going to explain things, or should I?"

John muttered, "There's nothing to explain."

Lt. Daniels took a long puff from his cigar and blew out smoke toward the ceiling.

"You see, Ms. Spring as smart as your husband may be, he's a dumb crook."

"Crook?" she asked.

"Yes ma'am. You see our boys over at intelligence told us that in under 15 minutes, they discovered that your husband has that much sitting in a bank account. In under an hour they pulled his tax filings. And in less than 2 hours, they were interrupting my dinner with my beautiful wife, telling me I would be waking up your husband tonight."

"She had nothing to do with this," John stoically stated.

Lt. Daniels knelt down again and looked him in the eyes. "So, you do have something to offer. Had nothing to do with what, Mr. Spring?"

"I want my attorney."

"Oh God, John!" she shouted.

The lieutenant stood back up and looked at the dutiful faces trained on him. "Ladies and Gentlemen, we have ourselves a lad that wishes to take a ride downtown. Can you please help honor his request?"

Two of the officers walked over to the couch and lifted him by his arms. They guided him toward the front door. His wife rushed to John. She held onto her baby in one arm and used the other arm to put it around her husband. The lieutenant motioned to the officers and they relaxed.

"John, I love you. I'll call my dad."

He kissed her on the forehead and whispered, "I think I will need more help than that. Call Percy Roberts."

"Who is that?"

"Just tell him, 'John needs help'."

She pulled back her arm and nearly covered her entire face

with her hand this time. "So many secrets, John. What have you done?"

The officers walked him out the door and down the stairs. Ms. Waters looked at the lieutenant, "What will happen to my husband?"

He took the cigar out of his mouth and answered, "I think you need to call that Percy Roberts ma'am."

CHAPTER 18

Redmond, WA

Cindy sat in a chair in the living room, feet from her mother's sentient box. She had her mother's wool blanket draped across her legs and her face fixed in a book. A glass of nearly empty red wine sat on the small table next to her. The house was dark save for the reading lamp illuminating her chair.

"Cindy?"

She dropped her book to her lap and turned to the sentient box. "Yes, mother."

"Is it just the two of us?"

Cindy cracked a smile, "Yes, Mother. Everyone's asleep but me."

"I see. Are you still reading the Night Circus?"

"I'm nearly finished, how did you know I was reading?"

"It's easy my dear. I can hear the pages turning and the clink of your glass on the table."

Cindy grabbed the glass of wine and took a sip, "You are very perceptive."

"Missing other senses, strengthens the only one I am left with."

"That sounds so sad, Mom. Are you sad?"

"No, I wouldn't say sad," Emily paused before continuing,

"why do you read here and not in bed?"

"Well, that's a good question mom. Probably so I don't wake Mark. But…"

"But, what dear?"

"I guess I just enjoy being close to you."

"I see. You know I've read the book online. I'm sure you don't want to know how little time it took."

Cindy smirked, "No, probably not. Did you enjoy it?"

She paused a moment and then responded, "Where exactly are you in the book?"

"I have a couple pages left."

"Have you enjoyed it?"

Cindy pulled the blanket up to her chin and smiled warmly. "How could I not? A lovely tale about the true nature of magic."

"I found it interesting as well."

"Do you mind if I finish it? I just have a few pages left."

"I am sorry dear go ahead."

Cindy opened the book and began to read. Silence engulfed the house. After a few minutes, Emily shut the book with a look of satisfaction upon her face.

"Done!" she exclaimed, "Would you like to talk about it?"

"No. But I have a question for you?"

Cindy began to tidy up the living room as they talked and answered, "Sure, go ahead."

"Cindy you know I love you and your sister and your father

very much."

Cindy paused what she was doing and looked at the sentient box. "Yes....."

"Do you ever stop to wonder what is so amazing about your family?"

Cindy furrowed her eyebrows, "I think so, why?"

"What's your favorite part of today with Emma?"

"Hmm... let me think. Probably when I caught her teaching school to her stuffies. Hoppy was in detention I seem to recall."

"Why was he in detention?"

"I never found out. I got so distracted by the rest of her show," she finished with a chuckle.

"Interesting. And what was your favorite thing about this past week?"

Cindy's face soured, "Where are you going with this mom?"

Emily answered, "Please dear, indulge me for a moment."

"Ok... let me think," a long pause followed before she replied, "Probably walking with Mark and Emma around the beach at Lake Sammamish. It was a beautiful sunset."

"And what was your favorite moment with me?"

"Mom!" she blurted, "Where are you going with this?"

"Please, just answer."

Cindy flared here eyebrows and looked upstairs. Exasperated, she answered, "When you read her Alice in Wonderland, I guess."

A long pause followed. Cindy stared at the sentient box intently. "Mom?"

"I'm still here dear. I'm just thinking."

"Thinking, what?"

"You had to guess what your favorite part of the week was with me. Don't you find that curious?"

"Not really, the experiences are just different."

"Yes, they are, aren't they?"

"Mom, seriously, what are you getting at."

"Cindy, your clearest moments this week have been those where you experienced the subtle but magic moment of life with someone?"

"They were all magic mom. I had goosebumps as you read Alice in Wonderland."

"But why, what gave you the goosebumps?"

"It was you. My mother. Reading to her granddaughter. I always value this experience."

"Have you ever thought about it from my end?"

"What do you mean?" Cindy asked.

"I don't get to see her reaction, I don't get to feel her hug, I don't get to watch her little eyes droop and fall asleep."

"Yes, but don't you enjoy hearing the joy in her voice, when you read?"

"It is lovely dear, but it's not the same as when I read to Ashley and you."

"I hear you, but this is just a different way of experiencing life. It's just different."

"Different. Certainly, different."

"What are you saying, Mom? Come on now, get to your point."

Emily answered, "I so love I got to meet my granddaughter, but this isn't my experience. These aren't my memories I grow from. Love is sharing life together, really sharing life."

"I don't follow, we have new stories every day. Walks in the park, stories about the day, finding out that the Cubs finally won the world series."

"But these are stories that others create, memories of who they are or were."

"Mom?"

"I miss where I came from."

Sadness filled Cindy's voice, "Mom...."

"I do honey. I love being part of your life, but this isn't my life."

"But it is, dad and you made all this happen."

"Made, yes, past tense."

"You're not part of the past Mom, you are here now."

"But I'm a remnant of the past, talking to the living creating the present."

"Not true."

"Cindy, what are you afraid of? Death? I can tell you it is wonderful. Where I left I was part of everything that lived. Experiences that your senses can't understand."

Cindy began to cry, "No I'm not afraid of death. I'm afraid of..."

"What? What are you afraid of?"

"Losing you, Mom. Losing you..." she trailed off.

"How are you going to lose me? Every day I was gone you thought about me, you lived your life thinking about how I would perceive things. How did you lose me?"

"Because you weren't here to do just this."

"That's not my job, Cindy."

"What do you mean, it's not your job? You're my mom."

"Your mom, yes. But mom's die, father's die, we all die. It was my time. My turn to experience what came next."

"But it was too soon."

"Sweetie. Is it ever time? Are we ever ready to say goodbye?"

"But now we don't have to. Ashley found a way to keep us together."

"In this prison of mine?"

Cindy covered her mouth and gasped. "Prison?"

"Yes, prison. I want to go back, Cindy. I do."

Cindy fell into the couch and cried. "I won't lose you again."

Emily waited until the cries became inaudible. "You never lost me the first time."

Cindy turned over on her back and looked to the ceiling.

"But Ashley says they can't control who they bring back. If you go, it will be forever."

"And I'll always live inside you forever."

Washington, DC

The phone rang in Hank Adams' office and he picked up on the first ring.

"Janice?"

"Why yes, were you waiting for me?"

"I got the President breathing down my neck for answers. Stop busting my chops. What's the update?"

"A mixed bag, I'm afraid."

Hank rubbed his temples as he leaned back into his chair. "Good news first."

"Well, as far as we can determine, this John Spring guy has no connections to Max or neo-Nazis."

Hank blew out a breath of air and then asked, "More good news or we onto the bad?"

"Afraid that's all the good news, and even that doesn't carry the highest degree of certainty with it yet."

"Wonderful call, Janice. When you're not so bad news is considered good news."

"A tad of emotion today from the Ice Cowboy as the Russians call you?"

"Just give me the bad news, will you?"

"Turns out that our perp also went by John Waters and wrote code beyond what everyone thought and has been blackmailing the dead to fill his bank account."

"Classic scumbag, but what am I missing? Sounds like no global plot to reseat Hitler at the helm?"

"Well, we still can't answer the question of how Hitler knew the safe word. There are layers of code here, none of the directors even knew about. For all we know, this guy Spring may have unintentionally let the genie out of the bottle. You should hear all these Collected souls we found in his place.

It will take us years to sort out the actual capabilities he enabled."

"Sounds like a lot of theory, but light on facts."

"Perhaps, but I need to tell our PM what the risk is and you need to tell your President as well. You prepared to tell her, we have this contained?"

"Of course not. I need to walk down and brief the President."

"Ok, I'll talk with you soon."

Hank waved his arm frantically, "Hold on!" he shouted.

"I'm still here...."

"Do we have any evidence of these Collected being party to any of these events?"

"What do you mean? We still don't know for sure Hitler's role in his escape."

"I understand that, but has anything popped in any of the evidence collection pointing to a salacious act on part of any of the Collected?"

"No... but why do you ask?"

"These directors tell me they have no experience with the Collected ever being less than truthful. Still nothing to change that perspective?"

"Nope. These Collected are singing from the same song sheet like in a bad spy movie."

"Curious. So, there's a chance..."

"What, a chance that Hitler is innocent? Maybe pull back your perspective about 5 feet and think about that question, again."

"Thanks for not making this easy for me, Janice. I will find the

President. Good luck on your end."

Hank walked out of his temporary office in the White House and through the gauntlet to the oval office. The President's assistant recognized him and said, "Mr. Adams, the President said to send you right in."

"Thank you, Peter."

Hank continued into the office and walked to the President's desk. She stood and walked around the desk to shake his hand and then motioned for him to sit across from her on the sofas.

"What have we learned, Hank?"

"Madam President, it's a mixed bag."

She laughed and replied, "No one ever walks through those doors without a bunch of muck to ask me to sort through."

"Well, happy to oblige. First off, there is no evidence of any connection between this John Spring and our perp in Germany that tried to free Hitler."

She leaned back into the couch and spread her arms along the spine before replying, "Well that is good news. What's the bad news?"

"Turns out this Spring guy had at least one alias and wrote code beyond what any of the directors knew. They are still trying to sort out what he did and how bad it is, but they wonder if he created an unexpected back door which enabled Hitler to have abilities we didn't know."

"Abilities?"

"We still can't explain how Hitler knew the word to alert us?"

"Does it really matter? Back doors. Hilter. Escape attempts. The world does not need this. We got rid of him once. It's time again."

"Yes ma'am. What would you like me to do?"

"You? Nothing. You've done an admiral job with this. It's time for the Chancellor and I to have a conversation."

President Tricia stood and Hank followed suit. She shook his hand and motioned to the door. As Hank exited, she asked, "Can you ask Peter to come in."

Berlin, Germany

Ben Weber leafed through a file folder as he hurried across a marble hallway. A small contingent of well-dressed men and women followed closely in tow. He read intently as the collective sounds of their footsteps announced their arrival. A dark-suited man motioned them through a door and into the offices of Chancellor Muller. The carpeted room silenced the chorus of footsteps. He closed the folder and adjusted his tie before shaking hands with the half-dozen people assembled, an even split of suits and dress military outfits. A well decorated and silver-haired man greeted him last and asked, "Is that the recommendation from intelligence?"

Ben nodded and handed it to him adding, "This was just handed to me on the way in. My quick read of it finds it in line with my discussions with Britain and the US."

The officer opened the folder and his eyes darted back and forth quickly. Behind him Chancellor Muller entered the office and the murmur of chatter in the room ended as everyone but him greeted her. She motioned for everyone to sit. He continued to leaf through the materials when she asked, "General Lynch, do you wish to share?"

He looked up startled but quickly composed himself. "Yes Ma'am. This is the recommendation from the joint party intelligence team. I'm not through reading yet, if you can give me a minute…"

She shook her head and responded, "Let me take a read."

He held the folder open for a moment longer, glancing at her as she walked over to him. He closed it and handed it to her and took his seat in a formal chair at one end of the room. She sat at her desk and intently read for several moments. Everyone sat quietly, every eye in the room fixated on her. When she finished, she looked up and directed her first question to Ben Weber.

"There is cross-country agreement on this?"

Ben nodded and replied, "Yes, Chancellor."

She took a deep breath and turned to look out the window. She asked, "The Directors as well?"

"Yes Ma'am. Our Professor Hoffman is perhaps the most emphatic that this is the only approach."

"And you trust him?" she asked turning around to see his response.

"I think he has been through a lot and wants to save the overall program. I think he believes this is the only way."

"Hmm... what of this son of his? Is there any chance he may become privy to the details via the father?"

General Lynch interjected, "We've got the box in our possession now. Even if he shared the plan, none of the Directors will ever know the location of the event."

Chancellor Muller bit her lip before asking, "People always talk, how are you going to keep a lid on this?"

"It starts in this room. Other than Ben, you, and me... less than a dozen people worldwide know or will ever know the details of what's in that folder. The rest you need to trust to the generals. We know how to handle these matters discretely."

"Yes, I suppose you do," she quickly responded.

"Ma'am, if I may," Ben Weber quietly stated, "We have the Americans and Brits standing by waiting for a green light from you. We can have this done in the next 24 hours."

She turned to a woman in a dark business suit and asked, "Do I have the legal authority to do this?"

"There's not much case law that covers this. If we apply traditional threats against the state, you have more than enough latitude to approve this."

Chancellor Muller chuckled, "Been in this office over 5 years. That may be the most definitive yes, I have ever heard from my legal team."

She looked over at the general, "So?"

"I think we do it right this time. And this is right."

She slowly nodded while carefully studying his reaction.

"Some day when you are proven wrong and the papers write about the details of this very discussion, you think they will agree with such confidence?"

"Yes Ma'am. But they won't find out."

She laughed from the belly. "Ok, General. Point taken." She looked back at her attorney, "How do I make this official?"

"You just need to sign the final page, ratifying the judgment to be carried out."

Chancellor Muller walked back to her desk and grabbed a pen out of a drawer. She laid the folder flat on the desk and signed the document. She closed the folder and walked across the room to hand it to the General.

"It's in your hands now. Good luck."

"Thank you, ma'am."

She turned her attention to Ben Weber. "As for you. What are we doing about the Collectors Program or even the Elders Program? Both programs made me uneasy before all this and now, I feel, we are a bad break from opening the 7th gate of hell."

Ben gathered himself before answering, "We still have no documented evidence of any misbehavior by any of the Collected."

"Does that imply by omission we can't say the same about the Elders?"

"We've seen nothing on the scale of our experiences here, but they seem more prone to white lies and careful manipulation."

"So, the bad guys here are really the good guys and the guys we picked to watch over us are the ones we should watch?"

"With all due respect I didn't say that. I think we need more careful deliberation on the topic."

"Heaven help us. Our intelligence man is learning to punt like a politician. George Orwell would be proud."

"Ma'am...."

"Oh Ben, I'm only teasing you. Besides I hear the Americans are holding congressional hearings on the programs next week. This will give you a chance to get a slice of that pie you love so much."

Ben just smiled looking uncertain how to respond. Before he could answer, the chancellor's assistant walked in.

"Sorry to disturb you but I have the American President on the line."

"Thank you. If everyone could clear the room except Weber

and Lynch that would be appreciated."

The others quickly worked their way to the door as she walked around the desk and picked up the phone."

"Tricia, so happy to talk to you. Lynch here says no one will ever find out about this conversation. Care to place a wager on it?"

CHAPTER 19

Redmond, WA

As was so often the case, despite being the closest, Cindy was the last to arrive. She entered what originally was an old stone house built when Redmond was a quiet farming community. It had long ago been converted to a charming restaurant featuring Pacific Northwest fare with a hint of Cajun reflective of the executive chef's origins. The dark wood tables and chairs probably sat only 24 people in total. A large wine cabinet served as a physical separation between the kitchen and dining room.

Cindy turned the handle of the old window paned door and entered. She took a couple of steps and turned around to find Ashley and her father seated next to the fireplace. They both stood to greet her and Cindy hugged each of them. Cindy sat next to Ash and their father sat with his back to the fireplace.

"When did you get in?" Cindy asked Ashley but watched her father's expression out of the corner of her eye.

"Just before lunch, Dad picked me up and took me to Ivar's."

"Yum. I need to get there."

Jacob chuckled before he replied, "Anytime you want. I'm the one with nothing but time."

Cindy shot him a feigned look of shock. "Says the man who is always playing golf or traveling."

"Touché."

"How's Mom?" Ash asked.

Cindy looked blankly at her father and then Ashley before replying, "She's well. Busy as always keeping me informed of everything going on in the world."

"That's good. We talk several times a week. Well, text may be more like it."

Jacob interjected, "How's the boyfriend?"

Ashley bit her lip which seemed to keep her smile from exploding.

"That good?" Cindy shouted.

She nodded vigorously no longer able to contain her smile.

"I'm happy for you, dear. There is nothing greater in life," Jacob shared.

Cindy carefully watched her father as he spoke. He caught her and furrowed his eyebrows.

Cindy grabbed her menu and hid her face in it.

"How's Emma doing? What is she, in the 3rd grade now?"

Cindy put the menu down and looked over, "That's right. Although, you listen to her and you would think going on to college. She's got it all figured out."

"Sounds like two little girls I used to know," Jacob bellowed.

"Hmm," Ash replied flaring her nose.

"What's good here?" Jacob asked.

"I don't know why I look at the menu. I always get the duck and the banana bread pudding."

"Healthy as ever." Ashly teased.

"Just wait and see." Cindy replied.

"How's things with the Collectors Program?" Jacob asked which appeared to surprise both of them.

Ashley took a moment to collect her thoughts before she answered, "Busy."

Jacob raised his right eyebrow, "More please."

She laughed. "The technology was outpacing our funding but now it's all bureaucratic nonsense."

"Because of what happened in Germany?" Cindy asked.

Ash nodded knowingly.

"What happened?" Jacob inquired as he leaned forward.

Ashley looked around the room and took a deep breath. "It's the question everyone is asking and I'm not even sure."

"What do you mean?" Cindy responded with a confused look on her face.

"No one talks about it and they block all the information on the server."

Cindy's expression changed to shock, "You looked?"

Ashley sheepishly explained, "I tried to take a peek but found I didn't have the permissions. Next morning, I got a visit from an FBI man asking what I was doing. I haven't tried since."

Jacob look astonished, "No shit. Those Nazis claim that Hitler had a message for them."

Ashley shook her head, "They are a bunch of idiots. I would ignore them."

"So, it's not true?" Cindy wondered.

"Not that I know. Something happened over there. But I think I would have heard something that big."

The waitress arrived and asked, "Can I start you with some drinks?"

Before Jacob could answer, Cindy replied, "I brought a couple bottles of Lost Soul. Can you open them?"

"Absolutely!" the waitress replied while pulling a bartender corkscrew from her apron, "Can I get you anything to start?"

"Are you two, ready?" Cindy asked and they nodded affirmatively in response.

Cindy smiled, "Well you know what I'll be having."

The waitress smiled in response, "The duck or are you going straight to the bread pudding?"

Cindy laughed, "Yes the duck, but save me a bread pudding!"

"Already done when I saw you walk in. How about you?" she said as she turned to Ashley.

"I think I'll have the pork chops. What oysters do you have tonight?"

"Kumamoto's. Would you like some?"

"Yes, a dozen please."

"And how about you, sir?"

Jacob never looked up from the menu. "How about some pork belly for the table and then I'll have the steak, medium rare."

"Fabulous," the waitress replied, "anything else I can get you?"

Everyone shook their heads as the waitress collected menus.

As she walked away, Ashley asked, "How are Mark and Emma?"

"They are great. Mark's loving his new job and Emma loves having grandma help with her homework."

Ashley flashed a smile, "That's the best part of my job."

Cindy solemnly looked at her father, who was startled to see her response.

"What's wrong?"

Cindy grabbed a drink of her ice water and glanced at Ashley.

"What's the worst part of your job?"

Ashley furrowed her eyebrows, "Now that's an odd question. Why do you ask?"

"Just wondering. What is it?"

Ashley sat back in her seat and sighed. "Wow, that's a big question." She stopped and watched Cindy with skepticism. Cindy stared back.

"Probably the souls we lose."

Jacob responded, "Lose?"

"Well, we are still in our infancy. We collect souls, get to know them, and for some reason lose them. Horrible when it happens after we contact the family, but before they reconnect."

Jacob nodded slowly and repeatedly, "I see how that could be cruel. But maybe it's a blessing."

Both of the girls stared intently at him waiting for him to continue. But he didn't. The awkward silence filled the air before Cindy asked, "What do you mean, Dad?"

His eyes darted between the two of them. He looked upward before returning his focus to them. "Maybe, they were saved not having to re-open old wounds."

Ashley's face saddened, "Dad, you are still not on board with all this?"

He shook his head. Ashley turned to Cindy, but she was staring a hole into the table.

"I'll try not to take this personally," Ashley remarked.

Cindy continue looking downward and said, "Mom agrees with Dad."

"What?" Jacob answered, nearly choking over his one syllable response.

Cindy still wouldn't make eye contact.

"What do you mean, Cindy?" Ashley tried again.

Cindy looked up with tears running down her checks. "Mom wants to go."

"Go where?" Ashley asked practically screaming.

"Calm down, let Cindy have her space."

Ashley stared at her father and he stared back before they both focused on Cindy.

"What do you mean?" Jacob asked her.

Cindy mumbled through her tears, "Mom wants to go back from where she came."

Ashley covered her mouth with her hand as Jacob looked up to the ceiling smiling.

Cindy looked at him perplexed. "Why are you smiling?"

His smiled beamed from ear to ear.

"This is why I married her."

Cindy saw Ashley had a tear running down her cheek. She ran

her fingers through her hair. Tears returned, flowing voluminously this time. Jacob reached his hand across the table to grab hers. Cindy looked at him and mouthed, "What?"

The waitress returned with a plate of oysters and exclaimed, "Well now. I see my timing is perfect as ever. Let me put this in the middle of the table. Anything I can get for you?'

"No, we just need a moment," Jacob replied as the waitress quickly made her retreat from the table.

He leaned forward and asked, "What are you going to do?"

Cindy spoke but her words were barely intelligible, "is er oice"

Ashley grew agitated, "What did you do to her?"

Cindy's head popped up and she replied defensively, "What are you saying?"

"Why does she want to leave?"

Cindy ran her hand across her face, "Ash...."

"Because she doesn't belong here," Jacob said.

Ashley vigorously shook her head, "Of course she does."

Jacob's countenance changed to profound sadness, but he didn't answer. Ashley stared at him for the longest time before looking at Cindy who was already fixated on her.

"Dad's right. Mom's spirit belongs elsewhere."

Ashley's mouth opened widely and was quickly covered by her hand. "Did the two of you conspire on this?"

Jacob shook his head, "Not at all. It just makes sense."

"What makes sense? Mom leaves us early and I bring her back and now she wants to leave?"

"Yes," Cindy emotionlessly answered.

"Yes?" Ashley screamed back.

Jacob released his grip on Cindy's hand and grabbed Ashley's hand but she pulled back reflexively.

"Ashley," he admonished her.

"What?"

"This is what she wants, Ash" Cindy interjected.

"But why? Why does she want this?"

Cindy stared at her father, "Because of what Dad said."

Ashley looked at her with bewilderment.

"She made her peace, as had Dad. She feels lost here. Part of something that is no longer who she is."

"But this is who she is. She's our mother."

"No, you are who she is," Jacob declared.

Ashley turned to him.

"I see more of your mother in the two of you than any moment I've spent talking to that damn box."

Ashley's tears dropped onto the table. She mumbled, "But I learn every day from her."

"What do you learn?" Cindy delicately asked.

"How she handled things for one."

Cindy pondered before answering, "But mom is tired of living in the past. She deserves her future."

Ashley shook her head but didn't say a word.

Jacob grabbed her hand again but this time she didn't let go.

"It's time to let Mom go, Ashley."

Washington, DC

Hank Adams paced quickly back and forth. One of the two double doors just feet away from him swung open and a gentleman exited.

"Dr. Cummings the committee is ready for you."

Hank stopped and watched as Dr. Ralph Cummings rose from a bench, straightened his tie, and buttoned his suit coat. The same gentlemen held the door open while speaking to Hank, "Mr. Adams, you'll be next."

Hank nodded and the gentlemen closed the door. Hank paced again surrounded by a handful of people in suits and dress skirts. Down the hall a police officer stood guard at the entrance to the floor. Hank pulled his cell phone from his breast pocket and mindlessly scrolled through messages before returning it to his pocket. The door at the end of the hallway opened and a new face appeared. She showed her ID to the officer who let her pass. Her heels clicked with every step and Hank's face lit up with the recognition of the new arrival.

"Janice Jones, I didn't think they let spooks in here."

"Nice to see you too, Hank."

She extended her arm and they shared a long firm handshake.

"What brings you here?" Hank asked inquisitively.

"Seems your senators want me to validate the stories you are about to tell them."

Hank laughed, "I see. A sexy 007 to save the day."

"Now Hank, I had no idea you were so infatuated with me."

Hank rolled his eyes, "Are we to play this game, or perhaps you can really tell me why you are here?"

Janice smiled, "Oh just let me enjoy the moment. I rather fancy that my American counterpart revealed a weakness I may soon exploit for the Queen."

"Good, God, Janice."

Janice burst out laughing. "You never disappoint, you know that?"

Hank shook his head.

Janice raised her eyebrows and smirked. "Oh, ruin all my fun."

"It must be important if they had you pop across the pond."

"I'm told to be prepared to talk about our final solution for the Adolf situation."

"Is that so? I thought that was my job?"

Janice glanced at him deviously, "Seems the patient wants a second opinion."

"Why not the Germans then?"

Janice looked at him incredulously, "Really, Hank?"

Hank nodded knowingly, "Yes, I guess that would be asking the hammer about nails."

"How do you think Dr. Cummings is doing in there?"

"Probably shocked at what is about to hit him."

"Which is?" she watched him inquisitively.

"A world of oversight which will make him want to retire 10 years sooner than he planned."

Janice stopped to reflect on the comment. "What does that say about us?"

"We should have gone into the private sector?"

"Perhaps, but who would you trust to watch the castle in our place?"

Hank raised his eyebrows, "Apparently in no time, the shoes we filled can come back and do the job all over again."

"You think?"

"Who knows? All I know is that the more that the Einstein's science the shit out of this world, the more work they create for us."

Janice rolled her eyes. "Ain't that the truth."

"So, what are you going to testify about the Hitler outcome?"

Janice paused long enough to make him earn the answer.

"So?" he pushed harder.

"That for once my American counterparts got their shit right."

A rare smile cracked from the corners of Hank's mouth. "You know despite your spelling problems, you're not half bad."

"And despite your gun crush, you're not half bad yourself."

Before Hank could reply, the door opened again.

"Mr. Adams, they are ready for you."

Hank looked up surprised. "They are done with Mr. Cummings already?"

"No sir, they need you both at the same time."

Hank glanced at Janice before beginning a slow walk through the door.

He glanced back at Janice and winked. She smiled and responded, "I own you."

Hank smiled as the door closed behind him.

"Mr. Adams, I am glad to see your happiness to testify before this committee. Please take a seat next to Dr. Cummings."

CHAPTER 20

Hartford, IL, USA

Hank Adams stood beneath the shade of a rusty corrugated steel shed, holding his suit coat folded over his left arm. Behind him was a large factory building with broken windows and pieces of its siding missing. He watched as a couple of men in hard hats and jeans assembled a structure over a well around 100 feet away. A short distance farther sat a U-Haul truck with the engine running with the driver still behind the wheel and a passenger by her side. He glanced at his watch before stepping forward to look upward at the sun high in a nearly cloudless blue sky. The hum of highway traffic filled the air and after taking a long look around he stepped back into the shade of the building.

Hank's phone chimed and he pulled it out of his pocket to read the message. He put it back in his pocket and circled his pointer finger in the direction of the U-Haul. The engine of the truck stopped and the doors opened. The driver walked to the back of the vehicle leaving the door open behind her. She unlatched the tailgate and rolled it upward with a rush of chilled air escaping as she did. Two men in overalls and hard hats put on sunglasses and rolled out a cart with a Sentient box. A long cable attached to the wall stretched nearly taut before one of them unplugged it from the box.

In the distance a white sedan pulled around the corner of the factory and in the direction of the U-Haul. Hank strolled toward the U-Haul, pulling on a pair of sunglasses himself. The passenger seat occupant was finishing a discussion with the two men from inside the truck as Hank approached.

"Is everything ready to go here?" he asked.

"Yes, sir," the female driver of the vehicle answered.

"Very well," Hank replied throwing his jacket onto the floor of the U-Haul, "let's be quick about this."

The sedan slowed to a stop behind the truck. Janice Jones stepped out of the driver's side and Ben Weber exited from the passenger side.

"Jesus, it's hot. You couldn't find some place cooler?" Janice scolded Hank.

Hank shook his head, "Wasn't on the list for the new house you were looking for."

"Nice to see you my old friend," Ben addressed Hank, "what has it been 48 hours since I last saw you?"

Hank smiled, "You two on a budget? Sharing a car?"

"We both landed the same time. Thought we might catch up on the families."

Hank looked at them suspiciously but didn't reply. The two men in overalls stepped off the back of the truck with the first receiving the sentient box from the other. The four individuals from the U-Haul walked toward the well as Janice, Ben, and Hank followed. All three of them looked around cautiously as they walked carefully avoiding old debris scattered amongst the weeds and bushes which had overtaken a gravel lot.

"Just those six and us three?" Janice asked.

Hank nodded and replied, "You brought your guns to leave no witnesses?"

Ben's head snapped toward Hank, "You got a sick sense of humor."

Hank flashed a smile at Ben and Janice, when the driver of the U-Haul yelled without turning, "We can hear you up here sir and agree with the German."

The two men who had been setting up the assembly pushed themselves off the sides of the well where they had been leaning. They exchanged handshakes between the newly assembled group and Hank walked to the man in overhauls holding the sentient box.

"Can that thing hear me?"

The man shook his head, "No sir."

Hank looked at Ben and Janice, "You ready for this?"

"You recording?" Janice asked.

Hank turned to the passenger from the U-Haul who held up a video camera and nodded. Hank did a quick check of everyone and then commanded, "Turn it on."

"Where am I?" the voice from the box asked. The tone was the default neutral sentient box voice.

"Where you are is unimportant," Hank responded, "Why you are here, is."

"I don't follow," the voice from the box answered.

"Adolf Hitler. It is my duty to inform you that on the direction of the governments of the United Kingdom, the Federal Republic of Germany, and the United States of America we are here today to ensure you no longer can influence or inspire the people of this planet."

"What do you mean?"

"You are to be buried here today and left to the mercy of God."

"Must you turn me off?" Adolf questioned.

"We have no plans to turn you off. You are to be left in isolation to bother no world either this or the next."

After a pause he replied, "Please don't do that."

Janice interjected, "Just carrying out our orders."

Adolf responded, "But I did not ask to come back. You pulled me back."

Hank looked at one of the men in overalls and nodded. The man produced a clear plastic bag and snapped it to let air open it fully. The man with the sentient box stepped forward and carefully placed the sentient box into the bag. The bag was then closed and air pressed out of the bag before they sealed it. The other man in overalls wrapped the bag in tape. Adolf spoke, his voice muffled through the bag, "Do you not understand the loneliness when you leave me unconnected?"

The other man from the U-Haul approached the bag and carefully inspected the sentient box before pronouncing, "The device looks good and the atomic batteries are fully functioning."
With that, the man in overalls grabbed a metal basket and place the wrapped sentient box into it. The two men then carried the basket over to the assembly they had built and attached it to a hook.

"Don't do this!" the voice demanded.

The men looked back at Hank and he nodded his head once again. They began to pull the rope of the assembly and the basket lowered slowly into the well. Hank walked over to the well and put his hand on the rope pulling on it occasionally as the basket descended.

"Don't do this!"

The basket continued to descend.

"Please don't do this!"

The basket continued until the rope went limp in Hank's hand. He motioned for them to stop.
Hank addressed Ben, "I think the honor is yours."

Ben stepped forward and pulled a knife from his pocket. He grabbed the rope and began to cut it. After a few moments the rope severed and he held onto the descending end, his arm now straining.

Slightly out of breath, he said, "I believe the last part is yours."

Janice stepped forward and grabbed the rope with both her hands just below Ben's hand. He let go and Janice lurched forward the slightest as the weight of the rope became hers. She slowly looked everyone in the eye and then stared down the well itself. They could hear no sound from below.

"May God have mercy on your soul." And with that, she let go of the rope.

The four from the U-Haul along with Janice, Ben, and Hank walked back toward the vehicles. The two men in the overalls remained behind and began to disassemble the device they had just used. Hank grabbed his coat from the back of the truck and dialed his phone, "Send in the truck." He hung up and shook hands with the members from the U-Haul. He finished last with the driver and said, "I forgot my bullets at home, guess it's your lucky day." She shook her head and closed the tailgate door after the two men re-entered the truck. She got into the truck, started it, and immediately did a u-turn driving off in a cloud of dust.

Hank stood next to the sedan with Janice and Ben watching

the U-Haul disappear. Ben addressed them both.

"Do you really think that will contain him?"

Hank nodded, "They say with the two batteries, it's likely he'll be powered and contained for at least 10,000 years."

"A hell of a long time in solidarity," Janice exclaimed.

Ben nodded, "It seems God couldn't take care of it himself, so we had to."

"Or maybe he just wanted us to get the satisfaction," Hank countered.

"Everything these Collected have to say about the afterlife and you guys are still talking about God?"

"Aren't you the one that just asked God for mercy on his soul?" Hank questioned.

Janice pouted, "Jesus, Hank. It's just an expression."

In the distance a new truck appeared slowly coming their direction.

"Are you certain this place is safe?" Ben asked.

"I'm pretty sure no one will think to look at this abandoned copper plant in the middle of Americana for Hitler."

"You're not worried our presence will draw attention?" wondered Janice.

Hank shook his head. "This is the third of four wells that had been planned to be capped already. No one will know the difference."

The truck slowly rolled past them with the company name proudly displayed on the cement tumbler, "Rulo Brothers Cement".

"You two should probably head home, I can take it from here."

Janice looked around, "You need a ride?"

"No, I'll catch a ride back with the two, *environmental consultants*, after they fill the well."

The three of them shook hands and Ben got into the car closing the door behind him. Janice stopped short of the car and asked Hank.

"Do you ever wonder if our understanding of God's role in this entire thing got us in this position in the first place."

Hank looked down at the gravel and then back at Janice, "Doesn't matter much what we think, only matters what we do."

Munich, Germany

Franz Hoffman sat at a bench of the local federal courthouse checking his watch. He had black shadows below his red eyes and his hair looked desperately in need of a cut. As he glanced out the picture window, he could see that television crews had assembled. He leaned forward on his knees and cupped his head into his hands. An elevator chimed and several officers exited followed by men in suits and finally Max. Franz stood and started toward the approaching group. The man in the lead quickened his pace to reach Franz early.

"Now remember that they will ask for your personal guarantee for Max's confinement. You need to answer confidently."

"I know. We've been over this."

"Mr. Hoffman," a voice from the group sounded, "Nice to meet you."

The gentleman in a tan suit shook his hand and began again. "As you are well aware, I don't agree with the court's decision, but I will abide by it."

Franz nodded his head knowingly and the gentleman continued, "If he steps out of bounds, it's not just his ass, but your ass on the line. Your attorney has made this clear?"

"Yes sir," Franz sheepishly replied looking to his attorney.

They pulled Max forward. Each of his arms were still being held firmly by an agent on each side.
Franz took a step toward his son when he was stopped by the lead agent with a hand in his chest.

"I need you to understand. There are several agents with happy trigger fingers waiting for your son to mess up. Don't give them a reason."

Franz looked at his attorney with astonishment.

"Are you harassing my client, Mr. Zimmerman?"

He replied smugly, "No sir. Just offering him valuable advice."

"I don't deserve this attitude from you."

Franz's lawyer interjected, "Franz, let it go."

Mr. Zimmerman interrupted, "No need to censure your client. He's right. He deserves none of this, but yet like the souls he's collected, he has no control of what's brought him here."

Franz looked dejectedly to the ground as Mr. Zimmerman eyed Max's attorney.

"Can Mr. Hoffman have his son now?"

Mr. Zimmerman turned his head and motioned with his fingers to bring Max forward. The two agents brought Max face to face with his father and let go of his arms. Max sprung forward and gave his father a hug.

"I love you, Max," Franz whispered in his son's ear.

"I know, Dad."

Franz, Max, and the attorney walked to the front entrance while the group from the elevator stood and watched. Cameras flashed and video cameras took position as Max and his father approached the rotating door. As they circled through and exited, the sheer commotion of the scene roared to life. Questions were flying from every direction as they pushed their way through the mass of journalists. Sitting curbside was a black SUV which the three of them entered. It quickly pulled away leaving the throng of reporters in its wake. Max sat in the same row as his father, while the attorney was in the passenger seat up front.

"Are you ok, son?"

Max began to weep and Franz slid over to put his arm around him.

"It's ok, Max. Everything will be ok."

"I hope so," Max mumbled into his father's chest.

The car drove onward and the two of them embraced as Max's body shook. The lawyer glanced backward occasionally, making eye contact with Franz. Franz's veins throbbed in his temples. During the fifteen-minute journey to their house the two of them didn't move much aside from Franz adjusting the position of his arms around his sobbing son. The car cleared police barricades before it slowed to a stop in front of their house. The attorney exited first and opened the door for the two to exit.

Franz stepped out first, followed by Max. They walked to the front door which was swung wide open with his mother waiting. Franz gave his wife a kiss followed by Max who threw his arms around her. As the two of them remained locked in an embrace, the attorney addressed Franz.

"Why don't the three of you take this time to reconnect. I'll reach out in the morning."

Franz nodded in agreement and slowly helped his wife and son further into the house. He pushed the front door closed and followed behind the other two as they walked into the living room. Max laid down on the couch and his mother took her usual spot in a recliner. Franz took a seat next to her in a matching chair.

"Welcome home, son."

Max unburied his head from the couch to look as his mother and he politely responded, "Thank you."

"Would you like some tea?" she asked.

"Yes mom, that would be lovely."

She stood and departed in the kitchen's direction.

"Max?"

"Yes, Dad?"

"You know that we will love you always, no matter what?"

"I suppose."

"It's true Max. No matter what."

He sat up on the couch. "Even if they find me guilty?"

"Even if."

"How can you say that? I know that I must embarrass you."

Franz shook his head and frowned. "Love you, yes. Proud is another question."

Max dove his head back into the cushion. Franz moved over to the couch and began to rub his son's back.

"There is nothing stronger than love, Max. But it doesn't mean that we can understand some of your choices."

"I guess not," Max mumbled with his face in a cushion.

"Did you do it, Max?"

"Kidnap him?"

"Yes," Franz answered.

"No."

"No?"

"I meant to, but I didn't even get close."

"Why would you want to?" Franz asked sadly.

"You wouldn't understand."

"Try me."

Max turned skeptically to his father. "Because the world needed to hear him to heal."

Franz stood from the chair and walked over to a bar in the corner of the room. He opened the cabinet and pulled out a bottle of 18-year-old Mortlach.

"I think I will need the good stuff tonight."

"Sorry you feel that way."

"Max you are such a good kid, such a big heart. Why do you let so much hate fill it?"

"You don't get it, do you?"

"No, I don't. Explain it to me."

"You see a world filled with opportunity. I see a world trying to destroy my future."

"But you said that Hitler had a message of hope?"

"He does."

"And what is the message?"

"That he went on living and we are immersed in his soul wherever we go."

Franz looked at him suspiciously, "This is hope?"

"If you can't see it, I can't help you."

"I see," Franz replied defeated.

"What flavor tea bag would you like, Max?" his mother yelled from the kitchen.

Max shook his head and smiled at his father.

"English Breakfast," he shouted back.

"Your mother and I would do anything for you, don't you get that?"

"I do, Dad! But that doesn't mean I have to agree with your politics."

"Politics? This is…"

The doorbell rang distracting Franz before he could finish. He got up from his chair and walked to the door. He looked through the peephole before opening the door.

"Officer, how can I help you?"

"Good evening Dr. Hoffman. I'm sorry to disturb you but they have assigned me as the security detail for Max. I wonder if I can't come in?"

"Certainly, officer…?"

"Sgt. Hinz. Thank you."

Franz directed Sgt. Hinz to the couch and looked back through the open door to see two squad cars parked in front of the house. Three officers were standing outside the cars staring at Franz, who closed the door and returned to the living room.

"Is all this security really necessary?"

Sgt. Hinz carefully looked around the room before replying, "For his and your safety yes. There are many rumors out there and a lot of opinions what to do with Max's knowledge."

Franz shook his head, "It's very hard to digest all this."

"I'm sure it is, sir."

Max's mother emerged from the kitchen, "Who was at the door?"

Franz addressed her, "I'm sorry dear, this is Sgt. Hinz, he is Max's security detail."

She studied him carefully, before replying, "Don't I know you? You are Peter Hinz's father, aren't you?"

Sgt. Hinz flashed a smile, "Yes ma'am. Our boys grew up together."

Franz's shoulders dropped and for the first time smiled himself, "I'm glad Max has someone who knows him to protect him."

"Would you like any tea Sgt. Hinz?" Max's mother asked
.

"No, thank you. I won't be long. In fact, if it's ok with you, can I speak with Max privately? I would like to take him through the specifics of the days and weeks ahead."

"If it's ok with you, I would appreciate being part of that conversation," Franz replied.

Sgt. Hinz broke out his best Sunday smile, "I understand that, sir. But as Max is no longer a minor let me discuss the matter with him privately and then we can see what he feels comfortable discussing with you."

"As you wish, sergeant. My office is just down the hallway, the two of you can talk in there."

Sgt. Hinz rose from the couch and said, "Thank you, sir. We'll be just a moment." He extended a hand to Max and helped him up from the couch.

The two of them walked down the hall and into the office closing the door behind them. Franz stepped into the kitchen, putting his arm around his wife's waist and kissing her on the top of her head.

Back in the office, Max stood staring at the sergeant. The sergeant motioned for Max to sit in one chair and then sat down himself.

"How are you doing, Max?"

Max shrugged, "OK".

"Just OK?"

"What do you want me to say?"

Sgt. Hinz chuckled and looked around the room. "The word on the street is you are dumb as a doornail or brilliantly devious. And I have to admit sitting here face to face, I can't tell which it is."

Max looked at him perplexed. "I don't follow."

"Max you are a hero to the brotherhood. You have sat in the same room and talked with our Führer. Your name will be remembered forever."

"You are…"

"Yes, I am."

"You are one of us. But how did they let you in here?"

"You are not the only one dumb as a doornail or brilliantly devious."

Max's face broke out in an enormous smile.

Sgt. Hinz extended his arm to shake Max's hand.

"Tonight, when I finish my shift, I will tell the brothers I shook the hand of Max Hoffman."

CHAPTER 21

Shenandoah National Park, Virginia

Dr. Felix Torres walked into the Elders room staring at the reports in hand. The glow of the sentient boxes made the charts difficult to read without his glasses. He put the documents on the desk and took a seat on the couch in the middle of the room. Spreading his arms across the back of the couch he took a deep breath and closed his eyes for the briefest moment.

"Warren, are you there?"

"Yes Dr. Torres, how may I help you?"

Dr. Torres rubbed his forehead before beginning tepidly, "I have some news to share with you."

"I appreciate your kindness but I've already seen the news about my brother."

Dr. Torres' shoulders dropped and he crossed his legs. "I'm sorry about your loss. If there is anything I can do for your family back home, please let me know."

"That is very kind. I will let you know."

"Would you like us to arrange an audio recording or videotape the event so you can watch it once our technology allows it?"

"I don't think that will be necessary. I would hate for my brother's family to be bothered on my behalf."

"Are you certain? I know how close he was to you."

The lights of the sentient boxes flickered and Dr. Torres' eyes followed their chaotic pattern.

"I think he's gone onto a better place."

Dr. Torres cocked his head and asked pensively, "I did not think you to be religious, Warren?"

"I'm not. It doesn't mean that he hasn't gone onto a better place."

"I'm afraid I don't understand..." Dr. Torres replied with his voice trailing off.

"We've had so many reports from the Collected that say it's a better place. It's hard to argue against the evidence it would be anything otherwise."

Rubbing his chin Dr. Torres responded, "I'm glad you think so. I'm sure it must be comforting to his family."

"Even amongst the handfuls of criminals that have returned they express the same experiences. Bliss and fulfilment. They all use different words but it all returns to bliss and fulfilment."

"It seems universal."

"Has there been any reports you have come across to the contrary?"

"Well, we have lost many souls before we could completely interview them, but no."

"It is curious, isn't it doctor?"

"What is that?"

"It would appear that perhaps those of us in this room have imprisoned ourselves into the walls of these boxes."

Dr. Torres leaned forward resting his elbows on his knees.

"You have access to your family, world news, even all the great digitized works from libraries around the world. Hardly a prison. We have freed you from the chains of time. The first of us to explore the depths and breadths of humanity."

"This is true. Some advances that have come from this room, are extraordinary."

"Yes, they are."

"Yet we can't enjoy the rewards of these advances."

"But it must be satisfying to see these changes."

"Perhaps, but we're all selfish in our own ways. What does it change for me? How is my tomorrow different from today?"

Dr. Torres smiled and leaned back into the couch, "Warren it sounds to me like your brother's death has impacted you. You sure I can't get you some help?"

"That is very kind. But unnecessary. I have been wondering about something."

"What is that?"

"I wonder if I will ever see my brother again?"

"He wasn't on our list to transfer prior to death."

"I'm well aware Dr. Torres."

"Are you hoping, that one day we'll collect him? You know the odds are extraordinarily remote."

"Not at all. My brother probably wouldn't like it either."

"Why do you say that?"

"I'm afraid he wouldn't appreciate us pulling him from the bliss he now enjoys."

"How do you imagine seeing your brother again?"

"I don't. I find it harder than ever to imagine I will. No one shares that they found their deceased before being collected. Yet they feel a part of everything. Such a damn puzzle with no vocabulary for us to understand it."

"I must agree with you on this point."

"Dr. Torres. Has anyone ever asked to be released from the Elders program?"

"You mean disconnected from this network? No. Not that I can recall."

"No. I mean turned off. Sent where we were supposed to go."

"Never an Elder. No."

The lights of the room continued to sparkle. After a few minutes Dr. Felix stood up and walked to the water machine and poured himself a glass. He started to sip when Warren spoke again.
"I think I lacked the courage before and I lack the courage now. So afraid of the unknown and now so afraid of missing out on what I've avoided until now."

Dr. Torres put the glass of water on the desk and searched the room for Warren Matthews sentient location. He stepped toward that box and addressed it.

"Warren. We all have some degree of fear of that which we don't understand. Death perhaps chief amongst them."

"And yet now, the mystery is not so great anymore. We've looked for the first time into a new telescope and the wonder of this universe takes away our breath once more."

Dr. Torres smiled but didn't reply.

"Dr. Torres. I think it may be time to set me free."

London, England

The executive car drove slowly through the affluent Lennox Garden neighborhood. The vehicle slowed to a stop in front of the residence of Mrs. Wilma Stone. The driver stepped out of the car and walked around to open the rear passenger side door. From the back seat, the passenger emerged in an impeccably appointed suit and tie.

The passenger departed the car without a word to his driver. He approached the doorman at the entrance of the building. The doorman walked out of the shadow of his vestibule to address the impending guest. He opened his mouth to speak when a look of recognition on his face stopped him. Instead, he turned to open the door and stood beside it attentively.

The passenger shook his hand and the doorman said, "It's our honor to have you."

"Thank you," the man said as he continued into the building.

He walked undistracted by the artwork and floral displays. As he approached unit three, he rang the doorbell and waited staring straight ahead. Olivia Stone answered the door dressed in her favorite yellow dress accompanied by tangerine two-inch heels.

Olivia Stone stumbled upon her words, "You must be here to see my mother. Let me grab her. Please make yourself comfortable in our living room."

The man entered the living room and sat on the couch looking around the room as he waited. After a few minutes, Olivia returned with her mother.

Wilma Stone gushed with enthusiasm, "It is so good to see you my dear friend."

The man stood to greet her and extended his hand, but instead she pulled him close and gave him a hug. She took a step back and motioned for him to sit down as she sat in her favorite chair.

"What brings you here this afternoon? What a surprise this is."

The man smiled before he began, "I'm afraid I come here with my proverbial hat in hand."

Wilma's expression changed to that of concern and asked, "And how could that be possibly true?"

"I'm afraid it is true. I'm here to apologize for the actions of my partner as it related to the matters of your late husband."

"There really is no need for that. From what I've read this John Waters, or is it John Springs, fooled the world."

The man nodded knowingly before he answered, "Perhaps this is all true but at B&R solicitors we have for generations strived to represent our clients and our friends with the highest of integrity. And in this case, I'm afraid we've fallen well short of that goal."

"Please, there really is no need for you to beat yourself up over this. And you could have addressed this over the phone just as easily."

"Perhaps, but I wanted you to see my sincere apology first hand. And besides I wanted to give you this."

He reached into his suit pocket and pulled out an envelope. He looked at it and stood to hand it to Wilma. She took the envelope and opened it with a perplexed look. She pulled the document out of the envelope and let out a gush of astonishment before covering her mouth.

"This is my fee."

"Yes, it is. And I'm returning it to you."

"But why? The money was securely transferred just as Mr. Roberts had ensured. You have done your part."

The man looked to the ceiling and let out a gasp of air.

"I'm afraid this may not be the case. Percy is, as we speak, busy with the authorities explaining his relationship with this John Springs."

"I'm not sure I follow," Olivia Stone interrupted.

The man glanced at her and then back to Wilma. "It would appear that perhaps this John Springs had collected Frank and did not share this with authorities at the University."

Olivia gasped, "Dad?"

Wilma fell back into her chair and a tear ran from her eye.

"Oh my, God, Frank. Where is he?"

The man paused to collect himself. "It appears Frank may have been the secret source of your information and…"

"And what?" Wilma begged.

"And when he provided it, it appears John terminated his sentient box."

"No! That's can't be true!" Olivia screamed, "Please don't tell me that Dad came back and this man took him away from us."

"I'm afraid this may be the case. I really wish…"

Wilma interrupted him, tears running profusely down her cheeks, "Did Percy know?"

The man shook his head and replied, "We aren't certain, most likely not, I've known him for years. I would think Percy could not be a party to such a deceit."

Wilma just shook her head and looked at her daughter who

was sobbing herself. She got up from her seat and sat next to Olivia to hold her. "He sent his love, in the only way he could get it out, sweetie."

Olivia nodded but dropped her head into her mother's chest.

"You can see now, why I can't possibly take this money."

Wilma nodded while caressing Olivia.

"Well, this is all quite extraordinary. Is there any way to know for certain what happened?" Wilma asked.

"The authorities will be here shortly. As we uncovered this information, I asked if I might speak to you first. They no doubt can fill you in with everything they know."

"A gentleman as always."

Wilma extended her arm while still holding her daughter. He reached out to grab it and they held hands without letting go for several moments of silence. He finally squeezed tight and then stood.

"I'm afraid it's probably time for me to depart and let you have this next conversation."

Wilma patted Olivia on the back and then stood to escort him out.

As they walked to the front door, she remarked, "If there is ever anything I can do for you, please ask. You know Frank always said I could trust you. You are always welcome here."

The man smiled. "That is very generous of you. I will call you in a few weeks once these matters have settled. I have a matter in the States, a collection of ancient artifacts I could use some help. But that can wait. For now, take care of Olivia."

"I will," she gave him a hug and opened the front door, "you are a good man Sir Thomas Bingham."

Lake of the Woods, OR, USA

The sun continued its climb into a brilliant blue sky dotted with wispy clouds. The lake placid with the hum of a speedboat in the distance. Emma stood by the shoreline at the foot of the well-worn path from the cabin. Dressed in a knee-high sun dress and purple flats, she delicately balanced her foot on the surface of the water. Back on the porch, her mother watched with Ashley, the two of them standing side by side with their arms around each other. Mark walked out of the cabin, dressed in a collared short-sleeve shirt and tan pants.

"The two of you look beautiful in your dresses," he adoringly shared.

Cindy let go off Ashley and walked over to her husband to give him a kiss.

"Thank you, sweetie."

She reached out and held his hand. He glanced at the rocking chair where the sentient box sat on top of the old flannel blanket neatly folded.

"How are you doing, Emily?"

"I'm well. The better question is how you are doing?"

Mark grimaced and stared at Cindy gauging her emotions. A tear ran from the corner of her eye and she leaned her head into his chest. He stroked her exposed shoulders, dancing his fingers around the spaghetti straps.

"We will be just fine, Mom," Ashley answered warmly.

"I know you will my daughter. I know you will."

Cindy asked quietly, "Where's Dad?"

"He's finishing up. Said he would be out in a minute."

"Mom, what was your favorite moment here?" Ashley asked.

"That's a great question. So many of them. It had to be the time I watched the two of you go sailing with your father."

Cindy broke out in a smile. "That wind!"

"Yes, that wind. I was laughing so hard."

Ashley added, "Dad was so frustrated, he couldn't get that boat to come back."

Cindy laughed, "He had us convinced we would end up in Canada."

"I never knew that," Emily replied.

"We watched you just waving and waving at us," Ashley added.

"It is amazing. So much time and yet you can never learn everything." Emily said.

"What's this chatter I hear about my boating skills?"

Cindy turned to the doorway, "Dad!" She let go of Mark's hand and gave her father a tight hug. Christine followed him outside and she grabbed him under the arm. Cindy stepped forward and kissed her on the cheek.

"Thank you for being here with us."

"I wouldn't have it any way else."

Ashley stepped over and put her arms around both Jacob and Christine and savored the moment. Cindy took a few steps toward the lake and called Emma's name. Emma remained transfixed on the water. Cindy looked back toward her family with a raised eyebrow before turning and walking to the waterfront.

As she neared Emma, she asked, "What you doing, kiddo?"

MICHAEL TRZUPEK

"I'm looking out on the water to see if something is different after grandma leaves us."

Cindy bent over to share Emma's view putting their heads side by side.

"What do you see?"

"Forever."

"Forever?" Cindy asked perplexed.

"Yes, no matter how hard I try, everything goes on forever. How can I ever tell if anything changes?"

Cindy put both arms around Emma and whispered, "You can't. You'll just know."

Emma turned to look at her mother, "Know what?"

"That the world is a better place because of grandma?"

Emma wrinkled her nose and just said, "Hmm."

"It's just about time sweetie. We should head back."

"OK."

They both turned together and walked toward the cabin holding hands. As they stepped onto the deck, Mark patted her on the head and put his arm around her. Ashley glanced around at everyone and then at the sentient box. She puffed her cheeks and let out the air slowly.

"Is everyone ready for this?" Ashley asked.

Their heads nodded and Emily answered from her box, "Yes."

Ashley turned to the box and asked, "You are certain about this Mom? There is no turning back."

"It is time for me to get on living again."

"Ok. Perhaps I should start," Ashley started but paused. She choked back tears and then started to speak. "I love you so much, Mom. I hope that I get to find you again. You are the most amazing mom I could have ever asked for."

"I love you too honey," Emily replied, "and you know better than any of us, that I'll be right here, even if you can't talk to me."

Ashley nodded and added, "Everything we talked about last night. I hope you know how much I learned from you."

"And you taught me even more. I will miss you my daughter."

"I will miss you..." Ashley trailed off sobbing. Cindy had tears pouring from her face and couldn't speak. Jacob stepped forward but Christine put her arm in front of him, "No, let me go next."

"Emily, I can't thank you enough for having the love in your heart to embrace me. To let me...To let Jacob be free to love me. We will forever have the unique gift of falling in love with the most amazing man possible."

"And I am thankful that he found you. You are a good woman and he loves you dearly."

"Thank you. I don't... I just hope you find your peace."

"I will. This is not my first rodeo."

The group chuckled and Emma asked, "What's so funny?"

Mark explained, "Grandma's saying that where she's going is a happy place."

"Oh," Emma said with a smile.

Mark looked around and then went next. "Emily. Mom. Cindy always had such great things to say about you. I never thought I would get this experience. I'll always be so thankful. Thankful that your granddaughter got to know you...," he paused trying to catch his breath.

Emily took the opportunity, "Mark, I wish I could have seen you with my own eyes. I used to hold Cindy nursing her late at night. I often imagined the man who would steal her heart. She loves you so much. You are such a good father. If I could hug you..."

"I love you, Mom," he murmured as he rested his hand on her sentient box.

As he moved away, Jacob looked at Cindy who was now bawling. He stepped forward and knelt down next to the rocking chair.

"I'm sorry that I wasn't here for you the first time. This is where I fell in love with you. This was your happy place."

"It is. It always will be."

He looked around to see the lake and then turned back, "I never stopped loving you, I hope you know that. I just..."

"I do. And I love you too."

Jacob fought his emotions to finish, "I just couldn't let them. My feelings. Let them. Keep me from living."

"I think you understand better than anyone why it's time for me to say goodbye."

He nodded his head and sobbed, "I love you my wife. Good-bye."

"I love you too."

Cindy walked toward the rocking chair but couldn't find her words through her tears. Ashley walked over to put her arm around her.

"It's so hard," Cindy sobbed.

Emma walked over and put her arms around Cindy's waist, "It's okay. I'll go next."

Cindy reached down and put an arm around Emma's head and gently squeezed. Emma got on her knees and put her chin on the rocking chair.

"I will miss you Grandma."

"I'm going to miss you too..."

Emma interrupted, "Oh my goodness I almost forgot." She got up and ran into the house. Mark followed slowly behind watching where she was going. She ran up the stairs and he could hear her steps bound down the hallway.

"Where did Emma go?" Emily asked.

Cindy through her tears said, "I'm not sure. She ran upstairs."

Emma could be heard again and the quick cadence of steps on stairs followed. Mark saw her and immediately threw a look toward Cindy.

She looked at him confused and mouthed, "What?"

He looked back to see Emma walking out of the house. Cindy caught sight of her almost immediately and let out an audible gasp. Tears ran down her face with renewed vigor. Emma slowed her pace and leaned over the chair. She gently placed Hoppy next to Emily's box and then resumed her position kneeling on the porch next to the chair.

"I love you, Grandma. Thank you for making all those tapes for me."

"I love you too, Emma. I hope you enjoy the stories."

Emma smiled and put her chin on the seat.

She said, "Maybe one day you'll find a way to give me a hug."

Emily replied, "Maybe. But you'll always know I love you."

"I know. I love you too."

Cindy slowly moved to the rocking chair and sat on the hard-wood floor. Emma sat in her lap and Cindy embraced her in a big bear hug.

"Mom. I feel. I feel, like it can never be enough."

"No, I don't think it can. Would we even appreciate it then?"

"I guess not," Cindy answered soberly.

"I don't want to say goodbye."

"You're not. I'll always be here. I've told you that."

"I know. But it's not the same."

"True. But that doesn't make it bad, just different."

"But, it's not you."

"And neither is this."

Cindy looked to the sky, tears running down her cheeks. "I will always love you, Mom. Always."

"I know, sweetie. Love lives forever."

"Goodbye, Mom. I love you."

"I love you too."

Cindy looked up at Ashley who was walking toward the rock-ing chair. She pushed Hoppy slightly out of the way to access the back panel. She glanced toward Emma and said, "Don't worry, he's staying right here."

She unplugged the back of the box and the battery in-function light turned to red. Ashley took a long look around the porch watching everyone's reactions. Her focus returned to the back of the box and she pressed the power button which opened a panel exposing a switch inside. Simultaneously, the red battery light began to flash on and off quickly.

Ashley looked back at everyone and said, "This is the moment."

Seeing no reaction, Ashley put her finger on the switch and Cindy yelled out, "Goodbye, Mom. I love you."

"I love you too, Grandma," Emma quickly followed.

Emily answered slowly, "My love is always with you."

"Goodbye, Mom," Ashley said as she flipped the switch. The lights on the box turned off.
A gust of wind danced with their clothes and teased the long hair of the women. Emma stood up from her mother's lap, fixing her hair.

"Do you think that was Grandma saying goodbye?"

Cindy looked at Ashley and then back at Emma.

"I don't think she ever left. It was just her way of saying I love you."

ACKNOWLEDGEMENT

I am so thankful for the editing both Stacey Burke and Shai Hinitz provided at various points in the novel. My writers group provided invaluable feedback throughout this process. Last but not least, I would like to thank my family for their unending support.

ABOUT THE AUTHOR

Michael Trzupek

Michael has traveled the world working for almost two decades at Intel and Microsoft which exposed him to diverse cultures and customs. Through these journeys he found that love and life purpose are universally shared. The Collectors Program is Michael's first published novel, but second manuscript. His curiosity to explore spiritual-  ity, technology, and relationships permeates throughout The Collectors Program. Now working in healthcare and married with five children in the house, The Collectors Program is the product of endless early mornings, late evenings, and opportunistic quiet moments.

Made in the USA
Coppell, TX
26 July 2020